I

KNOW
I SAW
HER

I KNOW I SAW HER

E.D. THOMPSON

HACHETTE
BOOKS
IRELAND

First published in Ireland in 2021 by
HACHETTE BOOKS IRELAND

1

Cataloguing in Publication Data is available from the British Library

Trade paperback ISBN 978 1 52937 039 3
Ebook ISBN 978 1 52937 040 9

Typeset in Garamond by redrattledesign.com

Printed and bound in Great Britain by Clays Ltd, Elcograf, S.p.A

Hachette Books Ireland policy is to use papers that are natural, renewable and recyclable
products and made from wood grown in sustainable forests. The logging and manufacturing
processes are expected to conform to the environmental regulations of the country of origin.

Hachette Books Ireland
8 Castlecourt Centre
Castleknock
Dublin 15, Ireland

A division of Hachette UK Ltd
Carmelite House, 50 Victoria Embankment, EC4Y 0DZ
www.hachettebooksireland.ie

For my mum and dad,
the mighty Myra and Robin

1

Someone is lying.

I saw her. I wasn't sure if she saw me.

Kevin says I couldn't have, she's at a friend's, not even in the same country as I was when I thought I saw her.

But I didn't *think* I saw her. I saw her.

Someone is lying.

This is a nice house in an avenue of nice houses. Who could possibly live here? At a glance, it is the home of a bank worker's family, or a shopkeeper's, maybe. An income bracket to match a substantial but not outrageous mortgage. People who put a bit of 1930s architecture ahead of a master bedroom with en-suite shower room in a shiny new development for the same money. Here, there is stained glass, and mature lime trees in full leaf all along the street. But look again. The windows of this particular house are dirty. The paint on the front door is flaking and a bracket securing the drainpipe has come away. There are slatted blinds on every window.

I observe all this from the driveway. I have just come twenty-five miles to County Armagh from Belfast International airport in a taxi. It is half past nine at night, but it is still light, and warm. I have come home. This is my house. Mine and Joe's. And I don't want to go inside.

I trundle my wheelie-case to the step, turn my key in the lock and step onto the coir mat, with a 'Welcome' message printed on it that actually makes me bristle with bottled-up anger. The house smells nice, though – wood polish and something good in the oven.

'I'm home!' I call.

There is a muffled answer from upstairs. Sounds like Joe is in the attic. I pick through the week's post, which is resting in a casserole dish on the kitchen table, as I wait to hear him land safely on the upstairs floorboards and thud downstairs. Charity appeals, mainly. One from HMRC, which I'll read properly tomorrow. A reminder from the optician, and supermarket bumph.

Joe appears in the kitchen doorway, in jeans, a t-shirt and bare feet. He is carrying an electric fan – that must be what he was hunting for in the attic.

'Hi,' I say, throwing down the post and opening my arms for a hug.

'So, how was Kate?' he asks, squeezing me tightly.

'Tired, I think,' I say. 'I wish you'd come with me. She'd love to see you. The kids would love to see you.'

Kate is my niece – well, my sort-of-niece – but we've always had something special between us. I first met her when she was thirteen and I was twenty-four and we just hit it off. I never thought of her as a child, exactly, and now she's thirty-nine and has three kids of her own.

'I've made a pie and a bowl of coleslaw,' Joe says. 'We can eat it now or wait a while, whatever you want.'

I've been travelling since the late afternoon and all I've had to eat and drink was a bottle of water and some crisps.

'Let's eat now,' I say. 'Then I need an early night.'

'Shall I open a bottle of wine?' Joe asks.

I hesitate. I haven't been sleeping well and I don't think alcohol is helping. I drift off easily enough, but waken a couple of hours later and can't get back. I've heard drink can do that. Yet I see in Joe's face that he wants my homecoming to be some sort of celebration, and he's been on his own all week.

I say yes.

As Joe gets out plates and big serving spoons, I think again, as I keep thinking, about Kate. By accident, really, I caught a slightly earlier train from Gatwick to East Croydon station and the taxi delivered me to their new place in a few minutes.

I was on the front doorstep, hadn't even rung the bell yet, when I heard Kate practically screaming at George, her husband. She was shouting: 'When will you stop kidding yourself, George? We're not "bohemian", we're poor. We're the fucking Cratchits. Hand to fucking mouth. And I'm sick of it.'

I would have crept away, gone for a walk or found somewhere for a coffee, come back later, but Kate looked up from where she was standing in the front room and saw me. She mouthed, 'Oh shit,' and put her head in her hands for just a second. Then she looked up again, waved to me, smiled and called, 'I'm coming!' What could I do? What could I say?

'So, all the little 'uns happy to see you?' asks Joe.

'They're not so little any more,' I tell him, with a smile. 'Well, Conall isn't, anyway. He starts big school in September.' Kate was worried about paying for his uniform. I know she went round some charity shops looking for a second-hand blazer, then came home and cried. I asked her to let me help. In the past, she would have brushed aside such an idea, but this time she accepted, tearfully. She was happily skint for years, but it's different now that Conall is old enough to feel embarrassed, plus, she's staring forty in the face and things aren't getting any better.

'Will they come over in August?' Joe asks.

'Kate and the kids will,' I say. 'Not George – he's got a part.'

'Great!' Joe says. 'What is it?'

'Oh, it's in one of those tiny shows in a room above a pub,' I say. 'Some Brexit satire.'

'But George voted Leave,' Joe says.

'You know George. Show him any size of an audience and he's your man. This food is so good.' And it is. Joe can really cook. But I'm conscious that everything we're eating was in the fridge or freezer before I left – obviously. That's why we're having coleslaw, for example, and not fresh salad leaves.

'Did you beat him at the game?' Joe asks, with a big smile.

'Oh, yes,' I say. 'I saw Miss Ramsey, my old history teacher, in Bella Italia, Leicester Square. Had a little chat with her, to George's consternation.'

George and I have this thing between us. It started when he and Kate hadn't been together long, when they were both at RADA. Kate had invited me to come and stay at the big, filthy flat a lot of them shared in Bloomsbury.

George was a Home Counties boy, who considered himself an authority on London, compared with Kate, who'd never been there before her drama college auditions. He delighted in giving me lots of advice about disguising my tourist status, which, if displayed, would surely see me pickpocketed on the Tube and variously taken advantage of.

He told me London wasn't like a provincial town where everyone knew everyone and people looked out for each other. Everybody was a stranger here. No-one said hello to anyone in the street. There would be no eye contact and no smiles. It was the sheer size of it. It was a genuine metropolis. It was just the way it was.

That was all right, until we were queuing in the British Museum gift shop for some postcards and who should I spot but Jane Ennis, who went to school with me and copied all my answers in French tests, which wasn't smart as I wasn't very good. We laughed and hugged and I smiled at George and told him it wasn't so different to a provincial town after all – you could still bump into someone you knew. George huffed and said it was a fluke, that he had never run into anyone from home in all his time there. And then, the next day, we found ourselves in the queue for the Tower of London with my old Girl Guide leader, who was delighted, but hardly all that surprised, to see me.

Ever since then, I have regarded it as a challenge to encounter someone I know when in London visiting Kate and George. It's childish, but it's very satisfying when I win, which I often do.

'Anyone else?' Joe asks.

'Well, I *thought* I saw Kim Kennedy on the train in East Croydon station,' I said. 'I was on the platform and she was heading for Victoria. But I've just seen Kevin out watering his hanging baskets – he doesn't seem like a hanging baskets kind of guy, does he? I wonder why he has them? – and he insisted Kim's at a friend's somewhere in County Galway, so I must have made a mistake.'

Joe shrugs and tops up my wine.

'You still won,' he says.

'I did.' I smile.

I didn't make a mistake, though. I did see Kim Kennedy on that train. So either she isn't telling Kevin the truth or he isn't telling me. Not that I suppose it matters, and not that it's remotely any of my business, but someone is definitely lying.

2

'How has she been?' I ask Linzi. 'Did she notice I wasn't coming in?'

'Notice?' Linzi says. 'She hasn't stopped complaining about it all week.'

Linzi is a care worker at Mum's home. She has the bloated face and enormous chest of a woman who eats and drinks too much, yet you can see that when she was seventeen she was probably a real heartbreaker. I'd guess she's late thirties now, although it's hard to be sure, because of the weight she's carrying.

'Sorry,' I say.

Linzi stops in the corridor and looks at me. 'You've nothing to be sorry for. You need a wee break. Everybody needs a wee break.'

We walk into the day room.

'Ruby. Alice is here to see you. Show her your nails, that the girl did for you yesterday. Show Alice your lovely nails, Ruby.'

Mum looks up, looks at Linzi, glances at me, looks at her nails.

'It wouldn't have been my choice of colour,' she says, apparently to the backs of her hands, stretched out flat in mid-air, just above her knees.

I sit down in the chair next to hers.

'Oh? What colour would you have chosen?'

It's always easier if there's already a conversation starter, rather than trying to begin talking from cold.

'I like pink,' Mum says, 'although when the girl did my colours she said I should always go for a baby pink and never a coral.'

'So you had your colours done, too?' I ask.

'That was ages ago, Ruby,' Linzi says. 'Do you still remember that?' Then turning to me, 'She has a powerful memory, Alice.'

Yes and no. Mum unfailingly remembers that I was to bring her some cinnamon lozenges, or emery boards or new pyjamas, and will bite my head off if I forget them, but on certain days she will have deleted her entire marriage to my late father and my whole childhood and youth.

Before I went to Croydon, I brought her a photograph of her on her seventieth, with her two older brothers, now deceased, all lined up in front of the fireplace. She said, 'Will you put that in a frame for Mummy? She would love one of the three of us together.'

'Mummy' – my grandmother – would have been 104 when that picture of her elderly children was snapped, had she not died twenty years earlier.

Once, Mum told me about the two hilarious men who had come to visit them in the day room the night before. They had played pranks and told jokes and generally been the best visitors ever. She hoped they'd come back soon. When I asked Linzi, it turned out there had been no visitors – they'd been watching Ant and Dec.

This from a woman who'd launched a small business, driven an expensive car, solved cryptic crosswords for fun and thought nothing of reading a book in an evening. She'd even more or less designed the bungalow I grew up in and how glad I was that she didn't know it had been sold to pay her care home fees.

After leaving Mum, I have to do a big shop. With no money coming in over the summer, I should drive to Lidl, but instead I go to Nicholson's, because it's nicer. Following the stultifying heat of the care home, the supermarket's air-con is delicious. It's too hot again today to think of cooking big meals, so I pick up eggs and cheese and salad ingredients and some wheaten bread.

I am hesitating at the dessert chiller when someone reaches across and sets a packet of two caramel choux buns in my trolley.

'You know you want to.'

It's Kevin Kennedy, carrying a punnet of strawberries and two bottles of wine.

I blush. Kevin Kennedy makes me nervous because I find

him attractive and feel in my gut that he knows this. There is absolutely no foundation for my suspicion. I have never come anywhere near flirting with him, or, I think, said or done anything to give myself away. Yet there is just something in the way he is with me, something like a gently mocking smirk just a millimetre below the surface. He knows. I'm sure of it.

'You haven't seen Elvis in the chilled meats, then?' he asks, with a lopsided smile someone, some time, has told him is sexy.

I don't immediately understand what he's getting at.

'Oh!' I say, twigging that he's teasing me over my supposed sighting of his wife at East Croydon station, when she's actually in the west of Ireland. 'No! And no Lord Lucan at the hot food deli.'

I immediately hate myself. Kevin was making fun of me and I not only let him, but I joined in. Weak, weak. I experience a tiny, despicable moment of hoping that Kim *is* the one who is lying – lying to Kevin so that she can be with her lover in London. I've no idea if this is likely. The Kennedys only moved into Parnell Park about eighteen months ago and I don't know them well. She is a lecturer, I think in travel and tourism, or something like that. Kevin, I understand, goes to Belfast three evenings a week to sub-edit for a newspaper. I'm not sure which one. The rest of the time, he seems to be at home. He's about my age, well-spoken and, I suspect, very, very clever, yet he doesn't appear to have a career. I don't think Kim is as bright as him, but she seems to bring home the bacon and is, I'd guess, ten years younger.

'Any plans for the summer, now school's out?' Kevin asks.

'No, not really,' I say. 'I finished a week before the end of term, because the teacher I was subbing for came back, and so I took the opportunity of popping over to London. How about you?'

'Actually, I've just been to the travel agent to book us a couple of weeks in Île de Ré,' Kevin says.

'Oh, I know it!' I say, delighted to be able to keep up. 'We stayed in Saint-Clément-des-Baleines, years ago. Whereabouts will you be based?'

'Saint-Martin,' Kevin says. 'Near the harbour.'

'Nice,' I say.

As I head for the tills, I think two things. First, Kevin Kennedy is too cool to push a trolley or carry a wire basket, so must have to go to the shops with considerable frequency if each trip is limited to what he can carry in his arms. Second, who books a simple holiday for two in France through a travel agent, these days? Why didn't he just do it online?

I wonder what Kevin knows about Joe. I have no idea how much most of our neighbours are aware of – I stopped considering their opinions on Joe and me way back. I had to. It may be that we are the talk of Parnell Park; it may be that we are of no lingering interest whatsoever.

Time to go home. I'll ask Joe to make us an omelette for lunch – he's much better at it than I am. If I spend some time with him first, then I won't feel so bad dragging the sun lounger down to the bottom of the garden and taking a while for myself.

It might be the heat, and all the bare flesh on show, but for the first time in years, I find myself thinking about sex these days and how I would quite like to have some. Kevin Kennedy has flashed through my mind in this regard, but in reality I suspect something cruel in him and think what I really need is someone kind. At fifty-one I'm not too old to have expectations, am I?

The indicator light on the Corsa is playing up again, after repeated repairs. I need to raise the funds for a newer car.

One reason to book a holiday through a travel agent is for the ATOL insurance, should anything go wrong.

Another reason is that a holiday booked through a travel agent is somehow more concrete, so would make a better present or a surprise. Or provide you with better cover, if, for example, someone was lying about something.

3

I was hanging on by my fingertips in school for the last few weeks. The truth is, I'm a dinosaur in the classroom. I trained with blackboards, not interactive whiteboards. Technology leapt in during my baby years at home and I never caught up. When I tried to go back, I struggled. Without a job, I couldn't seem to find the opportunities to go on the right courses to bring my skills up to date. Subbing was a lifeline, financially, so I kept on putting myself up for it, but I've been out of my depth for years. When I'm out of work, I'm terrified about the lack of income; when I'm in work, I live in a state of high anxiety.

I had a sweet spell last Christmas, where I was reading *Atonement* and *Tess of the d'Urbervilles* with the sixth form of an all-girls school. The only device we used was an electric kettle in the corner, and we took it in turns to bring in cake or cookies. We strolled through each lesson, yet a lot of learning went on. When that teacher returned to her rightful role I could have cried. I was back in the bear pit of early-morning phone calls from whoever, asking me to be in school by 8.30 a.m., to face God knows what.

Not all new approaches fill me with dread, though. Safeguarding training is a step forward. It is correct, in my opinion, that anyone working with vulnerable people, like children or the elderly, should be vigilant about signs of abuse or neglect. I have seen the eye-rolling when I submit paperwork recording a bruise here, a scab there. Yes, probably they are innocuous, but what if they are not? What if everyone who has one piece of a potential jigsaw puzzle fails to put it forward, and the picture doesn't emerge until it's too late?

That's probably why I phone the police. I make it clear that I'm not reporting a missing person or accusing anyone of foul play, I am merely giving my small fragment of what might or might not ever turn out to be a bigger jigsaw, just in case my little piece was vital. Just in case.

I suppose I know they will ask for my name and address, but I don't expect them to call round to the house.

When the doorbell rings, I am in the front room, reading.

I hear Joe thud out of the kitchen and scurry upstairs, give him a moment and go to answer.

Two female officers, in uniform, albeit shirtsleeves, are on the doorstep.

'Mrs Payne? Alice Payne? You spoke to someone this morning?'

'Yes!'

'Can we come in?'

I think of Joe, hiding upstairs.

'Would it be all right if we talked in the garden?' I say.

The women exchange a look, but the smaller one says, 'The garden's fine.'

As we walk round to the side gate, I notice their huge, heavy belts loaded with all sorts of gadgetry. How on earth could they ever run in those, I wonder, if called upon to pursue a suspect on foot?

Not used to guests in my garden, it only now dawns on me that there isn't really anywhere to sit. There is my scruffy sun lounger and a wooden picnic table, but I could hardly expect the police officers to sprawl on one or throw their legs over the fixed seating of the other.

'We're fine to stand,' says the taller woman, reading my thoughts.

'Mrs Payne,' begins the other.

'Ali, please, call me Ali,' I say.

'Ali, could you just tell us again where you believe you saw Mrs Kennedy?'

She hasn't taken out a notebook, I notice.

'Yes, of course. I was standing on the platform at East Croydon train station. Mrs Kennedy was sitting by the window on a train coming from Gatwick airport, heading for Victoria.'

'Ali, you say the train was coming from Gatwick – do you

mean it was coming from Gatwick direction?' The smaller one, still.

'Yes,' I say.

'Which means it was on the Brighton Main Line, so it could just as easily have been coming from Brighton, or Haywards Heath or Redhill, or anywhere along that route. The passengers on board weren't necessarily coming from the airport.'

They've been doing their homework.

'No.'

'And they could disembark at any one of a number of stations. They could have got off just up the road at Streatham, or at Balham or Clapham.'

'Yes, I see what you mean. I'm reading too much into it, to assume she was definitely making her way off a flight and into the heart of London.'

'Mrs Payne. Ali.' The tall one again. 'We have absolutely no reason to think that Mrs Kennedy has been the victim of a crime. We appreciate your concern, but we're satisfied that there's nothing to investigate here today.'

'I'm sure you're right,' I say. 'I knew I was probably being over-cautious, but I just thought I should let someone know. I did a first aid course at Easter, and the trainer told us, whatever the patient's problem, bottom line, if you're not happy, call an ambulance. I thought that was good advice.' No need to elaborate. 'And I wasn't happy, not entirely, so I called you.'

The officers exchange another look. I think: if they'd already decided there was nothing in this, why on earth did they come and visit me, instead of simply phoning? Am I a little matter to tick off the list on their way back from a real job? Or perhaps I'm an excuse to escape a hot and sweaty office for half an hour and they'll go for iced lollies for everyone now.

'Well, no harm done,' the tall one says.

'Enjoy the sun,' says the other.

They are almost back at their car when I run after them. Darius is leaning against my front gate, rolling a cigarette. I can't figure out whether he is supposed to be in charge of the window-cleaning crew who service the street, or is a mere hanger-on. He never seems to do any actual cleaning, and he always looks a bit too well-dressed for the work, but he sometimes wears the money bag and he knows all our names.

'All right, Alison?' he greets me. Well, he *sort of* knows our names.

'Fine, Darius. Thanks.'

'You're off for the summer now.'

'I am. It's wonderful.'

Darius smiles and lights his cigarette with a snazzy electronic lighter. He's always pleasant to me, even though I cancelled all window-cleaning years ago and am immoveable in that regard.

But I must not let the police officers get away. They are climbing into their car. They are leaving.

I grab the passenger-side door and speak in. 'It really was Kim Kennedy on that train,' I insist. 'I saw her, and she might even have seen me. She wasn't in Galway. Not then, anyway.'

'We appreciate your concern, Ali.' This from the taller

officer. 'But, as we said, we're satisfied there's nothing suspicious to look into.'

Sitting on the sofa, half watching the Channel 4 news, I imagine them ringing me back.

'Have you found her?' I am full of hope.

'Mrs Payne, is it the case that you make a daily visit to your mother, Mrs Ruby Fisher, at Mount Charles Nursing Home?'

'Yes,' I say. 'Why?'

'What age is Mrs Fisher, please?'

'Mum's seventy-six,' I say. 'Why are you asking me about Mum?'

'What is the reason for your mother living in Mount Charles, Mrs Payne?'

My hope plummets. This is the thing about living in a small town – yes, there is a veneer of professionalism, more than a veneer, probably, to be fair, but there's undeniably still a place given to gossip and small-mindedness.

'She has dementia,' I say. I suddenly feel terribly, terribly heavy.

'And at what age did your mother first show signs of dementia?'

I sit down on the stairs and cup my forehead in my free hand.

'She was fifty-one,' I say.

They don't ring, of course. No one has suggested I am losing my mind. But they still aren't listening, either.

4

Parnell Park wasn't our first home, when we got married. We started out in a two-up, two-down on the other side of the river, where we were very happy.

It was an illusion. I'd never have married my husband if I'd known what he was really like. When I met him, he was lovely – open-minded, unmaterialistic, warm, generous. Had this been his true personality, I think I would have loved him forever. But it wasn't. It was just a phase.

'So you're saying he tricked you,' said Connie, the relationship counsellor I went to see, on my own.

'No,' I said. 'I don't think it was an act. I think it was genuine, but it was a genuine *phase*. My mistake was thinking it was his whole self. It wasn't.'

As time passed, his underlying meanness re-asserted itself. I was already pregnant by then.

We bought 25 Parnell Park with a large deposit from Mum and Dad and a mortgage based on my husband's earnings. Such a nice house in such a nice, leafy street, I thought it'd cheer him up. We were finally living among the sort of people he regarded as suitable neighbours. I thought I might get my old husband back.

Briefly, he seemed happy. But it didn't last. Our car wasn't as good as the others in the driveways. We were making do with old furniture from our previous home. Just owning number 25 wasn't enough, he wanted to be seen to be keeping up with the Parnell Park Joneses in every visible way.

Foolishly, foolishly, I had always left the family finances to him, so I didn't know at the time that in order to 'make economies' so he could buy the Audi, he secretly cancelled his life insurance policy. Looking back, this was totally in character, for he was the one person who stood to lose nothing whatsoever by the change of arrangement, but when I discovered it I thought it a despicable act for a family man. It was, I suppose, the final straw for me. I would never feel love for him again.

I like to think I would have left him, when the moment was right, but I'm not honestly sure. I am not brave. I fear pulling down a deluge of stony consequences. It didn't matter anyway, in the end.

One place I could speak boldly was with Connie, who was professionally bound not to tell anyone.

'The real Joe is a prick,' I said.

*

Antoinette has heard me in the garden.

'Ali? Are you there?'

She knows I am.

'I'm here,' I say through the hedge.

'Come round,' she says. 'I want to talk to you.'

She'll want to book me to water her plants when she goes on holiday, that's my guess. I don't have pots or baskets, on the basis that it wouldn't work, having anyone prowling about our garden.

I flap up the path in my flip-flops.

'Ooh, rock chick,' says Antoinette, with a big smile.

She means my halter top. Why shouldn't I wear a halter top? – it's thirty-one degrees. I wait for her to ask about the plants.

'I see you had a visit from the police,' she says.

So *that's* what she wants to talk about.

'Yes,' I say.

'Everything all right, Ali?'

I remind myself that Antoinette is actually a good neighbour – she raps my front door if I forget to put the bin out and she'll pull the weeds up from round our gateposts when she's doing her own.

Suddenly, I think I have to trust someone, and Antoinette has lived beside us forever.

'If I tell you what it was about, do you promise to keep it to yourself?' I say.

Her face takes on a look of concern. 'Course I will, sweetheart,' she says.

'There's something not right across the road,' I say. 'At least, there's either something wrong there, or there's something wrong with me.'

'Across the road? Which house? The Wrights?'

The Wrights are an elderly couple. Sprightly, but elderly. Jim was something senior in the council. I don't know what Marjorie did. Their front garden is immaculate.

'No, not the Wrights. Next door. The Kennedys,' I say.

'What's up with the Kennedys?' Antoinette says. 'Apart from the obvious.'

'I'm not sure,' I say. 'That's why it's so difficult talking to the police about it. Well, it's just that I thought I saw Kim Kennedy on a train in London last week, but Kevin insists it wasn't her. He says she's in Galway. At first I thought Kim might be cheating, but do you think she's the type? You seem to know them better than I do.'

'You spoke to the police because you suspected Kim Kennedy might be cheating on her husband?' Antoinette says.

'No! No, that was just a thought I had at first. But there's something about Kevin, and now he's made a big show of booking them a holiday through a travel agent, as if to make it very clear that they're making plans – when did you last book a holiday through a travel agent, Antoinette? I'm not talking about a safari, I'm just talking about a couple of weeks in France.'

'I don't know anyone who doesn't book it themselves online these days,' Antoinette says. 'But if you saw Kim alive and well on a train in London, what are you worried about? If you're right, then he hasn't harmed her.'

'I've tried saying exactly that to myself,' I say. 'Oh, look, it's probably nothing. Forget I said anything. But what did you mean, "apart from the obvious"?'

'What?' says Antoinette.

'Before, you said, "What's up with the Kennedys? Apart from the obvious."'

'Oh, nothing much,' says Antoinette. 'I've just heard them a few times, when I've been walking Jinx at night.'

Jinx is Antoinette's sister's springer spaniel, who lives round the corner. She borrows him sometimes.

'What have you heard?' I say.

'Rows. Loud ones.'

'Just words?' I say. 'Or did you ever think there was violence?'

'I've heard the odd crash. I just thought they were a bit fiery, though. Some couples thrive on drama.'

'Well, I did my bit,' I say. 'I told the police what I saw, and there's not much more I can do.'

'Is it possible you just *thought* it was Kim?'

'Yes, of course.' No. She was three feet away from me. 'Look, forget about it.'

'And you'll stop worrying?'

'Yep.' Don't be kind to me or I'll cry.

I flap round to the back door, let myself in, and kick off my flip-flops to feel the cool tiles on my skin.

I didn't know the Kennedys rowed. Lots of couples row. Joe and I rowed until I realised that there was no point, because I did not move him, not in anger or in distress. Other couples use it, I understand, as a way of clearing the air or even as a prelude to sex. So it could be nothing.

Or it could be like a child with a note to get them out of swimming. Another tiny piece of a bigger picture.

5

Mum is having a good day. The hairdresser came this morning and gave her a shampoo and blow-dry and the new cook has turned out to be rather more gifted than the last one.

'We had eggs Benedict for breakfast,' Mum crows. 'I haven't had eggs Benedict since Michael took me to New York for our silver wedding.'

That's a genuine memory. All right, so it would have been more appropriate to call him 'your father' when talking to me, instead of Michael – but that was his name and they did go to New York to celebrate twenty-five years of marriage.

The sad thing is, it was just after they came back that Mum started having problems. We thought it was depression, at first. So did Dr Harbinson, Mum's GP. He gave her anti-depressants and she tried to walk a lot, even though she said she was having difficulties with balance too.

We all kept waiting for the anti-depressants to work. Dr Harbinson told us to give it time, these sorts of medication required a waiting period before delivering maximum effect. After a year he conceded it might not be simple depression after all, it might be the menopause, and Mum started on hormone replacement therapy.

The thing that Dad kept pointing out was that, when they watched *Cracker* and *NYPD Blue*, which would have been right up Mum's street, she struggled to follow the plots. He knew at gut level that something was wrong, but, like me, he listened to the doctor and trusted that the drugs would work.

'Here,' Linzi says. 'Don't you live in Parnell Park, Alice?'

'Yes!' I say. 'Do you know it?'

'Just across from the school? Runs from the main road to the park gates?'

'That's right,' I say. 'It's a great spot. No through traffic, because of the gates, but lots of dog-walkers on their way to the public gardens, so there's always someone about, which keeps the burglars away.'

'It's real old, isn't it?' Linzi says.

'Oldish,' I say. '1937. Someone told us that every house in the street is different in some small way, because the builder thought it would be boring to build thirty-two identical houses. It's mainly the porches and the windows that are distinctive, from what I can see.'

'They've real big gardens too, don't they?' Linzi says.

'Not huge, but they're bigger than anything you'd get with a new build. A developer today would say you could squeeze another house or two in there.'

'I know,' Linzi says, and smiles. 'No, the reason I'm asking is I know a girl who lives in Parnell Park. Kim Atchison. I was in her class at school, when my daddy got moved to Coleraine. We only went up there for a year, but I always remember Kim because we were in the same maths class and when the teacher made a Venn diagram of us, me and Kim were the only two in the middle bit because we were both left-handed and we both had attached earlobes.'

My heart had started to bang against my ribs at the word 'Kim'.

'I don't know any Atchisons,' I say. 'But there's a Kim Kennedy.'

'Does her husband work for a newspaper?' Linzi asks.

'Yes!' I say.

'Aye, that's her,' says Linzi. 'Long red hair?'

'Yes!' I say.

'Yeah, she was in my class,' Linzi says, smiling. 'People said her granda owned half of County Antrim, but she didn't seem that posh to me. I don't think they've any kids, yet – do they?'

'No. No, they don't,' I say.

'Not like me. I's pregnant at seventeen,' Linzi says. 'But our Alanis is brilliant with my younger ones. I wouldn't change a thing.'

'Have you seen Kim since you found out you were both living in the same town?' I ask, trying to keep the tremor I feel out of my voice but hoping, hoping, hoping that Linzi will be a conduit for some more information. I thought I had put this one to bed, but I haven't. I so haven't.

'No. I just came across her on Facebook,' Linzi says.

Facebook! Of course. That should have been the first place I looked. I joined up last year, gave it a few months, then retired, over-stimulated and exhausted. As someone who struggles to cope in a TK Maxx, I should have realised that the huge, messy vastness of a social network site would be too much for me.

Joe could help me. He could steer me directly to the relevant information. If it weren't for his social media friends, Joe would have no-one. Except me, which is the terrifying thing, of course, and is the reason I keep a month's worth of supplies in the freezer and Kate's number taped to the fridge.

I leave Mum to the promise of cod mornay and scalloped potatoes.

I must get home to look for Kim Kennedy's Facebook presence.

6

Joe is working out on the home gym in the little back bedroom when I return, but is happy to stop and help. He likes a project. I watch his face as he confidently fires up his laptop. He got his mother's blue eyes and his father's dark hair, a sensuous mouth apparently from neither of them, and is so much more beautiful than both. Apart from the obvious, to use Antoinette's phrase.

'OK. And the name you want me to search for?' he says.

'Kim Kennedy,' I say.

'Kim Kennedy, as in the woman from across the road?' Joe says. 'Why do you want to check her out on Facebook?'

'I just do,' I say. 'Any more information is on a strictly need-to-know basis, as there's a good chance I'm making a fool of myself and the fewer people who are aware of that, the better.'

Joe looks at me with his eyebrows raised.

'Indulge me,' I say.

I tuck myself in beside Joe on the sofa, so I can see what he can see.

'Just Kim?' Joe asks. 'Not Kimberly?'

'Just Kim, I think,' I say. 'I haven't heard anyone call her anything else.'

'O-K,' Joe says.

It is a matter of seconds.

Up she pops.

'That's her!' I say. 'That was quick.'

'You're already friends with her. You must have added her when you were on Facebook before,' Joe says.

This is entirely possible – I added absolutely everyone who asked; I thought it would be rude not to. I couldn't possibly keep track of them all then, much less now. No wonder I quickly found the whole thing overwhelming.

'This is great, Joe. Can you get me some more material? Another picture?'

'I can probably get you hundreds,' Joe says.

Another second and we're in again.

'That's definitely her,' I say. 'So, is this chronological? I mean, are these posts the most recent?'

'This one here is the very most recent. And ... if you scroll, like so, you can go back days, weeks, months, years.'

'Brilliant.'

'What's all this about?' Joe says, with a curious smile.

'You'd laugh at me if I told you.'

'If I promise not to?' Joe asks.

I don't reply.

'If I make you an iced coffee?'

Joe's world is so limited, I feel mean keeping any comings and goings of the wider sphere from him, so I tell him.

'You have literally no evidence that anything untoward has happened.'

'It never occurred to me the police would come here,' I say. 'I'd have gone to the station if I'd thought that. Anyway, they won't be back – they've decided I'm an unreliable witness.'

'Good,' Joe says. 'If I'd known you were going all Miss Marple over what sounds like a bit of extramarital activity, I wouldn't have helped you.'

'So you think it's an affair,' I say.

'It's the most obvious conclusion.'

'At least that means you believe I really saw her.'

'Of course I believe you – the science backs you up. Human beings have amazing powers to recognise the configuration of familiar faces, even from low-quality or poorly lit images. You weren't looking at a bad photograph, you saw the actual person. It's highly unlikely you got it wrong. That doesn't mean I think you should be poking your nose in, though.'

'I'm not being a busybody ...' I begin.

'I know you're not,' Joe says. 'Look, I understand why you're doing this. Because of ... before. But the evidence, this time, is non-existent.'

'Just let me take a quick look. To put my mind at rest. If everything seems normal, then I'll drop it.'

Joe sighs, sets the laptop down on the sofa beside me and goes off, I hope to make that iced coffee.

I'm just about to look at Kim's posts, when the telephone rings. It's the care home. Mum is distressed and is asking for me. The staff think she might have an ear infection and have called the doctor, but would I come anyway? What can I say? I change out of my shorts into a clean pair of jeans, brush my teeth and put up my hair.

The right indicator light fails almost all the way there, then suddenly rights itself when I go over an old pothole.

Mum is lying on her bed, weeping a little. Linzi's shift has finished, but Margarida is nice too.

'Your mum got sick about two hours ago,' she says. 'At first, we thought she just had the blues, but now we think she might be in pain. Maybe her ear. We've asked her, but she won't tell us anything.'

'Mum?' I say. I pull a vinyl-covered chair over to her bedside. 'Mum?' I sit down.

Margarida waits.

'I'm worried about your father,' Mum says. So she remembers who I am, right now. But she has forgotten that Dad is dead. 'It's too much for him, looking after me, the way I am.'

The first time she talked like this, like Dad was still alive, I thought I was supposed to put her straight. I told her – very gently, but I told her – that Dad had died two years earlier. I reminded her she had attended the funeral, talked about the music we'd had, the people who had said nice things about him.

31

She was horrified, heartbroken. It was as if she'd just been bereaved all over again. I resolved never to put her through that from then on. In our chats now, everyone she ever knew is still alive, as far as we're both concerned – Dad, my grandparents, Master Polly whose pet she was at school, Sheila, her childhood dog. They've all come back, I could almost say 'to haunt us'.

The doctor comes and I withdraw while he examines Mum, with Margarida's help.

It happens to be time for the tea trolley and I am given a cup in the corridor, where there isn't much to look at except the pattern on the carpet and a few faded framed prints of Regency ladies.

When the doctor re-emerges, he says there is some redness inside the ear, but nothing in her throat and her chest sounds clear. He will prescribe a course of antibiotics and some analgesia. Infection in the body can have strange effects on the elderly, particularly in institutions, he tells me, so I am not to be alarmed if 'Mum' – he refers to her as 'Mum' – seems confused or irritable. Margarida catches my eye at this and makes a barely perceptible comic face, as if to say, 'So what else is new?' but I see it, and appreciate it.

I hang around while Mum's medication is sorted out and Margarida gives her a tall glass with a straw in it, to encourage her to drink.

Mum sleeps then and Margarida tells me to go, I look tired. But she says it kindly.

I *am* tired. The heat makes it difficult to sleep and the light wakens me early.

On the way home, driving the same route I take every day, I can't remember which lane I need to get round the bottom of the town. I choose the wrong one, then panic and almost pull out in front of a BMW because the indicator light has picked that exact moment to pack up again and the driver can't see me signalling. I end up having to go round the whole thing again, getting the right lane this time.

There are six photographs of Kim on holiday in Galway, posted in the last few days. One is of her holding up a full pint of Guinness and grinning. It looks like it was taken at a table outside a pub. Another is captioned 'Session at Spiddal' and shows Kim with a *bodhrán*. There are others, but it is the last one that makes me flush. It is Kim smiling for the camera outside the university. I've been there myself, years ago, with Kate in fact, when she was still considering her options.

My hand is trembling a little as I click onto the picture for a better look.

'Joe,' I call. 'Joe, where are you?'

I lift up the open laptop and practically run to the hall.

'Come and see this,' I say.

Joe appears from the kitchen, holding a saucepan and a wooden spoon.

'Can it wait five minutes?' he says. 'This sauce will go lumpy if I leave it.'

I have to be reasonable.

'But only five minutes,' I say.

I can hardly sit down. I could flick on the evening news, but I don't actually want to be distracted.

Finally, Joe comes in.

'OK. What is it?' he says.

'Look,' I say. The screen has gone blank and I have to put my password in again to call up the photograph.

When Joe sees that I am back on Kim's Facebook profile, his interest dies. 'I thought you were dropping this,' he says.

'But look. Look at the picture.'

Kim is sitting on a bench. Behind her there is gorgeous pink cherry blossom.

'So what am I supposed to be looking at?' Joe says.

'It's cherry blossom,' I say. 'In July? I don't think so. This picture can't have been taken this week – it's months old. It's a scam, Joe, a ruse. I told you Kim Kennedy wasn't in Galway last week and this proves it.'

Joe is quiet for a minute.

Then he says, 'Let's say for just a moment that you're right, and there is something strange going on. It could still be an affair. Kevin might be the innocent party. She could be trying to pull the wool over his eyes with these pictures.'

'Or he could've posted them to make it look like she was where he said she was,' I say.

'It's possible,' Joe says. 'But why? For what purpose?'

'I don't know yet,' I say.

'I'm not saying it's nothing,' Joe says. 'But I still think the most likely explanation is an illicit trip with a lover. You'll just have to wait and see if Kim comes back safe and sound.'

This is Thursday. I saw Kim in East Croydon station last

Friday. I will ask Antoinette to ask Kevin when she is due back 'from Galway'. See what he says.

I will also trawl through those Facebook postings for anything, anything that might be a clue. If I can't sleep, I might as well be doing something useful.

7

The night staff reported that Mum slept well, Linzi tells me. They gave her an antibiotic and painkillers after supper and she was asleep by 8.30 p.m..

'It could've been working on her for a few days,' Linzi says. 'Sometimes I think the wee residents know there's something not right, but they don't know what it is, so they don't say anything. If they'd said something, we could maybe have done something sooner.'

Exactly, I think, but I'm not talking about Mum.

'Here, your daddy must've been some man,' Linzi says.

I smile.

'Why, what has she said?'

'She's been talking about him a lot just lately,' Linzi says.

'She told us he serenades her every night, and he grows roses for her and picks her one every day, and he fills in the crossword with "I love you, Ruby" and just leaves it for her to find.'

'That was all true,' I say. 'He was the kindest of men, and I didn't appreciate that not all men were until I married one who wasn't.'

Linzi's eyebrows couldn't go any higher.

'Ooooh, Alice,' she says. 'That's a bit of a conversation stopper.'

'Sorry,' I say. 'Ancient history.'

'Alanis's daddy was a tube,' Linzi says. 'But I got married again in my thirties and Lawrence is a good 'un. See if I'm working here till seven? He'll have fed the youngsters and have my dinner all ready for me coming home. Here, did you tell Kim Atchison I was asking about her?'

'Not yet,' I say. 'I think she's away at the moment. Her husband said something about her visiting a friend in Galway.'

'Good for her,' Linzi says. 'She was a bit of a loner when I knew her. She didn't really have friends. You sign in there and I'll bring you round to the room. You can take Ruby out to the courtyard if you want, get a bit of the sun.'

Even as I am walking the short distance to the day room, my thoughts stray back to Kim. There is nothing in the Facebook posts I scrolled through that would raise alarm in anyone else, but again I hear John, my first aid trainer, saying, 'If you're just not happy ...'

The thing is, there is a difference between Kim's older posts and the recent ones. The ones from months ago notify of her experiences at the gym, her attendance at a wedding, a christening, her head-of-department taking part in a half-marathon. She shares memes about the tedium of work and the joys of alcohol. Then, in the last few weeks, something subtly changes. The posts start to feature not what Kim has just done, but what she is planning to do. She and Kevin are looking at IKEA kitchens. They are buying paint for Kevin's study. (What does Kevin study, by the way?) They are thinking of getting a puppy, or would a rescue dog be a better idea? And it's all so normal, so unremarkable, that I know I am clutching at straws to say that this could be Kevin, deliberately painting a picture of a thriving marriage, of a couple with a future. Except there's something else. In the older posts, Kim writes of each 'special occasion' but she spells it 'occassion', with two s's. She also doesn't know the difference between 'it's' with an apostrophe and 'its' without. The author of the recent posts has no such problems.

'Hi, Mum,' I say. She is in her usual chair, looking at a magazine. A casual caller would think she is reading it, but Mum can't read any more. She still likes looking at the pictures, though.

'What've you got there?' I ask.

'*The People's Friend*,' she says. 'Mrs Simpson always passes it on to Mummy after she's read it.'

I raise it slightly and peek at the cover. It is *Take a Break*.

'Remember when you and Dad used to enter all the magazine competitions,' I say. 'You won a couple of Christmas hampers, and a radio, and a camera. You always wanted to win a holiday, but it never quite happened.'

'Mummy's taking me to Bangor,' Mum says. 'The boys are staying at home to help Daddy.'

Another genuine memory, I think – I remember when we cleared out Gran's things, seeing a receipt for a guest house in Bangor, and the itemised bill. My grandfather couldn't have left the farm. I suppose they were never able to have a family holiday.

'Would you like to go outside, Mum?' I say.

'Yes, I have a bit of weeding to do,' Mum says. 'I'd rather get it done now, before it gets any hotter. I have sheets to hang out too.'

I have decided to clip the small privet hedge at the front. This has nothing to do with horticulture and everything to do with spying. I have no idea what I imagine I can detect from simply being outside across the road from the Kennedys' house, but it is as though a magnet is pulling me out there.

The front of our house really is looking shabby. It's ten years since the masonry was painted, five or six for the woodwork. Most houses in the street have PVC windows now, but not ours. We don't even have double-glazing. I simply don't have the money for these jobs.

The truth is, we can't afford the maintenance for an older house like this. I have often wished we could sell up, trade her in for a smaller new build, but it's not as easy as that. With no savings, Joe must be entitled to some sort of benefits, I'm sure, which could make all the difference, but the process would be unbearable, so we limp along on my subbing money, which is more than enough for food and all the basics, and I am grateful for this, but there's really no immediate prospect of paying for scaffolding and a painter, or changing the Corsa.

There are voices coming up Kevin's garden path, and the creak of the metal side gate. I push my clippings together with my foot to try and make it look like a convincing pile.

It is Kevin and Antoinette and they are laughing.

Kevin doesn't stop at his gateway. He comes across the road to my side with Antoinette.

'Looking luscious,' he says to me, pauses, then adds, 'your box.'

The remark is designed to embarrass, and it works. He is playing on words – I am sure he knows all the hedges in the street are privet. I wish I could think of a whip-smart retort, but my brain seems to stall when Kevin is around.

'I hear you think I've murdered my wife,' he says.

Antoinette's hands fly to her face and her eyes widen in horror.

'Sorry!' she mouths at me. I see now that she has the look of someone who's had a couple of glasses of wine.

I cannot think of a single word to say. I feel morally obliged to look at Kevin, but I do so dumbly. I am trembling.

'I don't think I actually said that,' I say.

'What did you *actually* say, then?' says Kevin, but he seems more amused than affronted. 'What do you *actually* think I'm up to? Oh, yes, I remember. I'm making sure everyone knows Kim and I are planning a future together so that, when her dead body turns up somewhere, the police won't think it was me and the coroner won't record it as suicide and stop me getting my hands on the insurance money – isn't that your theory, *actually*?'

Just for a moment, I forget to be embarrassed, as I think how plausible this proposition sounds. But if it were true, Kevin would hardly be setting it out so neatly in front of me, would he?

He does the lopsided smile. He certainly doesn't seem anxious. Maybe it *is* Kim who is the liar. Maybe Kevin really believes she is in Galway.

'I'm going for a lie-down,' Antoinette says. 'It's too hot.'

'Me too,' Kevin says. 'I'm working later.'

They drift away and I soon decide I've had enough of the hedge-clipping charade. Before I can even go and look for a brush for the clippings, though, Kevin is back. He grabs my wrist. The amused look is gone.

'I didn't want to embarrass you in front of your friend, *Alice*,' he hisses, 'but just keep your nose out of my business in future. I'm not the one with blinds on all the windows. I'm not the one with something to hide, so just remember that, you nosey bitch.'

'I heard him,' Joe says, when I go inside. I see that the front-room window is open. 'He's got a fucking nerve, talking to you like that.'

'It doesn't mean anything,' I say, looking at myself in the mirror to see if it is obvious how shaken I am. 'It doesn't mean he knows anything about you and it doesn't mean he's up to anything re Kim.'

'It proves he's got a nasty streak,' Joe says. 'Well, there are two of us against one of him.'

He pads out to the kitchen in his bare feet. I hear the un-kiss of the fridge door opening and a clinking sound.

He returns with two large glasses of the Chilean white we've taken to. I see that he is livid.

'People like him underestimate people like us,' he says. 'Let's be smarter than him. If his wife *is* cheating on him in London, then he's getting what he deserves. But if he's up to something, let's get him, Mum.'

8

Bikkie is stretched out on her bed in her bra and pants. She has opened the window and positioned the electric fan a foot away from her stomach, but she is still too hot. It is Friday night and she would like to get drunk, but she knows she won't.

The sound of traffic rarely lets up. She can hear voices at intervals and, occasionally, a dog barking. Bikkie would like a dog, but she isn't allowed that, just like she isn't allowed to get drunk.

Someone is playing music on a car radio with the windows down. She knows it's an oldie by Roxy Music, but she doesn't know what it's called. She isn't meant to listen to her own music these days, just the radio. At least she can choose which channel and doesn't have to put up with the old farts on Radio 4.

She is hungry, but no-one wants to cook in this heat. She gets up, opens some crisps and munches vacantly. It is even too hot to think.

During a brief lull in the traffic, she hears the woman across the road setting up her rattling tin stepladder to water her hanging baskets.

Bikkie would like to grow something. Something better than a plant, though, something like a baby. But this is out of the question. Her boyfriend would leave her, simple as.

She undoes her ponytail and looks for her brush. She only washed her hair this morning and already it is sticky and inclined to tangle. She plucks out a single white hair and throws it away in disgust. Apparently red hair like hers can go straight to white – bypassing grey – prematurely.

How come Portugal can cope with this sort of heat, and Greece? Just like Lapland doesn't grind to a halt when it snows. She tried to point this out to her boyfriend but he looked at her like she was stupid and started mansplaining about how it's not worth us spending serious money on something that only happens for a few days or weeks every few years, when Bikkie actually believes it's because we're just a bit crap.

Perhaps she will put her hair into a French plait. *Très chic*.

A foot spa filled with ice – that would be lovely.

She goes to the window. Two overweight women are vaping across the street. Bikkie doesn't smoke, although her boyfriend does. She'd rather keep her treats money for clothes. And tanning. She'll need a new bottle of tan soon.

One of the women looks directly up at her window and she steps back behind the curtain.

She could watch some TV to pass the time. No doubt there'll be an episode of *Escape to the Country* – there's always an episode of *Escape to the Country*. She sets her phone beside her on the bed. He'll be texting soon. She wills it to ring.

When she is feeling the most lonely she thinks she will leave this boyfriend and look for someone else. But she loves him.

9

'Alanis, this is Alice, Ruby's daughter,' Linzi says. 'Alice, this is Alanis, *my* daughter. She's doing her Health and Social Care and she's in here with us for the summer.'

Alanis is gorgeous. Her hair is baby blonde, like her mum's, even if they've both had a little help with that, but it is nature that has given her a simply very pretty face, big blue eyes and the hint of dimples. If Disney designed a girl-next-door with just a nod to Barbie, the result would be Alanis.

'She's beautiful,' I tell Linzi.

Alanis laughs and looks at her mum.

'When you get to my age, you stop merely thinking things and come out and say them,' I say. 'There's no point

46

appreciating good service or kindness or beauty and just keeping it to yourself.'

Alanis digs her hands into the low pockets on the front of her navy tunic, which she is wearing with leggings, slender tan ankles and Converse. 'Here, Ruby's some craic,' she says.

'She's feeling better, then?' I say.

'She's been great this past couple of days,' Linzi says.

'She doesn't like sharing a table in the dining room, but,' says Alanis.

'Ruby doesn't like the way some of them get on,' Linzi says. 'I probably wouldn't like it myself, shouting and taking their teeth out. It's no hassle to let her have a table on her own.'

'How're things going with the new cook?'

Linzi lowers her voice. 'Alice, he's amazing. He did Spanish chicken last night, with peppers and chorizo, and tonight it's supposed to be spiced pork fillet with shallots and apple, so we'll see what that's like. He still purees up everything for the wee residents that need it, but the ones that can eat it are getting, really, restaurant-standard food. Aren't they, Alanis?'

'Do they notice the difference?' I say.

'*What?*' Linzi says. 'We used to say it was terrible, the amount of food we were scraping into the bin. See now? Clean plates all round.'

I beam. I love the thought of all the oldies guzzling their grub. I imagine them stampeding to the dining room on their walking frames.

'Anyhow, that wee infection seems to be sorted, but there's another few days in the antibiotic still,' Linzi says. 'Go on through, sure. Me and Alanis have a wee change to do, I'll see you later.'

Mum is out for the count. Sometimes she falls asleep in her chair with her head tipped back and her mouth open, snoring. I don't like finding her that way. Today, though, her head has dropped forward and she is stooped silently over her lap, her Christopher Robin bob covering her face, so that I think of a child poring, fascinated, over some intriguing specimen.

I could wait a while, see if she wakens on her own.

'Your mummy's sleeping.' Mrs Lappin, oracle of the baldly obvious. If I engage with her at all, she will entrap me with one of her charmless, featureless, uninterruptable narratives. Easier to waken Mum and sit with my back to her neighbour.

'Hey, sleepyhead.' I take Mum's hand and give it a squeeze. She doesn't jolt, exactly, but she moves. 'Mum?'

There are a few imprecise sounds, like words, but not words, then she sits up and opens her eyes.

'It's me. Alice,' I say.

I can see from her face that she is disorientated.

'Everything's fine,' I say. 'It's Saturday afternoon.'

'Have I missed my hair appointment?' Mum says. She always went to the salon on Saturday afternoons before going out with Dad in the evenings – mainly dinner, but they looked out for a good film too, even a theatre show now and again.

'No, no you haven't missed your appointment.' If I keep it vague, it isn't lying.

'I need to get my highlights done,' Mum says. 'This strong sun bleaches the colour out too quickly.'

'My son's coming home from Canada, Ruby,' Mrs Lappin says, half-extending her upturned arm in Mum's direction and bouncing it gently at her, a crushed tissue in her loosely formed fist.

I should move to protect Mum, or Mrs Lappin will use her special powers of boring to ossify my mother in her chair, but I have had a thought and working it out is immediately consuming me. Kim Kennedy has a fabulous head of red hair, but is the colour all her own? Is there anything useful I can learn from her pattern of appointments, even if I could track down her hairdresser?

'Let's go for a walk, Mum,' I say, standing up, knowing that Mrs Lappin needs one or possibly two care assistants to get her out of her chair.

'I can't go far,' Mum says. 'I have a pavlova in a low oven for tomorrow.'

Until four or five years ago, tracking down Kim Kennedy's hairdresser would have been a week's work, trekking round town, down side streets, up stairs. I am hoping that won't be the case today. This is because we now have Salon School, a huge, shiny, porcelain-floored ground-level premises staffed by a large team of qualified stylists and an even larger squad of trainees. Students get stacks of commercial experience alongside tutorials, leading to an NVQ, and customers get a sliding scale of charges, depending on how big a chance they're willing to take. I don't go there, because my hairdresser of twenty years is one of the few people I think of as a friend, but a lot of people do go.

The big glass doors are thrown open in the afternoon heat

and I take a quick look inside as I walk past. There is a smart-looking cookie on the front desk, a woman around my age. I don't fancy my chances with her. I linger on the footpath outside, and dig in my bag for my phone, but really I am assessing the situation. The woman looks at her watch, and I sense a possibility. I fiddle with my screen. One missed call. I check in case it was Joe, but it was Antoinette. The woman behind the desk is calling someone over, and my one-arm bandit spins up Yes, Yes, Yes as I see that she is very young and, I believe, left in charge of the front desk while her senior colleague goes on a break.

When the older woman leaves, I plunge through the open doors, then hesitate, pull myself together.

'Hello,' I say, pushing my hair out of my eyes. 'I wonder if you can help me. My friend has gone on holiday and she entrusted me with making a hair appointment for her, for when she comes back. I'm afraid I've lost the little card with the day and time – is it possible you could give me a new one?'

With not a thought about Data Protection, the young girl does something on the computer, and asks, 'What's the wee name?'

'Kennedy,' I say. 'Kim Kennedy.'

'No problem. Let me see. Kennedy, Kennedy, Kennedy – oops, I've gone too far. Yes, here it is. That's just a wee trim?'

'Yes, that's right,' I say.

'That's Wednesday morning, a quarter to eleven, with Olivia.'

'Wednesday of next week?'

'Yes. Here, I'll give you a new wee card.'

'I'll take better care of this one.'

When I get back to the car, I call Antoinette.

'Hi, it's Ali,' I say. 'I had a missed call from you. What's up?'

'Ali, hi,' she says. 'Just a quick update. I engineered a little chat with Kevin Kennedy today, as promised, to try and find out when Kim's due back from wherever she really is. He said she comes back next Thursday.'

'Did you say Thursday?'

'Yeah, that's what he said.'

'Thanks, Antoinette.'

'No problem. Like you said, I owed you one.'

I slide back the driver's seat. I need to think. If Kim is lying about where she is and Kevin is in blissful ignorance, why has she made herself a hair appointment a day earlier than she will return? It makes no sense. But if Kevin is scheming something wicked, and trying to make it appear that Kim has a whole series of things organised to look forward to, maybe he's lost track of the finer details.

My hairdresser said, when I first talked about my family, 'So your husband is called Joe *and* your son is called Joe?'

'Yes.'

'That's actually quite nice,' she said.

'I don't know if it is, or not, but it was pretty much put to me as non-negotiable and I was so elated after the birth that everything seemed wonderful, even that. It was only later that I thought it might be a bit strange.'

'And you don't get mixed up?'

No. I didn't get mixed up. Not when it was quite clear that there was 'Joe' – the Joe I loved, and 'Joe' – the Joe I hated.

10

Bikkie has gone for a walk. She is wearing a big floppy hat, sunnies and the gladiator sandals that always make her feel like a bit of a bondage babe. She wasn't meant to go to the pharmacy, but it is the only place round here where she could buy tanning lotion, so she went anyway, then treated herself to a Magnum from the corner shop to stop herself thinking about the trouble she could be in.

There is nowhere to sit down and eat her lolly, so she just keeps walking. Last night's text was confusing.

Yo, Girl. They is snappin' at my ass. Stay low bit longer.

You can do this. We can do this. Together forever.

None of this was her idea. In fact, she said it was crazy

from the start. But she can't seem to say no to him. He didn't lie to her – he set out the whole thing, didn't sugarcoat it, said it would be hard, said it wouldn't be quick. But the way he told it, she'd felt they would have each other every step of the way, when in fact he has left her out on a limb.

Bikkie is starting to doubt the whole thing. This morning, she more or less decided she's going to tell him to call it all off. Could it have gone too far already, though? This is what she doesn't know. If they were caught this early, could she still go to prison?

She gets trapped in one of those side-to-side shuffles on the pavement with another pedestrian as they try to pass.

'Sorry,' he says, and smiles – she thinks the word is 'sheepishly'.

Bikkie walks on. She has taken a couple of steps when a voice calls, 'Excuse me!' and she turns to look.

It is the sheepish man again, and he is holding something up.

'Did you just drop your phone?'

Shit, Bikkie thinks. Her boyfriend would kill her if she lost that. But as she gets closer, she sees that it isn't hers.

'I guess I'll hand it in somewhere,' the man says. 'What's the name of this street, so I can say where I found it?'

This street? Bikkie doesn't know. She only knows that it's round the corner from Kidderminster Gardens.

'Two strangers, eh?' the man says. 'I'll pop in here and see what they can tell me.'

It is a small café. Bikkie has walked past it before and

thought of going in for a cappuccino. The door is open and she can hear the Italian coffee machine from the street.

The man hesitates for a moment, seems to weigh something up, then says, 'I don't suppose you'd like to join me for a coffee?'

He immediately looks embarrassed and Bikkie thinks this isn't something he does every day. She knows she shouldn't, and she certainly can't tell her boyfriend, but then he doesn't tell her everything either, and she has had absolutely no-one to talk to for days.

'OK,' she says.

11

Kate rings from London. She sounds good. I can hear strumming in the background and she explains that Conall has managed to get himself guitar lessons from their next-door neighbour in return for some weeding.

'He's even re-strung Conall's guitar for him, so he can play it left-handed,' Kate says.

'You don't leave them alone, together?'

'No, no. They have the front room and I keep the door to the kitchen open,' Kate says. 'Also, bit of good news: George has managed to get himself a morning job as an administrator for a theatre group, so that's a few quid, and it won't interfere with his rehearsals.'

'That's fantastic,' I say.

'So, any progress with the August dates?'

What August dates? Kate and the kids are coming over, I know, but was I meant to be looking into something?

'The *Titanic* centre? You were going to check the date of Ruby's clinic to make sure you could come with us.'

I have absolutely no recollection of this, but I can see on the kitchen calendar that my mother's hospital clinic is scheduled in August, so I must have said it.

'Kate, I'm so sorry. I completely forgot,' I say. 'I promise I'll check it out and get back to you asap. Any thoughts on what else you'd like to do when you're here?'

'Pip fancies the zoo, but Conall and I aren't keen. We're pretty much in the zoos-aren't-OK camp. I thought we could have a day at the Ulster Museum. I know we went last year, but there's so much in it, and Cara wants to see the mummy this time. Maybe take in a couple of National Trust places too?'

'Do leave some time for just flopping about, though,' I say.

'Oh, definitely. Cara would happily spend the whole week curled up in an armchair in your book room, reading all your old Mary Plains, and Pip is hoping Antoinette will let him train Jinx again. And, of course, we want to have lots of time with Joe.'

Joe is brilliant with Kate's kids and they are brilliant for him. Because they have known him since they were babies, there was never that first meeting, that initial reaction. They've always known Joe with this strange face – I hate the term genetic *mutation*, but there it is, with its casual, devastating misguidance on when and how a face should grow – and so they are like an inner circle of chosen ones whom he lets in. He will write clues for a treasure hunt round the house, bake with Cara, invent quizzes for Pip. He and Conall will spend ages at night with the telescope. If things go very, very well, he might make it into the garden.

Of course Kate remembers Joe before. She's known him since *he* was a baby. She is the only person left, apart from me, who witnessed his extraordinary childhood trajectory. So clever, so popular, so beautiful. Great things were expected. And then this.

'Enough about us – how are *you*, Ali?'

'Still walking on air because I don't have to deal with that witch day in, day out,' I say. In London, I confided to Kate that I had been struggling big time with the classroom assistant in my last subbing post. She had worked with the permanent teacher, Mrs Lemon, for fifteen years and they had a certain way of doing absolutely everything. Tanya would never give me the heads-up, so that I could at least try and do things in the manner that was familiar to her and the children; she preferred to let me blunder on and only when the damage was done would she tell me the expected way to mark the register, or by what time it needed to be returned to the office, or the tune they usually used for the morning song, or that instruments were normally handed out – every little thing, really, that she could sabotage, she did, just by keeping her mouth shut until it was too late, and then smiling from the teeth out as she explained to me what Carol – Mrs Lemon – would have done.

'Put her out of your mind. I'm sure the next one you get

will love you and bring you coffee and a Penguin when you're on playground duty and make sure you never lose your red pen.'

'Red pen?' I say. 'Not these days, Kate. Apparently they're regarded as too aggressive. I use a turquoise Faber-Castell. I bought my first one in Ryman's, when I was staying with you in the flat in Crouch End, in fact, and now I'm addicted.'

I hear a smoke alarm start to shriek at Kate's end.

'Uh-oh.' Kate is shouting. 'I said Cara could make grilled cheese sandwiches for everyone. I'd better go and flap a tea towel about under the thingy for a bit. Sorry, Ali. Speak soon. Love to you both.'

'Everything OK with Kate?' Joe is passing through with a coffee mug on the way to the dishwasher, a paperback in his other hand.

'Yes, she sends her love,' I say. 'Listen, I had a bit of a bright idea earlier – at least, I thought it was a bright idea.'

'Relating to ...?'

'The Kennedy situation.'

Joe looks interested and I tell him what I learned at Salon School.

'Let the great mind mull it over while I make us a snack,' I say. 'I saw strawberries in Nicholson's and couldn't resist, and I went the whole hog and bought double cream. It'll just take me a few minutes to whip it up.'

12

'They say if you put cold water on your pulse points, it makes you feel better,' he says. 'So I've started running my wrists under the tap. I think it works.'

Now that they're face to face across the table, Bikkie sees that Dale is a little older than she first thought. He's nice-looking, though.

She's starting to relax. He hasn't asked her anything to scare her off, just stuck to the weather, the coffee, Wimbledon.

'Good choice,' he says, nodding to the corner. There's a jukebox and a couple of Mods hanging over it. They're playing *You Really Got Me*. 'Are you into music?'

There's a question. The answer is yes, she is. She is a total and utter diehard fan of Prince, and, if anything, she's listened to him even more since he passed than she did before. But not recently. It's not allowed, which means it's almost certainly not allowed to tell this man either.

'Not really,' she says.

'Oh, that's a shame,' Dale says. 'You're missing out. I'm a bit of a music nerd, myself. I have a room at home fitted out with shelves for all my vinyls.'

He stops and looks embarrassed, again. Bikkie thinks he is sorry he mentioned his place in case it sounds like he is trying to lure her there. She wants to reassure him.

'What's the one record you'd take to a desert island?' she asks, thinking some of that Radio 4 crap has rubbed off on her.

'Oh, don't make me choose,' he says, and Bikkie is delighted that she has made him smile. 'Don't they let you take a few?'

'To begin with, yes, but in the end you have to pick just one to save from the waves,' she says.

'That's impossible,' Dale says, but he has a go, anyhow, hesitating at Bowie, Elvis, The Beatles.

'For sheer songwriting genius, it's hard to look past Paul Simon,' he says, eyes off to the side as if he's trying to focus. 'But that's assuming we're talking about a track with lyrics. I'd be a big fan of Paganini, too, old Niccolò – I've actually adapted some of his stuff for electric guitar.'

Is he blushing? She thinks that he is.

'I really admire people who can play an instrument. I don't play anything at all,' she says.

'So what's your talent? I bet you've got one.'

But Bikkie doesn't. She wasn't all that bright at school, she can't run fast, she can speak a little bit of French and Spanish but not as much as she pretends, she's a crap cook, she can't knit anything more challenging than a thirty-centimetre square towards a patchwork blanket. The only thing people have ever expressed admiration for is her looks, which were purely a matter of luck. And they won't last forever.

She doesn't want to say any of this to Dale, though. Sitting here, with him, she's feeling steadily better. Where her boyfriend makes her feel like a hopeless little girl in need of constant supervision and direction, this man is treating her like a normal person, able to have a conversation, to hold opinions, to do for herself.

He is looking at her expectantly.

'I'm a pretty good show-jumper,' she says. She has no idea where the thought comes from – she has never been on a horse in her life, but there are no horses anywhere near here, so it's never going to be put to the test.

'Fantastic,' Dale says. 'Expensive, though, I'd say.'

'Very.'

'Where are your stables?'

She tries to think quickly of some place she passed on the train.

'Near Redhill,' she says.

'Don't really know it.' Ah, so he doesn't live locally. That's probably good. 'Don't really know this part of the country at all. Although, if things work out, that could be about to change. I'm here for a job interview, thought I'd take a week's holiday, look around a bit while I'm at it.'

'That's exciting. Have you had the interview yet?'

'Monday morning. Ten o'clock.'

'Nervous?'

'Yep. That's why I'm out walking so much, even in this heat. Trying to calm myself down. I'm glad I walked this way today, though.'

He looks directly at her for a nanosecond, then looks over her head towards the counter.

'Hey, do you want to get something to eat? I mean, not here – well, here if you want ...'

'I think they're closing,' Bikkie says, indicating with a slight tilt of her head a teenage girl starting to brush the floor. 'Look, I'm expecting a call this evening, so I have to get back, but' – she must be mad – what she is about to do definitely wouldn't be allowed – 'I could meet you on Monday, after your interview.'

Dale looks like she has just handed him a thousand pounds.

'There's a little park round the next corner, with a pond and a few ducks. I could see you there at one and you could tell me how the interview has gone.'

'If it's good, we can celebrate; if it's terrible, you can console me,' Dale says, then immediately looks worried that this presumes rather too much.

Bikkie just smiles. She genuinely hopes Monday morning goes well for Dale. Whatever else she's up to, she's not a bad person.

As she walks back to the flat, she wonders what it is about Dale that makes her want to behave better. The more her boyfriend calls her 'childish', or accuses her of being 'sulky' or, to use his wankerish word, 'churlish', the more she seems to act that way. With Dale, though, she's different.

13

The doorbell is ringing. I'm not even dressed yet. I look out the window, but I can't see who it is.

'Coming! Coming!' I clatter downstairs.

'Antoinette.'

'Morning, Ali. Sorry if I got you up, but I thought you'd want to see this, and I can't really hang onto it.'

She hands me a postcard. The picture is of a thatched, whitewashed cottage with a donkey standing by the window, laden with turf.

'Is it for me?' I ask.

'No, turn it over,' says Antoinette.

The first thing I look for is the addressee. It is Kevin Kennedy, 28 Parnell Park.

'The eight looks a bit like a three – it got delivered to my house by mistake,' says Antoinette. 'I think it's a holiday postie, not the usual guy. As soon as I saw it, I thought, I must show Ali, put her mind at rest.'

I don't feel good about reading the message, but I do it anyway.

'Hi, Kevin. Having fun in the sun – who needs Ibiza? Good music, good food, good swimming, good craic. Missing you. Promise to paint study when I get back. Love from Kim.'

'It's definitely from her – I know she makes the dot over the "i" in "Kim" into a little heart like that; I've seen it on their Christmas card.'

Me too.

'So she really is in Galway,' Antoinette says. 'I just thought you'd want to see for yourself before I stick it through Kevin's letterbox.'

'Thanks,' I say. 'I feel a bit foolish now.'

I make myself some wheaten toast and cut up a slippery nectarine. When Antoinette showed me the card, my instant reaction was, *Well, that's that, then.* But within seconds I was wondering how Kevin might have staged it. This thought appals me. It is as if I am so unwilling to be wrong that I will consider the most convoluted possibilities rather than accept the obvious. Kevin has been in Parnell Park all week – he could not have gone to Galway and sent a postcard purporting to be from his wife. And anyway, the card is written in her hand-writing, I'm sure of it.

I knock on Joe's bedroom door. 'Can I come in?'

Perched on the end of his bed, I tell him about the card.

Joe takes in a big, sleepy breath and stretches out his face. 'Still doesn't explain the cherry blossom outside the university.'

'I've thought about that – couldn't Kim just have posted a nice Galway picture from an earlier trip? Maybe she wanted to make a montage of local scenes and landmarks. In the light of this card, it hardly looks like damning evidence.'

'Well, I say we do something evil to Kevin anyway. He's still a cunt.'

'You know how I feel about that word. It's used by men who hate women. It's misogynistic. There is no male equivalent.'

'But sometimes it's the only word that will do.'

'Just call him a "dick", if you have to call him anything.'

'Not the same thing at all. Calling someone a bit of a dick can be almost affectionate.'

'Well, think of something else, then. I don't want to hear that word again.'

'You still won this year's round of "the game", though. Against George. Even without Kim – you still met your old teacher in Bella Italia, so you don't have to concede defeat.'

Under the shower, I decide it is time to move on. I have a whole, lovely summer stretching out ahead of me and it would be such a waste to spend it obsessing about the neighbours. Kim will come home on Thursday, she will laugh when Kevin tells her I thought he'd done her in – which is not strictly true, anyway – and we will tread warily round each other in the Park until the matter is forgotten.

It is a relief to draw a line under things. I listen to *Woman's Hour* while I get dressed, then go round the kitchen methodically, checking what we need from the supermarket. It's about time I did some cooking – I tend to leave it to Joe during term-time, but I'm sure he'd appreciate a break. Something with chicken and peppers, I think.

When I go outside, I find the weather has cooled and there is a breeze. Delicious.

I visit Mum, then drive past Lidl and straight to Nicholson's.

I might go to the cinema this week. It's any ticket for £3 on a Tuesday. I could invite Antoinette.

Chicken with red peppers and onions and plenty of paprika. And more strawberries for afters.

Joe and I are reading, with our bare feet up on the coffee table. We did have *Tupelo Honey* on in the background, but neither of us must have noticed when it came to an end.

The doorbell rings. Joe goes upstairs.

I pad across the parquet flooring, my feet sticking to it slightly.

'Kevin.' What now? I suppose he has come to gloat about the postcard.

'Ali. Look ... I know you don't invite people in, but could I have a word? Could you come outside? Or come over?'

I see no trace of hostility in his face, or amusement at my expense. I do not sense that he is trying to trick me, or readying to spring. He looks troubled. He looks genuine.

I wish I hadn't answered the door. I've just had my best day for a week, thinking about nothing but my shopping and dinner and reading my book, and I don't want to get sucked into anything resembling another episode of *Parnell Park*, the soap.

'Please.'

There is not even one small part of me that wants to know what this is about. I am not so much as mildly curious. But I cannot be unkind, and that 'Please' makes it impossible to close the door and resume my place on the sofa.

'OK. Let me just grab my keys and my flip-flops.'

There is a small sun terrace at the back of the Kennedys' house, with an unexpectedly ornate table and four chairs.

'Sit down.' It is a courtesy, not an order. 'Would it be all right if we had a glass of wine?'

He is being very tentative, quite unlike his usual confident self.

'Yes, of course.'

Kevin goes in the back door, re-emerges with two huge wine glasses, half-filled.

'I didn't ask – we don't have any white.'

'Red's fine.'

Kevin sits down opposite me, scratches his head. 'Ali, I owe you an apology. A big one.'

This is unexpected.

For better or worse, I am a sucker for contrition. Tell me you're sorry and I'll forgive you almost anything. Had my husband ever shown the slightest hint of repentance, I would have given him a hundred chances. I don't like to be disliked, by anyone. Even as I was suspecting Kevin, I much preferred to be in his good books than written out of them.

'Well, just to start with, I shouldn't have grabbed your arm like that, and I shouldn't have called you a bitch.'

It stings me again, just hearing him say it, even though he appears to be remorseful.

'You are nothing like a bitch. You're clearly a lovely person. You've never been anything other than welcoming to Kim and me since we came to Parnell Park. I was completely out of order and I want you to know that I've thought about it and I'm sorry.'

Should I apologise back? Is this the moment when I'm meant to say I'm sorry too, for suspecting him of some wrongdoing, for speaking to the police?

Before I can figure out an appropriate response, he's off again.

'But that's not all.' He takes a gulp of wine. 'I take it Antoinette's told you about the postcard?'

'Yes.' There's no need to say that I've actually seen it, read it.

'So, Kim was in Galway all the time. Swimming, drinking Guinness, having the craic.'

The penitent tone is gone again and that edge of menace has come back.

'And when she returns, she is going to paint my study, because she loves me.'

Kevin is looking at me as he talks, but something tells me that the hint of venom in his words is not aimed at me, this time. It is for Kim.

I cannot stop myself from glancing at his ring finger. There is nothing there. I try to find something else to look at in the garden. Did Kevin used to wear a wedding ring? Has he removed it, or did he never have one in the first place? I have looked for a wedding ring on a man's finger before, but only recently, and only those I hope are unmarried. Kevin wasn't available, so I wouldn't have checked.

'It was a lovely postcard, really – warm, affectionate. Unfortunately, the stamp had the queen's head on it.'

Kevin tips his wine back. It is all gone, already.

'When you thought you saw Kim in London, Ali, there's every possibility you were spot on. It's an Irish postcard all right, but she posted it in the UK – it's a British stamp. She's not exactly cut out for deceit, is she?'

I am stunned. Apart from Joe, nobody believed me about seeing Kim, and now that it seems I might be right. I don't want to be, because I can see in Kevin's face the beginning of the damage done by such betrayal.

What can I say? I never noticed the stamp – I was too caught up in the card itself. Is he sure? I can't ask that – of course he's sure.

'What will you do?'

'I don't know.'

'Has either of you ever ...?'

'Before? I never thought so, but I've spent all day looking back on a few situations and wondering. I don't know what I believe right now. Glass?'

I have been pecking nervously at my drink because I don't know how to behave in this situation and the result is that I have almost finished my wine. I don't particularly want a second one because I don't particularly want to be here, sitting with Kevin, learning what I am learning, but I cannot think of an escape strategy and at least another glass of wine would give me something to do with my hands.

'The thing is, I really loved her.' Kevin is bringing out two more, fuller glasses. 'She was beautiful, spontaneous, she made me laugh.'

'I'm genuinely sorry,' I say. 'I don't think people fully realise how much they harm someone's whole faith in the universe when they break a trust.'

'That's it exactly,' says Kevin. 'I can't stop going over things in my head – times she was late, times she went "for a spa weekend" with a friend from work; she went AWOL on Christmas Day, came home and said she'd picked up a puncture when she went to the garage shop for something, had to call out the AA to change the wheel – now I'm thinking: do I ever remember seeing any letters from the AA? And I don't. It might be nothing – it might be they email her instead of sending a letter, but the point is that I'm looking back at everything now and wondering. I can't switch it off.'

It is after a third glass of wine, lots of soul-searching from Kevin and very little contribution from me that it seems like an idea to put it out there about the photograph at the university.

'I knew it couldn't have been taken last week, because the cherry blossom was in full bloom.'

Kevin looks at me and nods and we just sit for a minute and don't speak.

'Did you mention that to the police too, about the photograph?' he asks.

'No. I hadn't spotted it then,' I say.

'Another?' Kevin is lifting my empty glass.

'No, I'd better not. Look, I need to go, while I'm still capable of getting across the road.'

'Sure,' Kevin says. 'Hey, I'll walk you back, you do look a bit wobbly.'

At my front door, I struggle to find the right words. 'I'm sorry,' I say.

'Me too,' Kevin says. 'For how I spoke to you, for myself, even for Kim, in a funny sort of way.'

He takes my door key from my hand and, as he leans in to turn it in the lock, I think for one mad moment that he is about to kiss me.

'Goodnight, Ali,' he says, stepping back. 'Thanks for listening.'

14

Bikkie is not happy. This morning her boyfriend texted her to say there was a change of plan. He needed time to think, to figure out what to do next. She was to keep doing exactly what they'd agreed, but must have her phone on all the time so he could contact her. She mustn't let it run out of credit or battery.

The call unnerved her. It was all right for him. She was the one taking all the risks, telling all the lies, putting up with all the hardships. He hadn't even told her why they had to alter their arrangements, what had happened.

Was there any way they could just drop the whole business? Walk away? But she doesn't even know if he's done that thing with the clothes yet, so how can she tell? If he's already done that, the police will be searching and that means they can't go back – it's either freedom or prison.

She'd had such a lovely day today. She'd met Dale in the little park. He'd brought bread for the ducks.

'Well, how did it go?' she said.

He grinned shyly. 'I don't want to seem cocky, but it went really well. Here,' and he gave her the plastic bag of bread.

'They're so cute!' Bikkie said, as the ducks waddled out of the water and up the grass to meet them. 'How many were on the interview panel?'

'Three. Two blokes and a woman. They were mechanics, she was HR. They gave me a practical task first, then questions.'

'How was the practical?' Bikkie asked. 'I don't know anything about being a mechanic, so don't say anything technical.'

Dale laughed. 'Don't worry – I don't know anything about show-jumping. It was an engine from a vintage motorbike. An old Triumph. I had to "do stuff" with it – that's not too technical for you, is it?'

Bikkie liked the way Dale couldn't quite manage to look at her even when they were talking. He threw little bits of bread to the ducks, and only stole quick glances in her direction. Was 'furtive' the right word?

An ice-cream van pulled up at the park gates, the chimes ringing.

'Want anything?' Dale said.

Bikkie said she'd take a Diet Coke, if they had any. When he went off to ask, she checked her phone. Nothing.

'I got you a cup.' Dale held up a paper beaker. 'I once saw a girl get stung in the mouth by a wasp that had flown into her can. Don't want that to happen to you.'

Bikkie shuddered at the thought of it, but it was so nice of Dale to want to protect her. Her boyfriend never seemed to think like that.

They sat down on a wooden bench near the water.

'You really take care in the sun,' Dale said. He meant her big hat and sunglasses. 'Very smart.'

'I'm so fair-skinned – don't let this sun-kissed glow fool you, it's from a bottle – I'm not really built for this weather, although I love it.'

'Most girls wouldn't admit they were faking it, even when their orange knuckles stand out a mile.'

If only he knew how much she was really hiding. Bikkie had been toying with the idea of a kind of holiday romance with Dale. He was only here for a week, so it wasn't going to go anywhere, and if he did start to get too attached, she could just melt away again – he didn't know how to contact her. For a moment, though, she imagined leaving her boyfriend, abandoning their crazy scheme, going to Dale. What if she left the flat, locked the door behind her and simply didn't go back? Could she live under the radar until it all went away?

What if she told Dale everything? Would he go to the police, or would he try to protect her, like from the wasp? But she'd be asking for a lot more than a paper cup, wouldn't she?

Dale had brought a rug. Now that the ducks had gone back in the water, Bikkie and Dale walked round to where there were some big, leafy trees, laid the rug on the ground and sat on it.

If he lies down, it means he wants me, Bikkie told herself.

Dale sat with his legs crossed, making a daisy chain which was obviously going to be for her. Bikkie propped herself up on her elbows and gazed ahead.

'When were you happiest, out of all the times in your life?' she said.

'"Which record would you take to a desert island?" "When were you the happiest?" You don't ask the easy questions, do you, Charlotte?'

She had lied about her name. She had to.

Bikkie giggled.

'OK. When I was about ten years old, my friends and I spent the entire school holidays building rafts,' Dale said. 'The sun was shining, I was with my mates, no adult interference, daylight from 5 a.m. until ten at night, making something. Loved it. How about you?'

Bikkie thought. There was nothing. Not when she was a kid, not when she was a teenager. She'd believed she'd cracked it when she met her boyfriend, who was everything she was not. But she mustn't be very good at being happy, because that wasn't a word she could use to describe their situation now. If her boyfriend was right, though, when all this was over they'd get their fairy-tale ending. They'd be minted. They could go anywhere, do anything. Life would be like a permanent holiday – *if* he was right.

'When I got my first pony,' Bikkie said. 'That's when I was happiest.'

Later, as they got ready to leave the park, Bikkie folded the rug and Dale carefully gathered up the bread bag, the Diet

Coke can, the paper cup and the sticks and wrappers from the two Soleros they'd had from the van.

He looked sheepish, again.

'I don't like leaving litter. We have to look after the planet.'

Bikkie'd thought she would like to kiss him for that.

Now it is evening and she is back at the flat. She is lying down with a cold face cloth on her forehead and the fan switched up full. The banging from the other room starts up again. She is not in the mood. When it doesn't stop, she lifts a sandal and thumps on the pipes that run along the bottom of the wall.

'Shut up. Just shut up.'

15

When I went to Mount Charles this morning, Mum was outside in the courtyard. Alanis had taken a group of the residents there to paint. I use the term loosely. She had put them in front of a pretty display of multicoloured sweet pea and they were making pictures. Someone – Alanis, presumably – had painted green stems on white pages and she was going round the oldies painting the pads of their fingers pink, purple and cerise, and plonking them on the paper. The effect was really rather nice. Margarida was following her with a pile of wipes, cleaning off the paint again before the residents got it on their faces or clothes or each other.

Mrs Lappin had snared someone else's inexperienced

visitor. They were sitting side by side and Mrs Lappin had her hand on the woman's arm. I knew the weight of that hand. I heard Mrs Lappin say, 'My mummy was one of the *Ballywalter* Nesbitts' and I knew it was going to be a long sermon. A little shard of conscience urged me to go over and try to prise the new visitor free, but I reasoned, selfishly, that she had to learn, as we'd all had to learn.

'I like your picture, Mum. You used to grow wonderful sweet pea.' I nearly said '... at the bungalow', but I wasn't even sure if she knew she wasn't still there.

'I did. I grew it from seed, too,' Mum said. I loved it when she was this lucid.

We didn't stay out for long – the sun was so hot and it's easy for the elderly to become dehydrated, which is bad news all round.

When we returned to the day room, the new cook had sent through jugs of water with sprigs of fresh mint in them.

With Mum safely in her chair, I grabbed Mrs Lappin's latest victim, lowered my voice.

'Word to the wise. It's OK to sit with your back to Mrs Lappin. Everybody's been there, everyone understands.'

The woman looked shocked, bewildered, then insight passed across her face and she smiled just a little. 'Oh, thank you. I'm new to all this. I didn't want to offend her, but I did really come here to talk to my aunt, and I've hardly got speaking to her at all.'

'Who's your aunt?'

'Phyllis. Over there in the purple blouse.'

'Oh yes, I know her. She used to work in the little coffee

shop near Hillsborough Park. My mum and dad went there sometimes. She remembered Mum.'

'She probably remembered their order.' The woman was delighted to have made some connection. 'She still has a mind like a trap, but she can't really get about now, and the arthritis in her hands is so bad she can't even feed herself, so we had to put her in here. She couldn't come to us – she can't manage the stairs and we don't have a downstairs toilet. I wouldn't ask it of Colin anyway. It's awful, isn't it, growing old.'

'Mount Charles was a good choice,' I said. 'Mum's been here ever since my dad died and I can honestly say she's happy. The staff are fab, it's a nice building and they've just got a new cook who seems to be a bit special. I don't know what I'd have done if Mum had been unhappy – it would've been terrible; it wasn't feasible for her to live with me, either. Luckily, it seems to have worked out pretty well.'

'Phyllis sometimes grips my hand when I'm going, and tells me not to leave her.'

'Ah. Yes, Mum used to do that too. I went home and cried. But it passed, if that helps. I think Mum thinks of the girls here as family now, so she's not so attached to me.'

We each drifted back to our own person. Margarida was massaging cream into Mrs Lappin's hands.

Antoinette doesn't fancy the cinema tonight – there's nothing she can be bothered to watch. She wants to go for a walk, though, once it cools down, and she'd like me to come too.

I call for her at eight, and she appears in cropped leggings, a running top and trainers. She looks great.

'Antoinette!' I say, and look miserably at how I am dressed. I am in jeans and a t-shirt, my one concession to our planned activity being my comfortable Earth Spirit sandals.

'It's not obligatory, Ali, I just felt like wearing the gear.' She pulls her front door behind her and puts the key in her bra. 'One Yale key is practical,' she says, 'a whole bunch would be a fetish.'

We wave to Jim Wright, who is putting weedkiller around his gateposts.

'Evening, Mr Wright!' Antoinette told me before that she cannot call the older residents in Parnell Park by their first names – even though they've all said she should – because she has called them Mr and Mrs ever since she was a little girl. Antoinette lives in the house she grew up in. She was 'a wee late one', much younger than her siblings. When her parents died, apparently she got to keep the place.

'Lovely evening, ladies,' Jim says, straightening up. He must be pushing eighty, but he's in good shape. When we first came to the Park, it quickly became apparent that all the residents deferred to him and he was the street's 'safe pair of hands' – in my case, this was almost literal as I felt sure that, if our house went on fire when we were in bed one night, I would shout out the window and Jim Wright would come with his ladder and I would pass Joe out to him and he would be saved.

'I heard there's to be rain tomorrow,' I say.

'Well, the farmers will certainly be happy to see it,' Jim says.

'The farmers are never happy,' says Antoinette. 'A couple of months ago they were telling us they couldn't graze their cattle because it had rained so much and they were paying a fortune for feed.'

'To be fair, I think it's been an unusually tricky year for them,' I say.

But Antoinette is only warming up. 'Mr Wright, explain this to me: we live in the Orchard County, surrounded by apple orchards, and very nice they are too. So why is it, when I want to buy a decent Braeburn, I'm paying fifty, sixty pence for it, yet I can buy a banana, which has come all the way from the Caribbean, for twelve pence? It makes no sense.'

'Ah, well, most of the apples grown round here are cookers,' Jim says. 'A lot of them go for canning.'

'But why?' says Antoinette. 'If we've got the right growing conditions, why not grow some nice eaters? People would love to eat a local apple.'

Jim seems a little unsure how to talk to a woman as opinionated as Antoinette. I try to help.

'How's Marjorie?' I say. 'I feel like I haven't seen her for ages.'

'She's struggling with the heat,' Jim says. 'She's better off just staying indoors. I'll take her out for a drive when I've finished this – she likes to see what height they've built the bonfires.' He smiles, with a look that says, 'What on earth does she get out of that?'

We walk to the open end of Parnell Park, which joins the main road.

'Which way?' I ask.

'Left,' says Antoinette. 'If we go round in a loop, we'll get the big hill out of the way first.'

We walk companionably, Antoinette pointing out all the houses with For Sale boards up and giving me the low-down on each.

'That one's four-bed, but one of them's tiny, two reception, kitchen-diner, utility, downstairs WC. How much do you reckon?'

'I don't know.'

'Guess.'

'A hundred and sixty.'

'One hundred and sixty? In your dreams. It's on for two-twenty.'

Antoinette admits that she checks the PropertyPal website several times a week.

'Why so?' I say.

'Why do you think? To dream, Ali. To imagine myself in a new house, with a new life, possibly with a new man, definitely with a conservatory.'

'If you want a conservatory, why not just add one onto number twenty-three? Why not add a new man to number twenty-three, for that matter?'

'I'm thinking of selling it.'

'Selling your house? Really? How come?'

'Oh, Ali. I've lived there for forty-five years. I mean, I've done bits and bobs to try and make it more contemporary, but the carpet in the back bedroom is older than I am. It's always going to feel like Mum and Dad's place. I mean, it's mine too. I had a very happy childhood there. But it's not *just* mine.'

'Where would you go?'

'I'm not sure. Sometimes I think I'd like to live somewhere that's nothing like Parnell Park. Somewhere where nobody knows me – where no-one knows anyone and everybody leaves you alone. Don't you ever find the Park a bit claustrophobic?'

I do.

'The problem is, to sell number twenty-three, I'd have to share the proceeds with my brother and sister, so I'd need to take out a mortgage to buy something else. I've never had a mortgage before. I know the whole world is living in mortgaged properties, but when you've never had one yourself, it seems like a big deal.'

'Could you downsize? Keep your need to borrow to a minimum?'

'That would seem the sensible thing to do,' says Antoinette. 'But when I go on PropertyPal and see all the detached houses with garages and en-suite master bedrooms, I can't get excited about the little two-up two-downs with a shower head over the bath.'

'Oh, I don't know,' I say. 'Those houses are really easy to heat, and they have chimneys, so you and your new man could snuggle up in front of a log fire, glass of wine on the go. It wouldn't be expensive to decorate either, with smaller rooms, so you could afford to give the whole place a makeover, put your own stamp on it.'

'You should write the blurbs.'

'I'd miss you, though.'

'You'd have to remember to put your own bin out.'

'You're a good neighbour, Antoinette. You take just the

right amount of interest in me and my life and you know just when to look away.'

'That works both ways, Ali.'

We say nothing for a bit.

'Would you ever consider a new relationship?' Antoinette says.

'He'd have to be very understanding. *Very* understanding. I'd like to have sex again. I'd like to meet a man with low expectations, tip-top personal hygiene and a once-a-week sexual appetite. And not a prick.'

'Would you bring him to the house?'

I look at her. 'No, Antoinette. I would not bring him to the house.'

'But if it turned into a proper relationship, would you hope, one day ...'

'If I started to think about the future, genuinely think about the future, I couldn't go on,' I say. 'The only way I can cope is one day at a time.'

'I wish you had someone.'

'I wish I had someone. But it's not looking very likely. Nothing stopping you, though.'

'Mmm. Even when you think you have someone, it doesn't always work out. Kevin told me he'd had you round to cry on your shoulder last night. He came over to mine today. What a mess.'

'It's funny, I always thought he was the dominant character in that relationship. Not that I'm claiming to know them well, but if you'd asked me, I'd have bet on Kevin having the affair rather than Kim. Didn't you think he was the more beloved?'

'Well, he's gutted. He says he never suspected a thing – it came right out of the blue.'

'Do you know if he's spoken to her yet?'

'He didn't say, and I didn't ask.'

'Do you think they'll try again?'

'I suppose that depends on what comes out in the wash. Was this the first time? How long has it been going on? How many lies has she told? Is she in love with the other guy? Does she still have feelings for Kevin?'

'Does he still have feelings for her?'

'I think he really does, big-time, but that's not the same as being willing to forgive her. That's a five-bed, by the way, seventeen-foot lounge, family room, kitchen-diner plus separate dining room, playroom and study in the attic with Velux windows, double detached garage – how much?'

'Two-six-nine.'

'On the nose!'

We are at the halfway point in the loop, which brings us past the pub.

'Fancy a glass of something?' I say.

'Didn't bring my purse,' says Antoinette.

'I'll buy.'

'Actually, I've got a bottle of prosecco at home, right in the bottom of the fridge, so it'll be really cold. Why don't we save your pennies and have that when we get back instead? It'll only take us ten minutes. We can sit out the front and be proper nosey neighbours and see who's coming and going.'

'A minute ago you were saying it was claustrophobic.'

'I know, and at times I hate it, and at times I want to know absolutely all the biz.'

'"All the biz" will probably amount to the usual dog-walkers, a few people out with their watering cans and the exodus of teenagers before the park gates shut. Don't get too excited. But I'm happy to drink your prosecco.'

With the promise of wine, we pick up our pace and I am soon flopped down on the garden bench in front of Antoinette's bay window. She keeps her privet lower than some, which gives us a good view.

'Cheers.' Antoinette clinks her glass against mine.

'What are we celebrating? There must be something we can think of.'

'How about this fabulous weather?'

'To the weather,' I say.

A car comes quietly up the Park, pulls up outside the Kennedys' house. I cannot help looking.

A man gets out. He is searching for a house number, I think. He spots us. 'The Kennedys?'

As we are on her property, I leave it to Antoinette to respond.

'Yes, you're there. The red door.'

'Thanks.' He waves.

The Park is so quiet that we can hear the doorbell ring on the opposite side of the street.

Antoinette and I look at each other and she whispers, 'We should really talk among ourselves so that we're not listening in, but I want to know who he is.'

I do too.

The Kennedys have a low wall, instead of a hedge, at the front, so we can clearly see Kevin open the front door and the man, after a greeting I can't make out, clasp him in a hug. The door swings shut again.

'What did he say?' says Antoinette.

'I don't know. I was going to ask you,' I say.

'I haven't seen him before. You don't think it's *him*?'

'The other man? You must be kidding. Why would he be calling on Kevin and giving him a hug?'

'A brother, then. Hey, Ali, that's one each for you and me.'

'I think those bubbles are going to your head.'

'Which one would you want? I'd have Kevin. I've always thought there was something sexy about him, ever since they came to the Park. He always looks like he's having a private joke, but I bet he's good at coitus.'

'Why? Why do you think that? You know nothing about his bedroom tendencies.'

'Some things you can't explain. But if you pretend you don't see it too, you're a liar, Ali. I'd say he'd think it was beneath him to masturbate – he'd expect relief via intercourse every time. Why buy a dog and bark yourself?'

'Antoinette!'

Antoinette laughs.

'Let's change the subject,' I say.

'All right. Look at us, two spinsters. Well, one spinster, one widow. Me an orphan, you practically one. What have we got to talk about, except loss and loneliness?'

'That's a bit grim.'

'True, though. I still miss Mum and Dad. I'm glad they went

87

as quickly and easily as they did. I wouldn't have wanted them to suffer, and I wouldn't have wanted to watch them go downhill for years – oh, Ali, I'm sorry! I didn't mean ...'

'It's all right. Mum's OK. Or I'm used to it now. I wouldn't have chosen a slow decline for her either, but it is what it is.'

'The way you lost your dad, though. That was cruel.'

It was. It was utterly, utterly horrendous and yet I utterly, utterly understood why he did what he did. But it nearly broke me. It *would* have broken me, if it wasn't out of the question for me to break; breaking simply wasn't an option, because of Joe.

'Everyone knew. Everyone in this whole sodding town knew what had happened, which made it even worse, if it could have been any worse.'

'Were you angry as well as sad?'

Was I angry? It was as if anger were a chemical element and I was it. I was incandescent. I thought it would never stop.

'Yes, I was angry.'

Darius drifts by. Surely it can't be windows time again.

'Evening, sweet ladies.'

Antoinette salutes him with her glass, and he lifts his straw cowboy hat and says, 'Wine is sunlight, held together by water.'

'Is that a quote?' Antoinette asks when he passes.

'Don't know. Let me google it.' I lift my phone and check. 'Yep. Galileo Galilei.'

'Very erudite, for a window-cleaner,' says Antoinette.

There is a creak from across the way and we both look up and see Kevin coming through his side gate, carrying a bottle.

'Sorry to interrupt, but I've just banjaxed my corkscrew and we don't have another one. Any chance I could borrow yours?'

Antoinette is on her second glass of prosecco, which must explain why she invites our newly cuckolded neighbour and his unknown visitor, instead of taking her corkscrew back to their place and their own company, to bring their wine to her place for a sort of impromptu soirée.

Kevin looks dubious, but says he will return to ask Kim's brother – ah, Kim's brother – if he would like to come to Antoinette's. If not, he will return the corkscrew tomorrow.

I think Kevin is just trying to get off the hook and we won't see him again, but I am wrong, and a couple of minutes later the two men are coming across the road, apparently to spend the evening with us.

Antoinette pulls me close and whispers, 'This could be the next man you marry.'

Kevin does the introductions, naming me as 'Alice', which I urge everyone to abbreviate to Ali, please.

Kim's brother is called Callum. He is darker than her, darker than Kevin too, and about my age, I think – certainly not older. He still has his hair. His eyes – I try not to stare, but his eyes are like sloes. He is wearing a black linen shirt. It suits him. I check – of course, I check – and he does not wear a wedding ring.

'We can't all sit in a row. Let's move round to the back – there're more seats and a table,' Antoinette says. 'Kevin, you guys happy with your red? How about you, Ali?'

'Red's good for me,' says Callum.

'Let me pop next door and grab a bottle of white,' I say.

As I rise from my patio chair, Callum stands up and I think he means to come with me, which panics me momentarily, because of course he can't. Then I realise that he is simply one of those men left over from the last century who think it appropriate to get to their feet when a woman is about to leave the company.

I smile in, I suppose, surprise, and out of the corner of my eye I see Antoinette give a little smirk.

Back at my place, I have to excavate the wine bottle from under a pile of peppers and carrots and iceberg lettuce and find it's already been opened and only a couple of glasses remain. Something sticky has leaked or oozed or possibly dripped onto the shelf, but I don't want to take time to check what it is right now. Joe and I are not house-proud. We do not fuss over spills or crumbs or piles of newspapers, and lately I can see that we have gradually dispensed with coasters and putting away clean laundry because, let's face it, who's going to see if there are rings on our coffee table or piles of clean knickers on the stairs?

I wipe the stickiness off the back of the bottle with a dishcloth, dry it on a tea towel, then jump when I turn round to find Joe in the kitchen doorway.

'Oh, good. It's wine o'clock,' he says, with a stretch.

'Actually, I was taking this next door to Antoinette's,' I say, anticipating the hurt shadow that will cross his face before he can hide it, and resenting the fact that I have to see it, absorb it. I do need to see other people sometimes.

'Oh! Girls' Night, is it?' He does a good cover-up.

'As a matter of fact, we're entertaining two men!' I say, using a sort of jokey voice.

'Ooh la-la! Gentlemen callers at Antoinette's,' Joe says. 'And where did you find them?'

'We didn't have to look very far. It's just Kevin Kennedy and Kim's brother. They broke their corkscrew.'

'Is Kim's brother in the picture re London and the alleged infidelity?'

'I have no idea, but I don't see how we'll get through the evening without it coming up. Anyway, I thought we'd agreed it was no longer merely "alleged".'

'You might have agreed, Mother, but I am yet to be convinced.'

'Is this still about the disappearing picture?'

'Disappearing, then re-appearing.'

This is because, despite the evidence of the stamp, Joe has continued to keep a watch on Kim's Facebook account. He told me this morning that, shortly after I returned from Kevin's last night, the cherry blossom picture was taken down. Then, several hours later, in the middle of the night, it was put back up again.

Joe is sticking with the theory that Kevin does indeed have Kim's password and that it is he who is putting up and taking down posts in her name. Why remove it and then put it back up again, though? Joe reckons Kevin took it down in a panic, when I pointed out the anomaly of the cherry blossom out of season, then decided it actually backed up his story of Kim faking the current Galway trip and decided it was useful after all.

I am of a mind that Joe is over-thinking things. He has too much time on his hands and his shrunken life thirsts for juice. It occurred to me this morning that I wish I could introduce him to Alanis. I wish she could fall in love with his intellect and he with her vibrancy and beauty. I wish they could drive to the beach on a summer evening like this and roll about in the dunes. I wish Joe had a sex life and I wish I had one too.

Stepping round the corner onto Antoinette's patio, I hold up my bottle, as if in triumph, as if I had won it in some battle of wits instead of merely pulling it from the fridge.

'Let me get some better glasses. Those flutes are a faff,' says Antoinette.

'Ali, I was telling Callum earlier, you and Antoinette are my confidantes. We can talk about Kim,' Kevin says.

'Oh, I see,' I say. 'Please don't feel you have to ... to talk about Kim. We can steer the conversation in other directions, if you like.'

'What, like the novels of George Eliot? The pros and cons of vaping?' Kevin hasn't lost quite all of his acerbity, I see.

Callum stands up to take a tray that Antoinette is bringing to the table.

'Thanks.'

She unloads wine glasses and dishes of crisps and cashews, sets the tray on the back doorstep and sits down beside Kevin. 'Well, pet. Have you spoken to her?'

'No. Not yet.'

'She's not answering her phone,' Callum says. 'Not to me, either. I'm thinking she's realised she's made the mistake with the stamp and she knows Kevin will have seen it by now.'

She might be panicking or …'

'Or she might be screwing her courage to the sticking place, to tell me it's over between us,' Kevin says. 'Do you mind if I …?' He takes a packet of cigarettes and a lighter from his shirt pocket.

'No – go ahead,' Antoinette says. 'I'll get you an ashtray.'

'Your head must be all over the place,' I say. 'I imagine you don't know what you want, right now.'

'I'm pissed off that she won't even speak to me,' Kevin says. 'I think she at least owes me that.'

I think so too, but I say nothing.

'Do you know Kim well?' Callum says.

'Er, no. Not really. I mean, we say hello almost every day, when we're getting in and out of our cars and we spot each other. I've chatted with her a bit at Jim and Marjorie's – that's the house next door to your sister's – at their Christmas party, and she was very friendly when you had your barbecue a few weeks ago, Kevin, during that first little heatwave, but we really didn't get past small talk, if I'm honest.'

'Barbecue?' Callum says. He looks at Kevin mischievously. 'How come I wasn't invited?'

'No riff-raff.' Kevin takes the ashtray from Antoinette.

I start to think: do I ever remember seeing Callum's car at the Kennedys' before? It's hard not to notice regular callers at any of the houses in a small place like Parnell Park.

'Callum's just moved back here a few weeks ago, after a long time in the land of the kilt,' Kevin says, as if reading my thoughts.

'Oh, really?' I say. 'Whereabouts were you?'

'Kingdom of Fife. I worked up and down the east coast, but Edinburgh would've been too expensive as a base, so we set up home in St Andrews.'

Of all the words in that sentence, it is the 'we' that strikes me, of course.

Antoinette's in there like a ratter. 'That's you and who else, Callum – your significant other?'

'Oh, she's significant all right, but not in the way you mean.' He smiles wryly and I relax again – I think I know what's coming. 'She's my daughter. My wayward, eighteen-year-old daughter.'

'Did she move back here with you?' Antoinette asks.

'Actually, she came here ahead of me, over a year ago, as a boarder in the sixth form while I tied up all my loose ends at work. She's not what you'd call academic, but she was all for it and at least I knew she'd be fed and looked after. And, to be honest, I was glad she was putting some miles between herself and a certain young man I didn't much like. Rebecca seemed to relish the fresh start. She helped me find a house for us and we did up her room – nice day-bed for Rebecca, sofa-bed for any friends she wanted to stay, then one day she was off.'

'You mean she's moved out?' Antoinette says.

'Well, nothing as considered as that. It's more like "whoosh" and she's gone – clothes, passport, contents of the housekeeping jar, away!'

Antoinette raises her eyebrows.

'You must be worried,' I say.

'You must be furious,' says Antoinette.

'She is a worry. She's been a bit of a wild child since she was thirteen, but things have changed since she became – legally speaking – an adult. The police aren't interested in looking for her any more, because she's not a minor, so there's really nothing I can do, except keep my phone on and hope to hear from her.'

I cannot help comparing our lots: Callum afraid because the world is so big and so wild and his daughter could be anywhere in it, me because Joe's world is so terribly, terribly small and I always know precisely where he is, and probably always will do.

'What about her mum? Could she have gone there?' I hope Antoinette is less transparent to Callum than she is to me.

'It's just Becks and me. Always has been.'

I silently applaud Callum for fending her off without feeling compelled to give an explanation.

We chat about this and that, sometimes between the four of us, sometimes in pairs. Antoinette and I agree that we need to get the hedge between our two gardens trimmed at the earliest opportunity. If we keep it manageable, we can use the guy who doesn't charge too much, who goes at it with a hedge trimmer, climbing a set of folding steps in shorts and flip-flops. He's terrifying to watch – he doesn't so much as wear goggles; a health and safety nightmare – but he is cheap. If we let it grow taller, we have to get the other guy, the one with a proper liveried van – and, in all probability, proper insurance – who charges an arm and a leg.

'At my new house, I'm going to have a tiny little rectangle of grass I can cut with a push-mower, a wooden fence and a nice brick patio, instead of this subsiding piece of shit,' Antoinette says. 'Low maintenance all the way.'

Kevin expresses surprise that Antoinette is moving, until I tell him that all it really amounts to is a nosey fascination with looking at other people's homes on PropertyPal, the way lots of us like to watch *Escape to the Country*.

'You don't think I'm serious? I might be serious,' Antoinette says. I note that that's a sentence with too many s's for a woman on her third glass of wine.

We agree, the three of us residents, that we have the trio of most neglected gardens in the Park. None of us realised quite how much was required to keep these plots in order, until it fell to us to do it.

'So hire somebody to look after them,' Callum suggests, then looks rueful that he has spoken, as if it occurred to him a second too late that perhaps none of us has the money to afford 'somebody'.

Thinking about it now, we three are probably the poor relations of Parnell Park. Antoinette and I have no mortgages, but she is managing on a single retail salary, and I don't imagine that pays particularly well unless you're well up the management ladder, which she isn't. I have a teacher's wage, but only on those days I work, and I'm feeding and heating two people as well as trying to salt away something for my retirement, which sometimes seems to be hurtling towards me. Kevin and Kim might have two incomes – well, one and a half, I suppose – but they may well have a biggish mortgage, and Kevin smokes, which is exorbitantly expensive now. If my house looks the tattiest from the outside, I can't imagine the other two are all that far behind.

'There speaks money,' says Kevin, but it sounds playful rather than embittered.

After a while, it materialises that we are running out of wine. Antoinette only had the bottle of prosecco, I can provide no more white and Kevin is out of red.

'Looks like we'll have to call it a night,' Callum says.

'Do you really think your sister and I would have bought a property without taking the precaution of ensuring it had an offy within easy walking distance?' Kevin says.

I am glad he has made this suggestion. I couldn't care less about having another glass of wine, but I don't want to go home. Not just yet. I cannot remember the last time I sat in mixed company, giving and receiving attention like this. Yes, there is the annual drinks do at the Wrights', but nobody really talks to anybody – I mean, we mouth things about the rates and potholes, but it's nothing-conversation. And Callum is pretty definitely not 'the next man I'm going to marry', to quote Antoinette, but he's nice. I like him.

'Do we all have to go?' Antoinette is flagging.

'We could phone a taxi and ask them to pick us up a couple of bottles,' Kevin says.

'I'll go,' says Callum. 'If it really is easy walking distance.'

'It is,' I say. 'Look, I'll come with you, if that's OK – I can show you the way.'

'Great,' Callum says, and as I stand, he pulls out my chair. *He pulls out my chair.* I do not know when someone last did that for me. Certainly not Joe – the Joe I hate.

I fetch a supermarket bottle bag from my car boot and we set off, saying good evening to the Wrights' grandson Weston, who is smoking surreptitiously – although he must be twenty by now, old enough to defend his choices – under the lime trees.

'How do you think he's bearing up?' I say, when we're out of Kevin's earshot.

'Hard to say with Kevin. He's not one to show his vulnerability.'

'You must be concerned about Kim too.'

'I only have so much worry to go round, and right now, with Rebecca off the radar, Kim's shunted somewhat into second place.'

'Of course. I'd be exactly the same. But you took time to come and see Kevin. Not all families are like that. Some brothers and sisters take their family members' side no matter who's right or wrong.'

'I think that's misplaced loyalty. Going way back, I wasn't too keen on Kim getting together with Kevin. I knew him first, and he was, frankly, a womaniser. Couldn't help himself, or didn't want to. If he'd messed her about even a tiny bit back then, I'd have come out on her side all guns blazing.

'I tried to talk her out of seeing him, but she was determined and, to be fair, the guy surprised me. As far as I know, he's been faithful. Up until yesterday, I thought they both had.'

'You must be shocked.'

'Completely.'

'And she really isn't answering your calls, or is that just what you're telling Kevin? I won't say anything.'

'No, I really haven't been able to reach her. Look, Ali, I'll be straight – Kim and I weren't really in touch much for years. Some family stuff happened. Big stuff, involving Rebecca. It's only in the very recent past that we've opened up the communication channels properly again, and even then it's far from sweetness and light. So I'm not going to pretend to you that we tell each other everything, but I am still her big brother and I believe she'd come to me if she was in real trouble.'

'Even though Kevin's your friend too?'

'I think so, yeah.'

When we get to the off-licence, we agree that I will choose the white and Callum the red. I take a Sauvignon Blanc from the cooler and he selects a Saint-Emilion.

'Will these be enough?' Callum asks.

'Antoinette and I are lightweights. I'm half afraid she'll be asleep when we get back, so as long as there's enough for you and Kevin we're fine.'

Callum collects another bottle of the Sauvignon and adds it to what we've set on the counter. 'If you don't want it tonight, you can keep it for another time,' he says. 'Consider it a thank you for kindly spreading the intensity of what could have been a very difficult evening.'

He insists on paying for all our purchases, even though I brought my bag and have cash.

A black and white cat is sleeping on the wooden counter.

'What's her name?' Callum asks the youth who serves us.

'Janet,' the youth says.

Callum laughs. 'Wonderful.' And he swings the bag down.

*

99

When we get back to Parnell Park, the party has moved to Kevin's place and music is playing on the Kennedys' record player.

'Antoinette wanted to dance,' Kevin says.

She has found her second wind and has pushed back the furniture to give herself more space.

'Kevin is refusing to dance with me,' she says.

'Kevin never dances,' Kevin says.

'I can vouch for that,' says Callum. 'I have known this man for more years than I care to remember, and I have never, ever known him to throw a shape on the dance floor.'

'No fun,' says Antoinette.

I haven't been in this room before. It has two large purple velvet sofas on either side of the original art deco fireplace – ours had been taken out and replaced by the previous owners with a faux Victorian job that is entirely incongruous and I am instantly jealous of the Kennedys'. Like my front room, this one has wooden parquet flooring and a large bay window. We have a window seat built into ours, which Kate's daughter Cara has always loved, whereas the Kennedys have their vinyls stored there. There are a couple of mugs on the hearth; a used ashtray and copies of the *New Statesman* and *Private Eye* litter a big, upholstered ottoman.

'I brought your glass,' Antoinette says, and indicates the mantelpiece. 'Yours is there too, Callum. Kevin, this music is crap, I'm putting on something summery.'

I don't much like the music either. I've never appreciated jazz, though I wouldn't disparage it – I've always thought it's a bit beyond me. Joe and I like Van Morrison, Bap Kennedy, Jimmy McCarthy.

Callum goes to the window, flips through the albums. 'Don't you have anything recorded later than 1945, man?' he says.

'If you want U2, you've come to the wrong house,' Kevin says.

'*U2?*' says Antoinette. 'Kevin, Kevin, Kevin, you're showing your age. It's Harry Styles and Lewis Capaldi now. U2.'

I suspect Kevin adores being thought out of step with the contemporary music scene.

'Doesn't Kim have anything younger?' Antoinette asks, which, I think, frankly, is tactless but it's probably the wine.

'Kim's music's on her iPod, which she took with her "to Galway",' Kevin says. 'I can do you a bit of Beach Boys – is that summery enough for you?'

Antoinette dances on her own for a bit and half-heartedly smokes one of Kevin's cigarettes. Kevin starts sorting through his vinyls, apparently correcting any albums that have been mis-filed. This leaves Callum and me on the sofa facing the window. For a while we just observe the other two, but then we start to chat a little – the wine, the weather, what's in the news. We're hardly drinking at all now. Out of nowhere, Callum says these must be lovely houses at Christmas, with the bay windows perfect for a Christmas tree, and I tell him that they are, that that was something I loved about our house when we first moved in.

Callum says, very, very gently, 'Ali, if you don't mind me asking, am I right in thinking that you lost a child?'

I think how strangely distorted, yet how very perceptive, this remark is, and just for a moment I believe I will cry.

'Not exactly. Not lost, exactly. It's complicated,' I say, and somehow using that stock phrase, putting it in a box that looks like lots of boxes other people have used, gives me back my composure.

'Sorry. I don't mean to intrude. I was sure you were a parent, that's all, yet you don't talk about any children. I'm not one of those people who thinks that only people who've had kids can really understand what it feels like to have kids, but ... well, actually I am one of those people.' He laughs at himself, which is nice.

We listen to the Beach Boys album until the end, by which time Kevin, who has drunk a lot more than anyone else, is sleeping, sitting up, on the other sofa and Antoinette is sitting beside him, her head on his shoulder.

'I think it's time we went home,' I say.

Callum insists on seeing us across the road. We take an arm each of Antoinette's, and when we get to her back door I say I'll come in with her for five minutes to make sure she gets to bed.

'Well, it was great to meet you both, even if the circumstances were a bit odd,' Callum says. 'Thanks for the chat.'

I would like just to stand and watch him disappear back across the road, but Antoinette is staggering and I'm afraid she'll fall.

I manhandle her upstairs, steer her into bed and take off her trainers.

Then I go home on my own.

Joe is still up. When I come in, I fall onto the sofa and strip off my Earth Spirit sandals. He gives me a hard stare, playing the stern patriarch to my errant teenager.

I stare back at him. 'What? It's not even one yet.'

'It's not the lateness of the hour, young lady. It's the company you keep.'

I throw a cushion at his head.

'I think we can put all that behind us now, don't you? I told you Kim's brother was there tonight, and he's putting it down as an affair, so that's good enough for me.'

'So Kim's brother is siding with Kevin?'

'I don't think it's a matter of taking sides – he and Kevin were friends before there was a Kevin and Kim.'

'Has he spoken to her?'

'No. She's not picking up. But I'm sure he will. He seems the caring sort. She's probably embarrassed. Ashamed. Just because you're the one in the wrong doesn't mean it's not painful for you too.'

'Mmm. Well, if he hasn't spoken to her, then you still don't know that she's all right.'

'If her own brother isn't concerned, why should we be?'

'Did he know about your ding-dong with Kevin? Did he know you'd called the police?'

'I don't think so. He didn't mention it, and Kevin seems to be happy to put it behind us.'

'And you don't think that's strange? That you call the police and he tells you to fuck off and keep out of his way, basically, and then the next day he's round here with some story about a stamp?'

'It wasn't a story. I saw the postcard. And, by the way, I

didn't *call the police* – I didn't dial 999 and demand they come round, I rang the non-emergency number and gave them my information, that's all.'

'Mum, when you saw the postcard, wouldn't you have noticed if it had completely the wrong stamp? Wouldn't it have jumped out at you?'

I don't know. I'm not sure. Sometimes I don't notice things, these days. I miss road signs all the time – I'm going to get caught doing forty in a thirty zone for sure, because I don't see signs.

'Did he show you the stamp? When he took you over to his place to give you the sob story, did he show you what he was talking about?'

'No. He just ...'

'I bet he didn't. Because it didn't happen. You read the card, Antoinette read the card, and neither of you spotted a British stamp in the corner? I don't believe that. Ask him to show you. Ask him to show you the card, *with* the stamp.'

'Joe, I really think ...'

'Ask him, Mum. Something is not right there.'

We sit and say nothing for a while. Ninety per cent of me says this is a run-of-the-mill domestic situation, that Kim will be back soon either to repair the damage or to pack her bags, but ten per cent still isn't happy. There's nothing big, but there's the travel agent, the change in nature and accuracy of the Facebook posts, the hairdresser's appointment, even that disappearing-reappearing cherry blossom photograph. And the postcard. Is Joe right? Would I have noticed an incongruous stamp? There is absolutely nothing in any of this that I could take to the police, so what can I do? Zip.

'OK, Smartypants,' I say. 'What if you're right – and I'm not saying you are – what do we do?'

'The brother,' says Joe. 'He's got to be our route in. He's not going to be driving home tonight, not if you've been drinking to this time. Just make sure you get back over there tomorrow morning, catch him before he leaves.'

'And do what, exactly?'

'Tell him you're worried. Tell him you think there's something funny going on.'

'But what if he blabs to Kevin?'

'Make him promise not to. Get him on your side, Mum. Use your womanly wiles. Use the fact that he cares about Kim.'

I am too tired to think any more. I say goodnight to Joe, kiss the top of his head and carry my sandals up to the bedroom.

As I am climbing into bed, something scratches my leg. Damn. A long, pointed spring has burst through the side of the mattress – just one more bit of wear and tear on our home that I cannot afford to put right. They shouldn't put pointed ends on bed springs – I could've really hurt myself. It occurs to me that I could swap the mattress with one of the other beds, but then we'll need all the accommodation when Kate and the children come, so that won't work either. I take a bath towel, fold it lengthways into a long, thick strip and place it over the spring, tucking it below the mattress and then again under the fitted sheet. This will have to do.

It is too warm for the duvet. A top sheet is more than enough.

I think of Callum, sleeping in the spare room at Kevin's house. I wonder if he thought of me at all, after I came home. I hope I dream about him. I hope he dreams about me.

16

He has texted again.

Nearly finished, Girl. Couple more days. Then we free.

She is going crazy stuck indoors, in this heat. Dale has gone to some museum – he asked Bikkie to go with him, but of course that was out of the question. CCTV everywhere and funny looks if she kept her big hat and shades on indoors. Not that anybody's going to be looking for her anywhere near here – that's the whole point – but you can't be too careful, in her situation.

She doesn't even like museums, but she'd gladly go anywhere to get out of this dive. Every morning, she makes her bed, stuffs her dirty clothes into the bin-bag. Her dad's a neat freak, everything just so, and some things just stick. It's still a filthy hole, though.

Sitting on her bed, the pillow propped up against the wall behind her, she files her nails with an emery board – she always does her left hand first, to get it out of the way, because it's trickier, then relaxes as she shapes the nails on her right. Like keeping your dessert course until last.

Bikkie didn't sleep last night. Not much, anyway. She was considering her options. She was trying to figure out whether, in fact, she had options. Her boyfriend will have got things moving at his end by now, so there is zero chance she can just walk away from this, but if she went to the police, today, voluntarily, gave them the whole story, would they let her off more lightly for doing so?

She wonders how bad life would be in a women's prison, because that's where she could end up. No boyfriend to look out for her there. She would be alone with a lot of very scary people, and they'd smell her fear from day one.

What if she could persuade the police that she was ill, mentally ill, not bad but mad? Would they put her in hospital instead?

How would she do this? Take off all her clothes and walk up the middle of the road? Swallow a handful of pills, then call an ambulance? Could a psychiatrist tell that she was faking it? It'd be a big gamble.

Because she isn't ill, she is a criminal, a schemer – these are all the things they will say in the newspapers if she is caught, beside some photograph someone has dredged up of her enjoying herself – they always use a picture of the evil-doers that makes them look like they haven't a care in the world, don't they? Just so that everyone will hate them even more.

Her boyfriend says they won't get caught, so long as she sticks to everything they've planned. But is he as smart as he thinks he is?

Sometimes it doesn't feel real and Bikkie can hardly believe this is actually happening. If it could all turn out to be a dream, she would gladly take that. She would rewind the tape all the way back to last Christmas – well, New Year's Eve, really, when they sat looking out to sea and said they were fed up being poor and her boyfriend told her it was worse than that – he'd been tricked, scammed, and it all came out about the binary options.

Binary options. She still doesn't really understand what that means, but it came down to this: one day he'd had an email from a friend, encouraging him to go online with some financial services company; the friend said it was a sure thing, he could make thousands in a single day.

Her boyfriend was supposed to be smart, but not when it came to money, Bikkie thought afterwards. He'd emailed the company and they'd phoned him back, told him the basics of how the deals worked, taken his card details so that he could invest a couple of hundred to test the water. Within minutes, he'd seen his account appear on screen and watched his balance grow before his eyes.

So he invested another few hundred, and another. The bottom line kept increasing. He was going to buy the friend who sent the email something a bit special for putting him onto this. The guy on the phone said he'd obviously come on board at exactly the right time, the markets were in his favour, but that wouldn't necessarily be the case tomorrow or next week. He should act now, reap the rewards, and then – the guy shouldn't really say this, but – get the hell out.

Her boyfriend authorised a credit card payment of twenty thousand pounds. Then the phone went dead and he couldn't get any reply from the email address.

The bank said that, as he'd authorised the payment, there was nothing they could do.

The Financial Conduct Authority could only offer sympathy, as the company was registered outside its jurisdiction.

The friend who'd supposedly sent the original email knew nothing about it – his contacts must've been hacked.

The boyfriend had wanted to present Bikkie with a heap of money; instead he'd run up a twenty-thousand-pound debt that neither of them had the means to repay.

Bikkie hadn't known what to say. She was shocked that he could have fallen for something as blatant as an internet scam – she'd heard him laugh at the stupidity of people sending cash to a Nigerian prince, or to pay a supposed winner's tax so that big prize money could be released from a lottery they couldn't even remember entering, because they never had.

She was angry with him because he'd brought this upon them both, when she'd had no say, and angry that he'd taken a lazy route to making money – anything rather than do a proper day's work in a real job, like everyone else. She is angry again now, even just remembering it. If it hadn't been for that stupid, stupid act, the chances are they wouldn't be doing what they are doing.

But Bikkie loved him, which meant she also felt sorry for him, protective of his ego, which must have been hammered by the experience.

For the first time, Bikkie makes a connection: here is why she agreed to this mad scheme, in which she's now up to her neck – she wanted to prove she still trusted him, still thought him clever, hadn't written him off as a fool. Because that was what mattered to him most – not so much his looks, though he fancied himself in that department too; not the career ladder, which he seemed to think was boring – that everyone thought he was so clever.

Bikkie has put her life in the hands of a man who recently made a colossal error of judgement to prove to him that she still thought he was clever.

That doesn't sound very smart.

17

There is no way to disguise the fact that I am sitting out here, on a deckchair, at the front of my house, where I have never sat in the sixteen years that I've lived in Parnell Park, to try and catch Callum before he leaves.

Kevin will be laughing at me, teasing Callum. 'You've got a bunny boiler on your hands there.'

The light woke me at around five and, after having my shower, I started watching the house, parking myself here – with a mug of coffee and a book for some tiny shred of cover – at 7.30 a.m., long before their curtains were open.

The dog-walkers, and some dogs without walkers, arrived five minutes later. I'd never seen the whole lot of them quite so close up. There was a small terrier zipping past, pursued by a dachshund, a crazed-looking Great Dane on a hugely long lead, a shaggy black and white mongrel skipping round him, an enormous creature that might have been a St Bernard, and a Dalmatian. It was like something from *Hairy Maclary* and for one moment I forgot myself and actually laughed. I wished Joe could've seen it.

Callum's car is still there. I knew he wouldn't drink-drive.

Perhaps he will come out, come across the road to say goodbye, mention that he's spoken to Kim and that she's fine, and all of this will just go away. I can concentrate on sprucing the place up a bit for Kate and the kids, and Joe and I can pick out a few good movies to watch on TV, instead of catastrophising about the people in our street.

Seeing Kate and family will be lovely. They give so much and demand so little. I am glad that we can provide free holiday accommodation, even if it's not a particularly exciting location, especially when it's clear things are very tight for them right now.

Kate and George aren't stupid, but they've never quite managed to turn what they're good at into much money. I don't think they've ever had what people call a road map, but then how could they, really? – acting is not like being an estate agent or working in a bank.

Kate had that one big break, as a junior doctor in a hospital thriller on BBC2, but then she got pregnant with Conall, and when he was born she was completely unable to leave him, even with George, to go back to work, and they wrote her out of the second series. I have the clippings from her 'heyday', snipped from the *Radio Times* and the *Belfast Telegraph*, tucked in among the photographs from back then. I've never told her that I kept them, much less shown them to her, because I don't know if it would make her smile or make her sad.

I've never exactly had what people would call a road map of my own either. Whatever I expected to be doing at the age of fifty-one, it wasn't this.

I hear a sound and look up. It's what I've been waiting for all this time, and what I've been dreading.

'Hi, Ali. Catching a few rays.'

'Yep,' I say, standing up and walking towards him. 'It's a little suntrap at this time of day.'

Callum has his car keys in his hand, a small holdall in the other. He is trying to leave and probably wishing he hadn't bumped into me.

'Listen,' I hear myself say, over the soup of embarrassment and reticence in my head, 'I won't keep you a minute, but do you think I could just mention something to you?'

'Sure,' Callum says, and he looks searchingly at my face with what seems like genuine concern.

'Could we walk up here a little?' I say. 'I really don't want anyone else to hear.'

'Let me just throw this in the car.'

We stroll towards the park gates.

'I'm not sure how to start,' I say.

'Just start anywhere. I'm listening.'

'OK. I'm worried about Kim. I'm not convinced that things are as they're being presented.'

'Worried about her how?' says Callum.

'It's Kevin,' I say. 'I don't know if he told you, but I saw Kim last week in London. Not to speak to, she was on a train and I was on the platform. But it bothered me when I mentioned it to Kevin and he said she was in the west of Ireland. I don't really know what I thought, but I wasn't happy and I spoke to the police ...'

'The police?' Callum says, and his eyes widen.

'I know. I know that to many people that would seem like an over-reaction, but I have some experience, I had an experience, I neglected to mention something that turned out ... to be significant. My first aid trainer, I remember him saying, *If you just aren't happy* ... I mean, I'm not making any accusations, I'm just a bit worried. I'm just ... a bit worried.'

Anticipating making this speech for the past three hours has made me worse, not better. I have never been so inarticulate.

Callum asks me if it's simply a bad feeling I have, or if there are actual details that are bothering me. I say the latter and he nods, but I haven't made this clear at all. I haven't said it's actually Kevin I think is involved. I would very much like to walk away right now, but if I don't clarify this, then there has been no point in watching the house since 5.30 a.m. and no point in going as far as I've already gone.

'It's Kevin,' I say. 'I think it's Kevin. I think he's up to something.'

Callum's face softens.

'Ali, no. I've known Kevin for thirty years. He can have a sharp tongue, but he wouldn't physically harm anyone.'

'He might not have done it himself,' I say. 'He might have got someone else to do it, while he has an alibi, here at home.'

It suddenly occurs to me that Kevin, who would otherwise have been alone in his house, has actively sought out company for the past two evenings – me on Monday night, to talk about the postcard, and three of us last night, at Antoinette's and then at his place. Was this so he had witnesses who could testify to his whereabouts?

Callum is calm. 'I don't think Kevin is organised enough to carry out a complex plan spanning two sides of the Irish Sea, and I think he'd wet himself if he came within a mile of a professional hitman. Believe me, I don't want to think my little sister is cheating on him, but it does look that way.'

'I haven't told you everything yet.'

'OK. Tell me everything that's worrying you.'

And it's made easier by the fact that we are walking, so I don't have to see his face as I spill out the complete list of tiny little reasons why I'm just not happy. Callum doesn't interrupt. By the time I have finished, we are at the far gates of the park and we can't go any further without emerging onto a different street.

I wait for Callum to say something.

'Everything you're telling me – Ali, it could have an innocent explanation. Kim could've made a mistake with her hair appointment. Kevin could simply have chosen the easy option in booking a holiday through a travel agent. If he was some sort of a psycho, I might be starting to wonder, but I'm not even sure that I would. It is deeply kind of you to care about Kim, and I can see you're embarrassed even bringing it up with me, but I know Kevin and he's just not that guy.'

I'm not getting through to him. Is this because he is too

nice to suspect that seemingly ordinary people are capable of badness – they are capable; I know – or because Joe and I have dreamt up a nightmare scenario out of boredom or some need for drama in our humdrum lives?

'Look,' – Callum is taking out his phone – 'I'm not trying to be evasive, but I want to get home, just in case there's any sign of Rebecca.'

'Of course! Of course you do.'

I am ashamed. Whereas my thoughts on Kim's potential jeopardy are pure speculation, Callum has well-founded worries about the whereabouts of his teenage daughter. Naturally that's his priority. I must seem a nuisance, like a fly buzzing round his head when he's trying to focus on something else.

'But, listen. Give me your phone number. When I hear from Kim, I'll let you know. Put your mind at rest.'

'Oh! Thank you.' I tell him my number and he keys it in. 'Would you let me know too if you find Rebecca?'

Callum looks at me like I have just done something really good. 'Sure,' he says.

We walk back the way we came, staying on safe subjects like the trees and the flowerbed displays. Callum tells me he's going to a recording of the *Brain of Britain* quiz for Radio 4 tonight, and I tell him that the Wrights went to see *University Challenge* being filmed when their grandson was on a team earlier this year. Callum laughs and says he feels good if he can even understand the questions on that one, never mind answer one.

When we arrive at Parnell Park, I see that Callum's car

is a Volvo, a nice one, with leather seats. It has a Macmillan cancer charity sticker on the back window. There could be many reasons for this, but I find myself wondering if Rebecca's mother was one of those heartbreaking cases who found herself with a malignant tumour during pregnancy and turned down treatment because it would harm their baby. Did Rebecca survive and the mother die? If so, Callum's late wife must live on upon a pedestal of nobility and selflessness that is unapproachable by other, mortal women.

As Callum drives off, I hope very much that I will see him again, but suspect that I will not.

It's still early enough to fit in a visit with Mum before the home has lunch. I swap my flip-flops for a pair of Dunlops in which I can drive safely.

The day-room windows are open when I arrive, and I can hear someone playing the piano. As Linzi lets me in, she is barely suppressing a smile.

'What's going on?' I ask, signing my name in the book.

'They're called Gary and Yvonne,' Linzi says. 'She plays the piano and he sings. The new activities co-ordinator booked them, apparently, but she's not here. Go on through, Alice.'

The day room is packed. It seems that every single resident has been led or parked here to enjoy the event. I spot Mum, who is watching the performers keenly as they murder 'Hotel California', Gary on lead vocals, Yvonne his backing singer but also playing what I now see is no ordinary piano but a keyboard with electronic drum function, among other things.

As they bring the song to a crude conclusion, Alanis, standing on the far side of the room, leads a round of applause, grinning mischievously from ear to ear. (If only she could meet Joe. If only he would let her. If only she could rescue him.)

There is no way to be beside Mum without blocking the other residents' view, so I lift a spare dining chair from the hall, carry it just inside the door and join the audience.

Gary's patter is cringeworthy. He introduces each new song with the words 'and it goes something like this'. He wears what looks like a suit he bought for a wedding, although he has removed the jacket and hung it on the microphone stand, and he uses the hand not holding the mic to emphasise key moments in the lyrics. I try to keep a neutral face as they give us familiar Abba and Doctor Hook songs, but not as I've ever heard them before, and then extracts from *Les Misérables*. It is hard not to laugh.

When they finish, with 'What a Friend We Have in Jesus', there is no ovation, standing or otherwise, no speech of thanks – the staff here haven't been trained in showbiz etiquette; this was simply dropped on them. Gary and Yvonne pack up their stuff. I lift my chair over beside Mum.

'Well, what did you think of that?' I say.

'I could take it or leave it,' says Mum. 'My husband was a good singer. What was his name?'

'Michael,' I say. 'Yes, he was.'

'Did you know my husband?'

'I did. I knew him well.'

'What did he do?'

'He worked for the tax office.'

'Did he? Whatever happened to him? I haven't seen him for a long time.'

Oh, Mum. 'Maybe he'll come tomorrow. I'll try ringing him.'

'Would you? Thank you.'

'How did you sleep?'

'Not well.'

Snap. 'Really? What was the problem?'

'Oh, the usual, making plans and I couldn't switch off.'

'Oh? What were you planning?'

'I was thinking about Mummy's kitchen. The back door's in the wrong place.'

'Is it?'

'Yes. When you think about it, it should be down at the other end, beside the table – that way the units could come round in a U-shape. You could put the kettle and mugs and tea and coffee in the corner and you'd have all that storage under the counter.'

She's right, that's a much more practical design, or *would* be, if my grandparents' house still existed.

'And do you think Gran would go for it?' I say.

'Probably not,' Mum says. 'Unless Herbie suggested it. Then she'd listen.'

Herbie is one of my deceased uncles.

'Maybe you should put your heads together, then,' I say.

'She always listens to the boys, but I'm cleverer than either of them, you know.'

This was possibly true.

'I left home when I was fifteen, and the first time I went

back, Mummy cooked me two lamb chops – two! It felt like she'd finally noticed me.'

I've heard this story before, and how her brothers used to rope Mum into playing cricket with them, but whenever it came her turn to bat, they always decided the game was over. This may have played some part in turning her into one of the most self-sufficient people I have ever met – she loved my father, but she never depended on him, emotionally. Had he been the one to fall to dementia, she would have coped completely. She would have made a go of it. She would not have burdened herself with taking too long a view and she would not have given up. I would still have had two parents. Do I wish that? Would it have been preferable? Doesn't matter.

'What's for lunch, today?' I ask. 'Do you know?'

'I thought I might make a salad. I've a basin of radishes from the garden – I love radishes in a salad.'

'Mmm. They have that hot, peppery taste.'

'The girl who does my feet is coming today.'

May or may not be true. The 'girl' is a qualified podiatrist.

'Is the music finished?' Mum asks.

'Yes, they've packed up.'

'Ruby?' It's Linzi. 'Ruby, we're taking people in to lunch now.'

'Oh, I'll get out of your way,' I say.

'I don't want to rush you, Alice, but your mummy likes to get the table at the window, so we have to make sure she's one of the first in.'

'No problem,' I say.

'It's thyme roast pork with cider cream sauce, Ruby. I'm going to get the recipe, it smells amazing.'

'Roast pork,' Mum says, all thoughts of radishes forgotten.

I shuffle to the dining-room doorway with Mum and Linzi, then another carer I don't yet know comes and takes Mum's elbow and guides her to her seat.

Linzi stands watching with me, her hands deep in her tunic patch pockets.

'I'm so glad she's happy here, Linzi.'

'I know. All the wee residents are pretty content, to be honest. It's a good care home. There's a waiting list, which is hard if it's your family's needing a place, but it means we're doing something right.'

'I suppose the staff do some sort of safeguarding training?'

'Oh God, aye. The whole package, every two years. The Health and Social Care Trust does it. And your AccessNI has to be through before you can set foot in the place. Social services wouldn't let you away with anything else.'

'Have you ever ... have you ever had reason to use your safeguarding training ... have you ever suspected ... not necessarily here, but ...' I don't know how to ask. But Linzi's there.

'Have I ever seen something and thought, *That's not right; that's what they were telling us about at our training*? Yes. Not in a care home, but back when I was out and about, looking after clients in their own homes. I used to do home-help. There was one wee client I worried about. It wasn't any one big thing, but there were a whole lot of wee things. Stupid things, really – I thought someone in the family was maybe bullying her, but I wasn't sure. I said nothing, but I just had that feeling. Then, when I was changing her for bed one night, I saw bruises on her arm and I knew to look at them they were from someone gripping her real hard. The other girls wouldn't do that, I knew they wouldn't – we're taught how to hold older people so we don't mark them. That sounds awful; I don't mean we're trying to get away with something, I just mean we're told how to do the job without hurting the clients. I said about it to my supervisor, who did' – Linzi lowers her voice – 'frig all. So I went over her head to the social worker, and she was really good. The wee client was examined and they found frigging bite marks on her ears, old ones and fresh ones, which had been covered up by her hair. It was the daughter-in-law.'

'So, if you hadn't pushed it, no-one might have found out.'

'I'm not saying the daughter-in-law would have done anything worse, but you just don't know. Sure how could you bite a defenceless old woman? That wee client had been a music teacher. She went into the Braemar home after that, where Alanis did her placement, but I think she's in the nursing side of it now and not the residential – she'd be a lot older than your mummy.'

I call at Nicholson's for a few bits on my way home. The Wrights' grandson is at the customer service counter at the front of the shop, buying cigarettes.

As I am queuing with my wire basket, my phone dings. It's a text from Callum to say that he's doing a test on my number and, in the process, ensuring that I now have his too. There is no news of Rebecca yet, or of Kim, but he'll text again when there's anything with which to update me.

My excitement at the fact that he has texted vies with my concern about his daughter or his sister, which makes me feel shallow and desperate. I reel in my desire to reply immediately and slip the phone back into my bag.

18

Poor Dale.

'I feel like Michael Jackson,' he says, waggling his right hand.

They told him at A&E that it's most likely allergic contact dermatitis, he explains, but he'll need to have patch testing by a dermatologist to confirm it.

Bikkie feels sorry for him, even though he says the steroid ointment and antihistamines are helping a lot. He does look stupid in those white cotton gloves, especially in this weather.

What's bothering her most of all, though, is that he has done more harm than just to his hands. He told her he knows how it happened: at the interview, working with the motorcycle engine, no protective gloves or barrier cream were provided, and he was too shy to ask for some. This, Bikkie is in no doubt, will have counted against him – it was a test, surely, to check out his approach to health and safety. How could Dale not have seen that? See? She's not the complete child her boyfriend takes her for – she would've recognised what was needed in that situation, and spoken up. Dale will not get the job now, which means he will not get the new life he wanted in London, for which Bikkie is sad.

They have met at the duck pond once more, as agreed the last time. It is 5 p.m., but it's still hot. Dale is wearing the khaki fishing hat again, but has swapped his regular glasses for John Lennon shades.

He is such easy company. He tells her about his visit to the National Portrait Gallery, the picture of Dame Kelly Holmes that everyone standing round thought was a photograph until he pointed out the little ticket that said it was an oil painting. He tells her there's everything from the Tudors and the Stuarts to, yes, Michael Jackson. Bikkie doesn't want to make a fool of herself – she doesn't really know who the Tudors and the Stuarts are, though she thinks one of them was Henry VIII – so she says nothing. Her boyfriend knows these things. He reads all the time, books. Bikkie only reads magazines and blogs. But whereas her boyfriend uses his greater knowledge to make her feel stupid, Dale seems to want to share, treats her as if she will understand and appreciate everything he says.

And she rises to it. She feels more mature in his company. At last. Perhaps this is how she deserves to feel. She imagines feeling this way all the time.

Dale has a quality of stillness. His body is relaxed, except when they accidentally brush against each other and she senses him bristle with embarrassment.

Bikkie would spend every day with him if they could stay round here, out of harm's way. But Dale isn't stuck here, like her. He is keen to see something of the capital city while he is visiting – Camden market, Covent Garden, St Martin in the Fields. He has asked her to come too, but she can't. Some scuzzy guys, with the opportunity of a few days with Bikkie, would turn their backs on sightseeing in favour of round-the-clock bed. Dale is so much better than that. Bikkie realises that what she sees in Dale is that he is healthy – his poor hands excepted – and balanced. Yes, he likes her, that's obvious, but he doesn't just give up his plans and shrink his ambitions for the week to be with her. She should be more like that. She should divide her time and energy between her relationship with her boyfriend and other activities. She should make friends with other females, she should start running – Bikkie pictures herself in leggings, with earbuds in – and she has always yearned for a pet; maybe she could volunteer at a rescue centre.

If she were in a relationship with Dale, it would be easy to live a better life, she feels sure. They would both go to work every day, come home, eat big salads and drink water from a Kilner bottle they kept in the fridge. They would walk their dog, maybe on the beach, they would redecorate the spare room. Dale would know how to fix things, like the landing light and the lawnmower, and one day she would give him the news that they were having a baby.

'Penny for them.' Dale is looking at her. 'Penny for your thoughts?'

'Can't tell you. Just daydreaming. Silly stuff.'

'Aw, now I really want to know.'

'Dale, do you have a girlfriend, back home?'

Dale looks down at his gloved hands.

'Charlotte, if I had a girlfriend back home, or anywhere, I would not be sitting here in the park with you.'

'Because it would be disloyal?'

'Because it would be dangerous. I don't mess about, Charlotte. I don't take chances with other people's feelings.'

Bikkie is delighted. Further proof, if it were needed, that some people are just good.

'Do you always do the right thing?' she says.

'Always? That's a pretty high bar. I always *try* to; I don't always succeed.'

'I bet you've never cheated on anyone.'

Her boyfriend has cheated. Once, he took another girl into the bedroom for sex when he and Bikkie were at the same party. That had been a new low. His defence was that he'd been off his face, but how was that supposed to make her feel better?

'Nope, I've never cheated. Have you?'

'No.'

It's the truth. Bikkie has been with lots of men, has regretted more than half, probably, but she has always ended things, or they have, before she has moved on. Was this on principle, though, or more that she couldn't deal with life getting complicated?

She changes the subject. She wants to know more about Dale; she feels that she wants to know everything.

'Why do you limp?'

'Ah. Ha ha. Thank you for waiting so long before bringing it up. Motorbike accident when I was seventeen. Not my fault – I was not going too fast. I was not being reckless. An old guy pulling out of a country junction, just wasn't looking for a bike.'

'Does it still hurt?'

'Sometimes. You must have had quite a few tumbles yourself, show-jumping.'

Suddenly, Bikkie decides. Her whole life may be built on lies right now, and there might not be much she can do about that, but this one was constructed just for Dale, and she wants no further part in it.

'I'm not a show-jumper. I made that up to try and seem more interesting. I've never owned a pony and I've never even sat on a horse.'

Dale bursts out laughing. He shakes his head.

'If I'd said I was a gymnast, you might have asked me to do a cartwheel,' Bikkie says. She is laughing a little too, now. 'I didn't see how show-jumping would ever be put to the test.'

'Hmmm. The fact that you're telling me this could be seen as encouraging,' Dale says. 'If you thought you were never going to see me again, you'd have no need to come clean.'

Bikkie ponders this. Men have chased after her before, countless times. Sometimes she's been interested, sometimes not. Always she has felt that the man's desire for sex with her was only marginally below the surface. Always, she now realises, and she's never quite grasped this before, she has felt like prey. The thought makes her feel a little queasy.

It is not the same with Dale. He isn't tipping drink into her, trying to rush her into bed. He likes her, wants to talk to her for its own sake and not just as some trade-off for taking her clothes off later. He is willing to share little windows into his life and wants to peep through hers too; she is in no hurry. She doesn't think she has ever had this specific kind of attention before. It is sweet.

'Uh-oh. You're not confirming that, then.'

She hadn't realised he was reading anything into her silence.

What she should say is that she likes him, but her life is messy and she wouldn't be good for him. She should set him free now, walk back to the flat, lie low until he's gone permanently. He would go home, right home to where he's come from, put her in a little box which would be re-organised further and further towards the back of his mind over the months and years until he thought of her almost never. Then he would meet some other better, cleaner, healthier woman – she might not be as pretty as Bikkie, but she wouldn't be as messed up. *They* would have the salads and the Kilner bottle and the dog frolicking in the waves and the baby, and he'd be happy.

'Do you have any kids, Dale?'

'No.' Dale pauses. 'You?'

'No.'

If Bikkie let anything happen between her and Dale, she fears what her boyfriend would do to him. Not that her boyfriend is a hard man – he wouldn't fight Dale, even when he saw the limp – yet there is something seriously nasty about him at times.

But that sweetness is too good.

'Let's just see what happens,' Bikkie says, looking over at the ducks and twisting her long hair around her finger.

Maybe an hour later, they are still in the park, lying flat on their backs on the rug, their hats over their eyes and noses.

'Ever know anyone who went to boarding school?' Bikkie is asking.

'Nope. I always thought that was a particular form of cruelty favoured by the upper classes.'

'I read all those Enid Blyton books about Malory Towers and St Clare's and I just wanted to be part of that world – pranks on the mistresses, midnight feasts in the dorm with macaroons and ginger beer and sardines pressed into ginger cake; I can't imagine that's a great taste combination, but if Darrell and Sally adored it, then I wanted to try it too. They always seemed to be having so much fun, everyone had a special friend and a special talent, and any bullies always got their comeuppance. I had no idea what lacrosse was – I still don't – but it didn't stop me dreaming about playing for the team.'

She could say more, but she can feel Dale grinning beside her.

'Wouldn't you have missed your mum and dad, though?' he asks.

'I didn't have a mum then; it was just me and Dad.'

'Whoa. Now, you can't expect me to let that one go – you didn't have a mum *then*?'

'Well, I didn't know her back then. She wasn't in my life.'

'And she is now?'

'She could've been, if she'd wanted to. I found her. She couldn't stop me – it was my legal right.'

Bikkie sighs. What harm can it do talking about this now? She has more or less decided to go to the police anyway, so it doesn't matter if Dale puts two and two together later as they cannot have a shared future beyond the next few hours. She can't go on like this. It has to end.

'I take it she didn't greet you with open arms.'

'She did not.'

'That must've hurt.'

'I went in not expecting much. I mean, she was just a kid when she had me. I thought she'd have a whole other family and I'd be the guilty secret, the skeleton in the closet, but I thought it would be *our* secret, hers and mine, and that she would start to meet me quietly, send me a birthday card or even a present. But I didn't mean anything to her, I was less than nothing. She couldn't wait to get rid of me. Again. Fuck her.'

'Yeah, fuck her,' Dale says, so much to Bikkie's astonishment that she starts to giggle and sits up.

'What?' Dale says, pushing his hat off his eyes, but he is tittering slightly too.

'That is so unexpected, from you,' Bikkie says.

'Stick with me, baby, y'ain't seen nuthin' yet.'

And they just look at each other and laugh.

19

Joe has made us a chilli. It's good. He's brushing up on recipes he means to use when Kate and the children come. Joe will devise the menu plan and the list of ingredients and I will shop for them.

Conall is the picky eater. He doesn't like sticky foods to touch each other, but Kate says he's much more adventurous when Joe's the chef, which helped him progress from eating his meals on two separate plates to being able to cope with burritos and curries with rice and even once a stir-fry. Cara is the spice queen and Pip is the hoover, gobbling down everything without comment. I buy him treacle bread and soda farls just to top up on through the day and he devours the lot. There isn't a pick on him – he must have some crazy metabolism.

'How about having a Christmas dinner one day?' Joe says. 'We don't get to see them at Christmas, so we could nominate a date and do it when they're here. The kids could hang up stockings the night before and we could have presents and carols and then roast turkey and all the trimmings. What do you think?'

I think Joe is lonely. I think he needs to have friends his own age to go to Christmas parties with, in December, and late nights on the beach in this weather. He needs to eat in Nando's and Pizza Express, instead of cooking for his mother every night. He needs company. He needs to love and be loved by someone other than me.

'Oh, I don't know. If it's still as hot as this, I don't think we'd be able to nail the atmosphere.'

A wasp is buzzing in the window. Every year, there is a nest in the nearest lime tree and every year they come in through the windows and find themselves trapped by the slatted blinds. I can't move the blinds to release them, and I've got myself stung, before, trying to shoo them out by poking a magazine between the slats but only succeeding in making them cranky, so now I just leave them. They will escape, or they will not.

My phone dings. It's Callum. He's home and he's thinking about what I said. He doesn't want to come across as dismissive of the points I made, but he reckons I should stop worrying. Kevin can be a bit of a tool, but he's not dangerous.

'What's up?' Joe.

'Nothing, nothing.'

'Is it from Kate?'

I consider saying yes, but then I'd have to make up some message. I am cross that I cannot have anything for myself, however small, even as tiny as this text, without having to share it with my life-starved son.

'It's from Kim's brother.'

'Any news?'

'No. Just that he thinks there's nothing to worry about.'

My phone dings again. To save time, I read this one out.

'For what it's worth, I think Kevin's up for a reconciliation. I think he more or less confessed to me last night that he may have strayed, himself, in the past, so he's not claiming any moral high ground, but he's still gutted. I suggested Relate. Another text to follow ...'

'Maybe he's right,' I say.

'Mmm,' Joe says, and I feel his reluctance to relinquish his grip on this little bit of drama, yet he is a scientist, he always seeks to follow the evidence, and the evidence now seems to be pointing to a simple case of marital infidelity.

Ding. Another text.

I have not breathed a word of our conversation to Kevin, and will not. When all this is ancient history, you'll still have to live across the road. My lips are sealed.

'What are you texting?' Joe says, as I start to tap my phone.

'I'm just thanking him and agreeing to draw a line under it,' I say.

I set down my phone beside me on the sofa and pick up my book.

Ding.

Now that we've got that out of the way, how would you feel about coming out with me for a drink? We could steer clear of Kevin and Kim and talk about other things – for example, I'd love to get some advice on working in schools that I could use on Rebecca when she re-appears – I understand that she's never going to be a teacher, but she might make a decent classroom assistant. I think she'd be good with kids and young people (and, as the prospective granddad somewhere down the line, I like the idea that she'd be able to look after her own sprogs during the holidays).

My smile grips me all the way from my lips to my stomach and I am so grateful that Joe is distracted by trying to find a news update on TV.

'I think I'll put on the immersion for a bath,' I say, winning myself an excuse to go into the kitchen on my own.

I key in: I'd love that, evaluate and change it to I'd like that.

Just this once, I am not going to examine the fact that this relationship cannot go anywhere, that I can never bring Callum back to my place, can never pour him a glass of wine from my fridge, never cook him a meal in my kitchen, never hold hands on my sofa, or gaze into his eyes, here, or let him carry me upstairs to bed.

Just this once, I am going to cherish this little bit of excitement, enjoy it for what it is, trust that it will bring me some measure of joy, if I let it.

Callum texts back: Friday?

I respond with: Sure. Sevenish?

Callum texts: Sevenish it is. Tell me where you'd like to go and I'll book you a taxi — I don't particularly want to run into Kevin and there's no hiding place in Parnell Park. That OK with you?

That is more than OK with me. I, too, would prefer to keep this development private.

Someone is rapping on the front door.

'Alice!' It's Antoinette, shouting through the letterbox. 'Alice, it's bin night! OK?'

I rush to the door, open it and pull it almost closed behind me as I stand on the step.

'Thanks, Antoinette. I'll drag it round now.'

'Watch the steps, in your flip-flops.'

'I will. Antoinette?'

'Yep. Is something up, Ali?'

I lower my voice. I don't want Joe to hear me. I do want to keep this private, but I have to tell *someone*. 'Callum's asked me out for a drink.' I am blushing.

'Ooo-ooh!' Antoinette says, in a sing-songy voice. 'How did this happen?'

'He took my number, so he could let me know when he heard from Kim, to put my mind at rest.'

'Slick hoo-er.' Antoinette delights in a bit of vernacular.

'Then he texted me, to ask if I'd go for a drink with him.'

'That's fab. He is seriously good-looking, even if he doesn't have that whiff of danger, like Kevin, that we all secretly dream about.'

I am so glad, now, that I never, even slightly, acted on my attraction to Kevin. If anything had been going to happen, it would've been that night with the red wine and the postcard, when I thought he was going to kiss me. If he had ...

'Where are you going?'

'I don't know yet. Maybe somewhere out of town, where we're not going to bump into anyone we know. Promise you won't say anything to Kevin.'

'Course I won't. Get you!'

Antoinette is so happy for me. She issues no words of warning, drops no fly in the ointment, does nothing to steal the sparkle from this delicious moment, and I love her for it.

'By the way,' she says, 'guess who had the estate agent round today.'

'Oh, you didn't,' I say.

'No, I didn't,' says Antoinette. 'But Kevin Kennedy did. And it was a bit of a covert operation.'

'What do you mean?'

'Well, he didn't go to any of the firms in town – he used a little place thirty miles away, and the bloke parked around the corner. Nobody was supposed to know, clearly.'

'So how do *you* know?' I say.

'Because I did pretty much the same thing about a month ago. I told you I was thinking of moving, but I didn't want it getting back to my brother and sister – they who would share the spoils – until I'd done a bit of research. So I didn't go local, I went well out of town to a name I'd seen on PropertyPal. It was the very same guy I saw going into Kevin's with his tablet this afternoon. When he came out, I stuck on my sunglasses and hat and followed him back to his car, parked round in Richmount Drive. Just thought you'd like to know.'

I'm not sure I did want to know. As I shut the door, I decide not to share this titbit with Joe, but just to have my bath and forget about it. I remember this morning's *Hairy Maclary* scene with all the dogs and it makes me smile again. Parnell Park is a quiet suburban street in a small town, with privet hedges, power-hosed paving and an amusing cast of canine characters. It is hardly likely to be the lair of a wife-murderer.

I catch sight of myself in the mirror of the hallstand, stop and look at my face. I imagine Callum standing opposite me, studying me. First, he would tuck away that long lock of hair that has fallen over one eye, putting it behind my ear. He would trace, with his look, the arch of each of my eyebrows, smile at the just discernible childhood freckles that still pepper the bridge of my nose, he would follow the sweep of my cheekbones, the outline of my chin until his eyes stopped on my mouth and I would know he was about to kiss me.

How long has it been since I was kissed, properly?

I hold my breath now, contemplating that first touch on the lips and the electricity that will shoot through my body.

We will end up in bed. I know it.

20

Bikkie and Dale are still in the little park, but they have moved to a bench just inside the gates. A chip van pulled up a while ago and now the aroma of hot food and vinegar is wafting in their direction.

'Man, that smells good,' Dale says. 'Want something?'

They agree to share a bag of chips and are soon spearing the contents with little wooden forks.

'Look, we're doing this all wrong,' Dale says.

Bikkie just looks at him – what's the right way to eat a bag of chips?

'I'm right-handed, you're left-handed. We should swap sides,' Dale says.

Ah. They exchange places and it makes sense.

'My so-called mother is left-handed too, so I guess I got it from her,' Bikkie says.

'Yeah? Lefties are meant to be good at maths and spatial awareness, so excellent at parking the car.'

'I am good at parking,' says Bikkie. That's one proper, adult thing she can do that her boyfriend can't: drive a car. She couldn't wait to get her licence and can't understand why he hasn't bothered.

'And maths?'

'Not so much.'

Over the past hour, during the gaps in their conversation, Bikkie has reached a decision. She will go to the police. She will tell them everything – where she has been holed up, what she has been doing, what she and her boyfriend planned. Every day of this ordeal has eaten away at her belief in him, her love for him, even. Every hour spent with Dale has shown her what life could be like, should be like. She doesn't care any more about being 'minted' – her boyfriend's word – she just wants to be a decent person, the sort of human being Dale believes her to be. She cannot live the rest of her life in fear of that knock on the door. Her boyfriend is toxic. There's something wrong with him. She sees this now.

She will go to prison, she knows, but not forever. When she gets out, she will start again.

But first, first, she wants one last day of freedom. If Dale asks her – and she hopes he does – she will spend it with him.

21

Tonight I am exfoliating, smoothing on body lotion, painting my toenails, plucking my eyebrows, plastering on a face mask, my clean and conditioned hair piled under a towel turban.

Of course I want Joe and Kate and Cara and Conall and Pip to have it all – love and success and, yes, probably wealth, but somewhere along the line, I have stopped having such expectations for myself. I would settle – I would happily settle – for part-time companionship and occasional nights away. And even that, even lovely Callum, I would trade in a heartbeat if Joe could get his life back.

I lie on the bed, in my dressing gown, having taken care not to catch an artery on the crappy mattress spring, thinking I will ask Antoinette to pick me up one of those rolled-up foam mattresses the next time she goes to IKEA, and wondering where Callum and I will go on our first date. Because it is a date. An attractive man has asked me out for a drink, I have said yes, and he is sending a taxi for me – this constitutes a date.

It's best not to smile, or I'll crack my mask.

'Mum?' Joe is rapping softly on the bedroom door.

'Mmm,' I say, trying to keep my face muscles slack. 'Come in, but be warned, I'm wearing a face pack, so don't be alarmed.'

I hear the bottom of the door sweep over the carpet and sense Joe standing over me.

'What on earth ...?' he says.

'It's a mud pack. It's good for my skin,' I say, trying to keep my face still. 'Watch out for the pointy spring.'

I feel Joe sit down on the end of the bed.

'OK, I know you don't really want to talk about this any more, but there's been a development.'

'Oh, Joe, no. I thought we'd agreed we were done with the whole Kennedys situation.'

'Just hear me out.'

'Do I have to?'

'Yes. You do.'

'Does it concern Facebook?'

'No.'

I sigh.

'Will you listen?'

I don't feel like I have much choice. 'OK.'

'Right. Kevin Kennedy left his house about an hour ago,

with a laptop in a laptop bag. I saw him put the computer in the bag on the front doorstep, slip the bag strap over his head, then set off down the Park. Then, a few minutes ago, he returned with the laptop bag, checked up and down the street, saw no-one and *folded* the bag – so it must've been *empty* now – and put it in Jim and Marjorie Wright's bin, which is sitting at the kerb for tomorrow morning.'

My brain hasn't quite left the crisp hotel sheets – what is Joe saying?

'The guy just dumped a computer, Mum, and disposed of the bag in someone else's rubbish. Doesn't that strike you as suspicious?'

'Why would he dump a computer?'

'To get rid of whatever searches a layperson makes in order to carry out a crime and not get caught, presumably. Google searches, contacts with dubious people, access to the dark Web, I don't know.'

'Couldn't he just delete his history?'

'Might hide it from you and me, but a police investigation would soon get past that. It's odd behaviour, you'd have to concede, dumping a laptop and even disposing of the bag. Mum? You don't find it odd?'

'Antoinette told me tonight that Kevin had the house valued today on the quiet.'

'What? Well, now, this is really starting to mount up. With mortgage protection insurance, if one of them dies, the mortgage is cleared instantly, isn't that the case?'

'Yep.'

'And the surviving partner will own the house outright – so Kevin wanted to know how much he stands to make.'

'Or he's thinking of a new start for Kim and him, if they're going to put some affair episode behind them.'

'Maybe,' Joe says, but I can see he doesn't buy it.

'Mum, you need to put on your clothes and go and get that laptop bag from the Wrights' bin.'

'You've got to be kidding me.'

'I'm not kidding. It's evidence. The police aren't listening yet, but the only way to change that is with something concrete. If the bin lorry takes it away in the morning, it's gone forever, but you can stop that.'

I wish I had never seen Kim Kennedy on the train in Croydon, and then none of this difficult, puzzling, worrying, complicated and frustrating trail of crumbs would involve me.

I want to shout: *If you're so convinced, then* you *do it.* You *put something on your feet and sneak across the Park and fish some bag from a smelly bin, and leave me alone.* But Joe stops breathing every time the postman comes – what does he fear most? People's fear, or, worse, their disgust? – so instead I sigh again, check my watch, and say I'll think about it. Joe assumes this means I'll do it, but I genuinely haven't decided. I just want him to stop pressing me.

22

Bikkie knows why Dale has chosen this setting for their picnic. It is because he reads her like a book. She's in trouble, and he knows it, even though he's said nothing. He hasn't so much as hinted anything, but she's sure he's figured out something's not right. And so he is sparing her the crowds of people and their prying eyes and has suggested somewhere where there are no CCTV cameras just waiting for her to take off her hat and shades. Does he suspect this is her last day, that she has reached the end? It wouldn't surprise her – there is something in him which seems to sense these things.

He hasn't brought the rug today, but it doesn't matter – the grass is perfectly dry. Bikkie supposes he had so much to carry he couldn't manage the rug as well. She is curious to know what's in all the plastic bags.

'How're the hands?' she asks.

Dale glances at his white gloves.

'The itching's getting better. The hardest part is keeping these things clean.'

They look immaculate, Bikkie thinks.

'I don't know when I last had a picnic,' she says. Her boyfriend wouldn't lower himself. He likes hot food, not sandwiches.

They're not quite sure where to sit – they have the place to themselves, it seems. Climbing down the grassy hill, at the bottom they find a river, higher and faster than Bikkie would have expected after all this warm weather. If she were to fall in, just tumble off the bank, she would be swept away and would never have to explain herself. Dale could melt back into wherever he came from. That would be that.

There is a wooden footbridge over the water. Bikkie stands on this and peers into the depths. The water looks so clean and cold, almost inviting. Even though she has made up her mind, she still fears the future. Not just prison, but afterwards. Will her boyfriend track her down, punish her, take revenge? Will all this ever really end?

She has heard of people being given new identities in some part of the country where nobody knows them. But this must be expensive and she supposes the authorities would have to be absolutely convinced that her boyfriend posed a threat, and he's so good at fooling people he'd probably get round them.

'How about over here, under the trees?' Dale says.

'Sure,' says Bikkie, hoisting up her maxi dress an inch or two so she doesn't trample it as she climbs the few feet.

Dale sets down his bags and waits for Bikkie to sit first.

'Are you a good swimmer?' he asks. 'Just so I know whether to jump in after you if you fall, or if you'd end up saving *my* life.'

Bikkie smiles. 'I'm not bad, actually. I've been swimming lengths every week at the pool for a while.' Her boyfriend's idea, *again*. Is there anything at all in Bikkie's life that actually came originally from her? She's starting to wonder.

'Tell me three things about you that I don't know,' she says, leaning back on her elbows. 'Three things that separate you from the herd, that are just yours.'

'And you'll tell me three things about you?' says Dale.

She says she will. She'd better start thinking.

'OK. I whittle.'

Bikkie splutters with laughter. 'You what?'

'Whittling. You've never heard of whittling?'

'No,' Bikkie says. 'What is it? And are you sure I want to know?'

'Perfectly innocent,' Dale says. 'It means carving things out of little pieces of wood. You must have heard of this before.'

She really hasn't. 'Does it require special tools?'

'Just one of these.' Dale pulls a folded knife from his hip pocket.

'What's that?'

'Really?' He opens it out. 'I thought all kids had one of these, at some time. It's a penknife.'

'Not me. I wasn't a very girly girl, what with having no mum as a role model, but I think Dad would've gone apeshit. Aren't they illegal?'

'You're thinking of a switchblade – nasty bit of work; you don't want to mess with one of those. Was your dad very protective of you?' Dale folds the knife shut and sets it down.

'I can see now that he probably was, but I didn't think of it that way, at the time. It just seemed that he stopped me doing all the things I really wanted to do. He always had to know what I was up to and who I was with. I never did sleepovers – I think he was wary of having other kids at our place overnight with no woman on the premises, in case people talked.'

'That's understandable,' Dale says. 'Can't blame the guy for trying to safeguard his reputation, especially with a little girl depending on him.'

'I know, but it didn't help me to get in with the in-crowd, if you know what I mean. I wasn't exactly Miss Popular to start with and that made me even more of an oddity. He wouldn't let me stay over at anyone else's house either.'

'I can see how hard that would be for a young girl, Charlotte, but I also get where your dad was coming from. I might do exactly the same.'

'I think he tried to loosen up when he realised I wasn't a child any more, but I probably didn't help myself by having a couple of "bad" boyfriends and Dad started trying to control my life again. It drove me away in the end.'

'You'll see things differently when you have kids of your own. Then you'll go back to him, I bet.'

What will her father say when she is arrested, remanded

in custody, taken to court in a van with blacked-out windows? Will he disown her, or will he find her the best lawyer he can afford, call for mercy, point the finger at the boyfriend as the real culprit?

'So, what kinds of things do you whittle?'

'All sorts. Birds, animals, Christmas shapes.'

'Christmas shapes?'

'Bells, trees, angels.'

'You could do a whole nativity scene.'

'I could do. It'd take a while.'

'This is only July – plenty of time.'

Could she be sentenced by Christmas? She doesn't know how long a case takes to come to court or how long a trial is likely to last. Would there even be a trial, if she pleads guilty? There'd be no need for a jury, would there? Unless her boyfriend makes things difficult. But how could he? – he's in this up to his neck.

She hasn't given her boyfriend any clues that she has changed her mind. She's just played along with his texts. She doesn't want him talking her round, getting her to fall in again.

'Your turn. Tell me something I don't know about you.'

Bikkie thinks. She takes off her hat and pulls her hair up at the sides of her head.

'I have attached earlobes. See? Somebody told me twice as many people have unattached earlobes, but I don't know if that's true.' She lets her hair fall again. 'My mother – my biological mother – has them too. I noticed them when I met her. I wanted to find out all the things we had in common –

I'm nothing like my dad, not to look at, not in personality. When I was little, I sometimes wondered if he was my real dad at all. But I couldn't have imagined the truth. Bitch.'

Dale gives a low whistle. 'Man, she's really hurt you.'

'I spent my entire childhood fantasising about what she would be like. Even though I knew she'd basically abandoned me, I built up a picture of her as kind and caring. I dressed her in an apron and had her baking biscuits. Mad. But whatever she'd been like – if she'd been a bit hopeless and messed up, or if she'd settled down after she'd had me and brought up another family – I'd have accepted it. I just wanted to know her – I wouldn't have cared how successful she was or how many other people I had to share her with.'

Bikkie is sitting up now, hugging her knees.

'It was easy to find her, with dad's help, once he realised I was determined. And guess what.' She looks straight ahead of her. 'She was my dad's sister, Dale. An unmarried expectant mother. A woman I didn't know existed. I was going to be put in care when I was born. But Mum's older brother, who had nothing to do with it, stepped in and persuaded social services to let him keep me. My granddad, who had threatened to cut my mum off if she kept me, cut off my dad-slash-uncle instead. So I was brought up with no mother, no biological father and no extended family, by a dad who was really my uncle – pretty screwed up, huh? But I still yearned for my mum.

'I wrote her a letter. I bought a new pen to write it with, and Basildon Bond notepaper. I wanted to put my whole life in that letter, tell her everything she'd missed, but that might have frightened her off, so I just sent her a few lines to say who I was and that I'd like to meet.'

'She agreed to see you, though.'

'She didn't have much choice. I had her address, so I suppose she thought it was better than me calling at the house.'

'It wasn't like *Long Lost Family*, I take it.'

'No. Not much. She was the ice queen. I thought I'd get a hug, at least, but she didn't even shake my hand. I thought there might be a whole lot of brothers and sisters, but now I'm glad she didn't have any more children, or she'd have messed them up too.

'We met in a hotel bar and I went in wanting to order a bottle of champagne; even a couple of glasses of prosecco would've done. I wanted us to clink our drinks and have a toast to new beginnings, to being reunited, to our future together. But it wasn't a celebration for her – it was an ordeal she had to get through. She drank two of those little bottles of red wine and I had Diet Coke.'

'How long did you sit with her?'

'An hour? I couldn't stop looking at her, trying to take in every detail. She wouldn't make eye contact, just stared off to the side.'

'You can't pick your family.'

'Sadly, no. When I saw how much I looked like her, I couldn't understand how she didn't feel anything, no bond. I remember thinking: you should have been there to tell me how to cope with growing up as a ginger.'

Dale looks surprised. 'Is that how you thought of yourself

as a kid? A ginger? That's practically a term of abuse.' He looks at her, the old sheepishness replaced by something bolder. 'You're like a Pre-Raphaelite goddess, Charlotte.'

Neither of them says anything for a moment.

'Oh, I bought you something, by the way. Do you want to see it?' Dale says.

'A present? For me? Why?'

Dale takes the hat off his face and looks unsure. 'It's nothing expensive,' he says. 'Just, I don't know, a token. I saw it and I thought it would go with your hair.'

'With my hair?' she says. 'Now I'm curious.'

Dale sits up, dips into one of the plastic carrier bags and takes out a smaller paper bag. He hands it to Bikkie. She grins at him, takes off her sunglasses and sets them on the ground beside her.

'Watch you don't step on those when you stand up,' Dale says.

Bikkie slips her hand inside the paper bag and slides out a small, flat package, wrapped in yellow tissue paper. She looks at Dale and raises her eyebrows.

'Well, open it! The suspense is killing me,' Dale says, with a laugh.

Bikkie turns it over carefully in her hands and releases the contents. She finds a long silk scarf, emerald green with splashes of amber. She really likes it.

'It's beautiful,' she says.

Dale looks like he wants to tell her something – perhaps that *she* is beautiful? – but decides against.

'Put it on me,' Bikkie says, handing the scarf to him and

standing up. Dale rises from the grass and stands behind her. He takes the scarf in his gloved hands and places it around her neck, wraps it, really. For a split second, with the gloves on her throat, Bikkie thinks she feels him tighten the scarf and her heart starts to beat faster, but as soon as she raises her hands the scarf slackens again and she feels foolish, almost laughs.

'That OK?' Dale says.

Bikkie pulls a compact mirror from the pocket of her denim jacket, flips it open, smiles in delight, though the mirror is shaking slightly.

'Thank you,' she says.

23

In bed with the windows open, I heard the country lodge parading past the end of Parnell Park just after 7.30 p.m. this morning, or at least I heard the pipe band that led them. I was already awake, so I caught them faintly at first, thought maybe the sounds were coming from town, then I realised they were growing closer.

No-one flies a flag in Parnell Park and I have little idea whether most of my neighbours are Protestant-slash-unionist or Catholic-slash-nationalist or something else. Antoinette's Catholic, but she's dragged me into town before now on the Twelfth to see the district parade – just curious, I think. Men who knew her father stepped out and shook her hand as they passed. And if Marjorie Wright was asking Jim to take her on a tour of the bonfires the other night, then I'd guess her background's Protestant, although this is by no means certain – perhaps she just fancied a middle-class safari of estate-life.

Parnell Park is the sort of place you choose to live if the question of your neighbours' religious background is of little defining interest to you, compared with the handsome lime trees, the stained-glass windows, the quiet. And if you can afford it, of course.

I left it until 10.30 a.m. to set off for Mount Charles, so the roads would be clear again. Margarida let me in.

'The place seems very quiet,' I said. The residents in the day room were all sleeping or looking at the television.

'Linzi and Alanis have gone to the field with Lawrence and the little ones, and also the activities co-ordinator, the hairdresser and the student have gone to see the parade.'

I was amused to hear Margarida speak with apparent familiarity of 'the field' – the colloquial but entirely accurate name for that place where the tired Orangemen of the entire district remove their jackets and sit on the grass with a ham salad sandwich and a cup of tea before their homeward walk.

'So you're having a low-key day.'

'Yes, low-key. It's just me, the Polish girls and the Lithuanians.'

'But you'll get time off in lieu.'

'Sure. It suits us fine to work today and tomorrow and then take the extra days when we want to go home. Ruby, Alice is here to see you.'

'Thanks, Margarida. Hi, Mum.'

She didn't look at me. Ah, one of her difficult days.

I sat down next to her, angled my chair companionably. 'What's up?'

With her Christopher Robin bob and her chin on her chest, she looked like a sulky child.

'Someone's taken my teeth.'

I almost laughed. This was clearly something she'd heard another resident say.

'Someone's taken them?' I said. 'What makes you think that?'

'I left them in the glass beside my bed and when I put them in again this morning, I knew straight away they weren't mine.'

'Really?' I said. 'That's dreadful. But you've decided to wear them anyway.'

'Well, I haven't much choice, have I? How am I supposed to eat?'

'There is that. Tell you what, I'll speak to Margarida, ask her to organise a thorough check, and make sure you have your own teeth by teatime. How's that?'

'I know who took them.'

'Oh?'

'Nan Black.'

Nan Black was at primary school with Mum, seventy years ago. I'd seen photographs. She was a foot taller than Mum and had plaits – Mum had a bob back then too, but instead of a fringe her blonde hair was clipped off her face with a huge, floppy bow. I didn't know if Nan was still alive. I did know she wasn't a resident of this home.

'And what would Nan Black want with your teeth, Mum?'

'What do you think?' Mum said, but she declined to elaborate.

Mum doesn't have dentures. She has a full set of her own teeth. The dentist comes to the home and inspects them every few months and she never needs to have any work done because she doesn't have much of a sweet tooth and she lets Linzi or Margarida or whoever clean them every night.

I decided to change the subject.

'It's a bit more overcast, today.'

'It needs to rain. The farmers are crying out for it.'

Aha. A blink of reality.

'Did you hear that on the news?'

'It was in the paper. You can see for yourself – but Mummy might have burned it already. If she hasn't burned it, it'll still be under the cushion on that seat where you're sitting. Get up and look.'

I got up, checked for a newspaper I knew had never been there and which Mum had never read, but it gave me an idea.

'Would you like me to bring you some new magazines, next time I come?'

'Yes, please. I'm a great reader, always was.'

'Which ones would you like?'

'*Woman* or *Woman's Own*. Not *The Lady* – your auntie Doreen used to buy *The Lady*, I cannot imagine why. Advertisements for butlers and groundsmen and French-speaking nannies – Doreen worked in the co-op.'

'I think they've probably modernised it a bit now,' I said, although I didn't really know.

'Or the *Picture Post*. Yes, bring me the *Picture Post*.'

I stayed until lunch was served.

Now I've popped into the big garage shop to look for Mum's magazines and something tasty for Joe and me. I think perhaps pork chops cooked in cider – they even have an off-sales in this place now, so I can pick up everything in one go.

'Can I take that basket for you? It looks heavy.' It's the Wrights' grandson. I know his name, but just now I can't remember it.

'I'm Weston ...'

'Yes, Weston. I know who you are. That's very kind of you. Thanks.'

The weight is mainly in the two large bottles of Magners – one for cooking, one for drinking.

'Have you more to do? I can follow you round and you can pop in whatever you want. There's no rush.'

'I just need to decide which magazines to choose for my mother. She's in a residential home and she can't read any more, still she seems to like looking at the pictures. But I can't keep you – you must have things to do.'

'Not really,' Weston says. 'I'm on a bit of a hiatus. I finished my degree at the start of the summer and now I have to decide what to do next. I've been accepted for a master's, but I'm not convinced I actually want it right now. I'm thinking of going travelling.'

'Oh, how exciting. Where?'

'Not sure. Somewhere off the beaten track. And cheap, ideally. I'm not one of those Trustafarians.'

'Will you go with friends, or a girlfriend ...?'

'On my own.' He says it too quickly. I suspect there is a girl, but for some reason he's keeping that to himself. 'At least, initially. I hope I'll make some friends along the way.'

Would his parents disapprove of him travelling with a girlfriend? I can't remember their names either, now. She's the former Miss Wright – now, there's a handle to be saddled with – and I'm sure her first name has two syllables, emphasis on the first syllable, but what is it? Not Lynsey, not Wendy, not Susan. I give up. I'm losing it. The husband's name is short, like Tom or Bob, but neither of these. None of this is the point, though. What I'm really thinking is that they must be about my age, so sexual conservatism to this extent seems unlikely, but who knows?

'If your mum likes pictures, this one looks good.' Weston has set down the wire basket and is flicking through a glossy magazine. 'It has lots of big images, plenty of faces, but other things too.'

It is *Good Housekeeping*.

'It'll do,' I say. I grab a *People's Friend* as well. Perhaps Mum would like me to read her some of the stories.

At the till, Weston swings the basket into the cradle in the counter and I thank him. He goes to the next till and buys a packet of cigarettes. As a parent, I would be more distressed by those than by the possibility of unmarried sex.

'And these,' I say, lifting a packet of breath mints and dropping them into my basket. I don't bother to hide them from Weston. He's charming for a young man, but it'd still never occur to him that someone my age might ever be kissed.

I do it again, on the way home – get in the wrong lane even

though I drive this route practically every day, get trapped and panic slightly as I cannot figure out my exit strategy. The traffic isn't heavy, so it's not as traumatic as it might be, but I don't take it in my stride. When I get it straightened out, I pull off the road altogether and try to figure out what went wrong. Was I daydreaming? Was my mind on something else? The truth is I don't know. I cannot recall what I was thinking about at all since I paid for my groceries at the garage. Is this how it starts? With little periods of absence from my right mind?

When I get home, there are flowers on the front step – a proper bouquet, wrapped in cellophane and coloured paper. I feel trembly, but nice-trembly, as I set down my shopping bags and lift the flowers to smell them and, of course, to see if there's a card.

They are a mix of pinks and creams, roses and lilies and other sorts – I'm not sure what. They smell wonderful and yes, there is a tiny white envelope attached.

I open the front door, lift my shopping into the hall, carry in the bouquet and listen for Joe. The sound of the cross-trainer creaks overhead. I'm all fingers and thumbs as I try to open the tiny envelope. The card, which I tug out, is printed simply with 'For You' in gold, swirly script. On it is written, presumably in the florist's handwriting, 'From Callum'.

The whole time I am cooking the pork chops, peeling the potatoes, steeping the scallions in warm milk and melted butter, I am dancing round the kitchen to Van Morrison. I can't keep the smile off my face. When Joe appears, he's bound to ask. I've had flowers before, but always on the last day of school, from kind parents who want to make me feel appreciated, I hope, or perhaps just because they think it's expected. Term ended nearly two weeks ago, though, so that's clearly not where these came from. I could've put them in the bin, saved any questions, but that would've been a sin – they're beautiful and fresh and, on closer inspection, they're even Fair Trade, for goodness' sake. I resolved to enjoy them and deal with whatever Joe thinks.

I hear the low bark of the Great Dane followed by the chirp of the little Yorkshire terrier and rush from the kitchen to the front-room window, spoon in hand. I'm hoping for a re-run of the *Hairy Maclary* experience. To my great joy there are no fewer than eight dogs in all shapes and sizes lolloping along Parnell Park, some with humans, some on those extending leads, some, including the rascally terriers from round the corner, running free.

'Joe, look! Quick!' I shout. 'Out the front window!'

He can see through the slats. They won't see him.

A moment later, he comes galloping downstairs, grinning.

'Did you see them? Aren't they fab?' I say.

'I think I counted nine. Have they all agreed to go walkies at the same time, do you reckon?'

'I'm not sure if all their owners even know they're out there. I see two of those little terriers behind a gate most days. I think they've escaped.'

'Nice flowers,' Joe says, noticing them in a vase on the hallstand. He goes over, takes a sniff, sees the card.

'Who's Callum?' he says.

24

Bikkie cannot believe it, when Dale lays out the picnic foods on the grass. He has brought a crusty loaf and some ham and cheese and apples, but these are not the main event. Dale has remembered what she said about Enid Blyton and the midnight feasts in the dorm. He has gone and bought ginger cake and sardines and – where on earth did he get them, round here? – macaroons!

Then, ta-da! – from another plastic bag he produces bottles of ginger beer!

Bikkie can't help herself – she hugs him.

Dale looks thrilled, pushes his John Lennon sunglasses up the bridge of his nose.

'Can we drink it here? Is it alcoholic? Are we allowed?' Bikkie says.

Dale looks around. There is no-one.

'Who's going to stop us?' he says. 'This is Crabbie's ginger beer – the good stuff. Four per cent by volume.'

'I've never had it before,' Bikkie says. 'Oh, no. They've got those tops you need an opener for.'

But Dale is ahead of her. He has thought of everything. On the ground he sets a combined bottle-opener and corkscrew, which he carefully lays alongside a serrated, long-bladed bread knife and a shorter, sharper-looking fruit knife, with a four-inch blade and a red handle. As Bikkie watches his gloved hands move, she thinks of a surgeon laying out his instruments and for just a moment it makes her shiver.

'Your turn to tell me another thing about yourself,' she says, and the weird feeling passes.

'All right,' Dale says, popping the top off the first bottle and handing it to her, then popping another for himself. 'I have a tattoo.'

'Really!' Bikkie says.

'You're surprised. Didn't think I was the type?'

'I don't know that there is a type any more, is there? I mean, everyone seems to have one these days.'

Is he hurt? She didn't mean it like that.

'I only meant ...'

'It's OK. I know – it used to be the preserve of the armed forces and real hard nuts, now teenage girls have them across their shoulder blades. Times change.'

'So what's yours of? Can I ask?'

'You can see it if you want – do you want?'

'Better tell me where it is, first.'

'On my right shoulder.'

'Then show me.'

Dale opens a button on his chest, then pulls his shirt over his head. Bikkie sees the wolf. It is beautiful, but its fangs are bared.

'You don't like it,' Dale says.

'No, I do like it, but it's just not what I expected.'

'Should I cover it up again?'

'No. Leave it,' Bikkie says, and he does.

'How much did it hurt?' she asks him later, when they are digging into the bread and ham and cheese.

'The tattoo? Not that much. Not as much as I expected. How much did it hurt to get your ears pierced?'

'Painless,' Bikkie says through a mouthful of bread. She wipes her lips with the back of her hand. 'I had it done with a gun-thing. Hardly noticed. I went a bit woozy the first time I had to change my studs, but I soon got used to it.'

'Any other piercings?' Dale asks.

'No,' Bikkie says.

He gives her a mischievous look.

'No!' Bikkie says again, and she pretends to bat him with the ginger cake.

'You're good fun, Charlotte,' Dale says.

Bikkie smiles at him. She's had compliments from men since she was fourteen, but this is different. There is a warmth to Dale's words – what he says and the way he says it. She hasn't forgotten that he called her a goddess, and that was almost frightening, but saying things like this, things like she's fun to be with, makes her feel good to her bones. Her boyfriend never tires of telling her she has no sense of humour, and when you hear a thing often enough, you start to believe it. But thinking about it now, the things he did and said weren't all that funny. Too often they were cruel or dismissive and that's easy to do if you're cold. She wonders if she will have to face him in court. When she gives evidence, will he be there, staring her out as she stands in the witness box – although, will she be in the witness box? Surely she will be in the dock.

It must be a sense of dread creeping from that thought into the reality of the picnic, because she gets a bad feeling, seeing Dale's gloves on the corkscrew part of the opener for no good reason, twisting, twisting. Bikkie imagines it going into the side of her neck.

Snap out of it.

'Ready for another ginger beer, Enid?' Dale is holding up a bottle.

'Think I'll have some more bread, first. I'm not used to drinking alcohol in this heat.'

'Then I'll join you.'

As he saws through the tough crust, to make two more thick slices, Bikkie actually has to look away and try and think about something else. Prince songs. She will replay in her mind all the lyrics to 'Purple Rain' and by the time she has finished she will be eating the bread – and it is just bread,

Dale was not sawing through bone – and everything will be back to normal.

Why is she so jittery?

Is it because they haven't seen a single other person the whole time they've been here? What does she really know about him? Only what he has chosen to tell her, and she has no way of checking any of it. There are two voices inside Bikkie's head now – the one that says Dale is exactly what he seems, a nice guy, a thoughtful, gentle person who has given her a taste of normality at the craziest possible time in her life, and the other voice, the one that says play it cool, don't let him know you're scared, but get away from him, get away and then run.

'Hey, dreamer. Your turn. Tell me something more about yourself.'

Yes, of course. They were playing a game. Three things each to show their true personalities.

'It's not that easy to think of things,' Bikkie says, trying to keep the wobble out of her voice. 'I'm not a very interesting person.'

'Well, I know that's not true, for a start.'

She isn't a great thinker at the best of times, but right now Bikkie is attempting to juggle two lines of thought at once. She is trying to answer the question and at the same time devise a way to remove herself from this situation without arousing Dale's suspicion.

'I'm a massive Prince fan.' That much doesn't matter now. Leaving clues, risking discovery, all the things her boyfriend warned her against – none of these things matter, since she's going to the police soon. As for the more urgent need to escape Dale, maybe she could suggest they go for a walk, pack up the picnic stuff and try to steer them to somewhere more public. Would that seem odd? Would he guess what she was up to?

'Prince, eh? The little guy in the purple suit.'

Bikkie bristles at this. Prince was legendary, not a 'little guy'.

'He was a phenomenal talent,' she says.

'I know. I'm kidding. I haven't listened to that much of his stuff, but like any good pub-quizzer, I know he won an Oscar and – I *think* – seven Grammys?'

'Correct!' Bikkie's smile is back 'Do you really go to pub quizzes, or is that just a figure of speech?' This is so-o-o normal. She doesn't know what was going on in her head a moment ago.

'Sure I do. Did I not tell you I'm one of the Boundary Shot Boys? – pretty unbeatable team of six. We shock and awe in saloon bars and village halls for miles around – well, around where I live, anyway. I'm the specialist on music and the US, as it happens, so pulling out a few facts about Prince Rogers Nelson, born 1958 in Minneapolis, Minnesota, died 2016 in Chanhassen, also Minnesota, isn't even a stretch.'

Bikkie's jaw drops. Dale chuckles.

She hasn't been to Minnesota or indeed ever to the US at all, but she'd like to go. Her dad – the dad who brought her up – used to take her to France. He spoke the language a bit, but Bikkie's French never really took off – she thinks perhaps her biological father was somewhat dim; that would explain a lot.

Dale has done a coach tour including Los Angeles, Las Vegas, Yosemite, the Grand Canyon, San Francisco. Bikkie finds the thought of standing looking into the impossible vastness of the Grand Canyon terrifying. She is used to things on a smaller scale – small town, small life, small horizons. Her dreams of greater happiness might have included an idea of something bigger and more being better, but not too much bigger, not too much more.

'You can't go through life being afraid, Charlotte,' Dale says, seeming to read her thoughts.

She already knows this, but it doesn't make the feelings stop, and right now she has plenty of things about which to feel frightened.

'Aren't you scared of anything?' she asks. Surely there must be something.

'Course I am. I'm afraid of losing the people I care about,' he says, looking into the distance. 'When you get right down to it, that's all that matters – relationships.'

Bikkie thinks that if Dale is right, she's royally fucked, as she doesn't have a single healthy relationship in her life. And she suspects he *is* right. So why didn't they teach *that* in school? Why didn't anybody tell a twelve-year-old Bikkie how to choose a trustworthy pal, how to keep a friend, the value of just staying in touch, the way to identify the right person to fall in love with? Oh, how much more she could have done with that than with neurons, Roman numerals and noble gases bouncing about randomly in her head like the beads in a maraca shaken by a child.

'Would you like to have kids?' she says, surprising herself.

'Sure. Would you?'

'Yes,' Bikkie says, thinking that, depending on the length of her sentence, she could be in danger of missing that boat, which would make her very sad indeed, and for which she could never forgive her boyfriend. Not that she wants to have a child with him any more – it is amazing how quickly her feelings for him are changing; maybe she just needed time away from him to see him for what he really is – but she would very much like to have a baby, a sweet, milky, toothless bundle to cherish and hold and live for.

'You'd be a great mum. Any little daughters would want to dress up in your clothes and shoes and copy everything you did and any little sons would want to marry you when they grew up.'

This is nice to hear, if bittersweet.

'Hey, time for the next round of delights,' Dale says, glancing at his watch. 'Ready for a Malory Towers special? – sardines pressed into ginger cake, didn't you tell me? I can't say it floats my boat, but what do I know?'

He fishes out the tin of sardines and there is a ring pull in the corner of the can to open it. Bikkie notices that the tin looks a bit old – has he bought them in some neglected corner shop where the stock doesn't shift for ages?

Dale pours off the excess oil from one corner of the can into the grass, spears two fish with the fruit knife and plonks them onto a slice of ginger cake.

Bikkie lifts the can to her nose and takes a sniff.

'Ugh! Are they meant to smell like this?' She's doesn't think she's had tinned sardines before.

'I think all tinned fish is a bit strong-smelling – nothing to worry about,' Dale says. He pushes the sardines into the ginger cake with the flat of the blade and holds it out to her.

'You go first,' she says.

'No can do – I'm allergic. But you get stuck in.'

He watches as Bikkie takes a nibble.

'Wimp,' he says.

'Sod it,' Bikkie thinks, 'I've got bigger things to be frightened of.' And she takes a mighty mouthful and screws up her face as she chews.

'Well?' Dale says, with a smile bordering on a smirk.

'Disgusting!' Bikkie says.

'But you're going to finish it.'

'Just watch me.' And Bikkie, relishing a feeling of defiance, gobbles the lot.

25

Of course I spend all afternoon trying on clothes, attempting to decide what to wear for my big date tomorrow. I have a bunch of outfits I call my 'school uniform' which I swish to one end of the rail: a definite no. I have comfortable things I wear for travelling to Kate's and getting about when I'm over there and some tops and cut-offs I wear in our garden. I do not have anything seductive.

I do not have *anything* seductive! This is how long it has been since I have entertained the slightest idea of romance, since I have had any expectations of making a connection that could lead even as far as dinner, as far as the pub! And I'm not at all sure what something seductive would be, if I did have it. I'm a bit long in the tooth for an off-the-shoulder gypsy dress and I don't have a flat enough stomach for a pencil skirt. What is a fifty-one-year-old woman supposed to wear on a first date these days anyway?

Antoinette, when we went on a very mild pub crawl at Christmas, wore a pair of black leather trousers and a sleeveless, sequinned top and she looked fantastic – but she has that Italian-type figure, long-legged and slim, yet busty. I'm not that shape, and I'm probably five years older, so there's no point in asking her to lend me anything.

'How come he asked you out – how come not Antoinette?' That was Joe's response when I explained about the flowers. It cut me to the quick that he said it – I thought it a somewhat cruel thing to ask – but I'd wondered exactly the same thing. Antoinette is younger, prettier, more extrovert – why would Callum choose me, of the two of us, if he was open to possibilities?

'We just seemed to hit it off,' I said. 'Antoinette was a bit drunk and silly, whereas I was only slightly tiddly and thus retained my ladylike charm.' I know men like sexy women, but they still want someone they can talk to as well – at least, I'd better hope so. I'm not exactly a natural beauty, but I have good hair and I still fit into the same size Levi's I did before Joe was born. And I have turquoise eyes, which used to get a mention, long, long ago, before the Joe I hate, but the colour hasn't changed.

It's just a drink, so maybe a dress would be too much. How about simply jeans and a really nice top? Clean hair, dangly earrings, a bangle. Do I have a really nice top, though? I swish my options along the rail again. No, I do not. There are two good shops at the top of the town, on opposite sides of the street, called ... Something and Something Else. What, though? I can picture the girl who runs the first Something – I say a girl, she's probably even a little older than me, but she's got good taste and the garments are stylish and classy. Her name is as elusive as that of her shop. And the Something Else on the other side of the street – bigger and a little cheaper, but still a step up from the more basic high-street names. No good, can't remember what it's called either, but I'll take a look in both.

Half of me thinks this forgetfulness is probably completely normal for someone of my age, with fifty-odd years' worth of index cards filed inside my head and the retrieval system having to sort through so many – every taste, touch, smell, sight, sound, room, holiday, song, novel, person, visit to the optician, dentist, hairdresser, every single experience – to find the right ones. No wonder it's sometimes a slow process. The other half is worried.

In the changing rooms, I overhear a woman I identify as the Wrights' daughter talking about Weston's plans to go travelling.

'We've told him to try and line up a job to go out to, at least to get him started,' she is saying, through the curtain. 'But Weston just wants to pack a rucksack and go.'

'Go on his own, Rosie?' asks the manager, whose name I can't remember.

Rosie. Yes.

'Yes,' the mother says. 'We're not too happy about that either. He's very independent, and I know the world's a smaller place now, with mobile phones and Zoom and what-have-you, but he doesn't even want to go to any of the big cities, he says he wants to go to the most remote places. Why? What does he think he'll do there? How will he find work? Weston's never actually had a job – all the time he was at uni we tried to suggest he could get something part-time, but he said he had to concentrate on his studies, which is hard to argue with. He did a bit of gardening for his granny and granda, but we thought he could have got a few hours in a coffee shop or some store, but he wouldn't hear of it. We don't know anything, of course – we're just old fogies. No, Brenda – this is too tight across the bust. Could you reach me in a sixteen?'

Brenda.

I see that the summer sale is on, so it's a bit hit and miss as to whether I can find something in my size. I whizz past oranges and greens that would do nothing for me, give a second look to a wine-coloured blouse, but don't like the collar, push aside a denim shirt with a diamanté unicorn and then find something I very much like – it's tan, which is perfect with jeans, slim, to show that I haven't let myself go, and just a little bohemian in style. And it's in a size ten.

As I stand at the cash desk, Brenda is asking Rosie whether Weston is, broadly speaking, a sensible lad. His mother says that this, at least, is of some comfort: he barely drinks, has never done drugs, not so much as a cigarette, so she has no worries on that score.

'Hello, Alice. How are you? Sorry, I'm keeping you back, talking,' Rosie says, noticing me.

I deny any imposition, still stuck on wondering if I have actually seen Weston both buying cigarettes at the garage shop and smoking them under the lime trees in Parnell Park, or whether this is another trick of my mind. Wouldn't his mum smell smoke on him, on his hair and clothes? Wouldn't she have been bound to find a packet or a lighter?

Brenda concedes that children are a worry, whatever their age – her daughter is about to have a baby, and the whole prospect of childbirth is in itself a big source of concern – but if your kids have their heads screwed on, that's half the battle.

I am a few feet away from them, but I do not chip in. I have nothing to contribute to this conversation. I never comment openly upon anyone's children or anyone's child-rearing strengths, weaknesses, successes or failures. Joe – the Joe I love, the Joe I would die for – has no life, which makes me a dud at the most basic level as a mother. For isn't this our primary maternal function – to give, sustain, support and protect the life of our young? And I have fallen very short.

Back home, Joe is taking the pastry he made this morning from the fridge – he is going to bake a quiche. I kick off my sandals and put up my feet with the *Good Housekeeping* magazine I bought for Mum. Flicking through the pages, it seems that everything is about achieving success, particularly in the face of adversity – there are women who have responded to irretrievable marital breakdown by establishing highly remunerative small businesses, others who have beaten cancer and put two fingers up to the chemotherapy they've left in their pert-arsed wake by taking on a triathlon; and why have a crappy vacuum cleaner that merely sucks up most of your crumbs when you can have a gold-award model that also grabs *the dust you can't even see*, along with allergens, pet hairs and – I don't know – head lice eggs? Germs? Bad breath? Everyone smiling out from these pages – and they are all smiling, that is clearly the rule – looks absolutely perfect. Not just the models in the ads, but all the real-life women. Perhaps it's because part of the experience of sharing your positive life story with *Good Housekeeping* is that you get a makeover you'll never forget, and that's a generous gesture. But perhaps it's about maintaining a magazine fantasy where we can all succeed, all be beautiful, groomed, strong, every one of us blossoming, with clothes that suit us and the right lipstick, just like we can beat illness and misfortune and re-invent ourselves better and better, all of the time.

'What are you laughing about?' It is Joe, calling from the kitchen.

I am laughing at the thought of Mum, for whom this little treat was bought, flipping through these pages; she couldn't care less about Miranda's heroic struggle with altitude sickness as she ascended Mount Kilimanjaro to raise funds for her local air ambulance, she couldn't care less about the top three kitchen blenders or – oh, my! – the star ratings of various intimate vibrators; Mum couldn't care less, full stop. She couldn't, care, less. She'll just enjoy the different colours as she turns the pages.

I'd like to read a magazine for losers. People who've fucked up their life, fucked up the lives of others and not been able to figure out any kind of plan to put things right. People who hate their house but can't move. People snared in relationships that are killing them, but they can't get out. People trapped by poverty, by duty, by illness and disability, by shitty, shitty luck, even by love. Where are those magazines? I'd read them from cover to cover.

'I thought we might have some spinach with this, as a change from salad,' Joe says, sticking his head round the kitchen door, a tea towel over his shoulder.

'Mmm,' I say. 'There should be some in the freezer, if you have a poke about. 'Were there plenty of eggs?'

'Yeah.' Out of the corner of my eye, I can see that he is still leaning against the door frame. 'I was thinking.' He is hesitating, which means he already suspects I'm not going to like what he's about to say, which in turn puts me on edge. 'What if Kim Kennedy has another Facebook account? Under a different name. One she might not have told Kevin about.'

I sigh. 'Oh, Joe. Let's not start all this up again.'

'It could be under her maiden name, maybe somewhere she can post things for her girlfriends to see.'

I imagine Alanis posting pictures of her blonde, pretty self, laughing, showing those perfect white teeth and those dimples, squeezed up tightly to Joe, the Joe I love, the Joe with whom I am trapped, the Joe who is trapped with me, but who is not trapped in this imaginary posted photograph, because it is Joe as he should be, young, handsome, free, arms round his girl, the one he makes promises to, the one he makes love to.

'Atkinson, I think,' I say. 'Or Atkins, maybe. One of the carers at Granny's home went to school with her, briefly. I think she said her name was Kim Atkinson, back then. Or Atkins.'

Once the quiche is in the oven, Joe sits down in the front room with his laptop. There is more than one Kim Atkinson, but none of them is ours. Similarly with Kim Atkins.

'How sure are you about the surname?' Joe says.

'Honestly? Not very.' In fact, not sure at all. At this minute, I feel it is quite possible I have dreamt the whole Linzi-Kim-school connection and none of it is even real.

'Could you ring the home and check?'

No! I cannot call someone at work to ask about a piece of trivia-slash-gossip. Mount Charles is certainly very friendly and relaxed, but it is nevertheless a professional environment, not a phone-a-friend facility.

'I'll ask Linzi when I visit Granny tomorrow,' is the best I'm willing to offer.

'OK.' This isn't quite the response he wanted, but he is reconciling himself to it. 'Wine?'

He doesn't mean: Will we have wine? Because of course we will. He means: Is it an acceptable hour to start?

'Oh, yes, I think so.'

26

The picnic food is eaten and the ginger beer all drunk. Bikkie wipes the last almondy crumbs of macaroon from her lips.

Dale has told Bikkie his third thing: that he is a keen angler, can gut and clean a fish and cook it on a fire he has made himself. Bikkie is struggling to find something more of her own to share. On top of this, her jitters have come back. She is watching Dale clean up ever so carefully, as he always does, lifting each item of picnic litter in his gloved hands, placing it in one of the carrier bags he brought along. There is something about those white cotton gloves. How does she know he has dermatitis at all? He's never taken them off to show her. What if it's just an excuse to wear gloves all the time he's around her? Wouldn't that be a clever way to avoid leaving evidence, if he were to harm her?

She remembers the gloves on her throat as he placed the scarf around her neck. Why buy her a scarf? A scarf could be a deadly weapon. Why not a bracelet or a pair of earrings?

'There's a bottle bank just up the road. I can drop these off as we pass by,' he says.

Even this spooks Bikkie – the bottles touched his lips. Between the half-dozen of them they would carry both his and her DNA and this could link them, so he cannot bring them home but must dispose of them away from where either of them has been staying, mixed up with dozens of other people's.

He didn't bring her here for her benefit at all – the remoteness was not to ease her anxieties, it was chosen as a perfect crime scene. Some time soon, and it must be soon, because they are preparing to leave, he is going to hold one of those picnic knives to her throat, or the corkscrew, or he is going to strangle her with the scarf, and he is going to rape her. And while she wishes this were not true, she believes she can survive it; but after the rape, does he mean to kill her too?

'You must have something, Charlotte. Winner of the Butlins knobbly-knees competition, kicked out of the Girl Guides for smuggling vodka into camp – anything?'

Bikkie wishes she had been a Girl Guide – then she might be able to hatch an escape plan. She wants him to stop asking her questions – her brain is fogged with fear and she can't think. She doesn't know if she could outrun him, even with his limp – not in a maxi dress and sandals, and especially when the limp might be another trick – and not one single walker, tourist or local has passed them during this whole day. When his back is turned, she looks around for a rock. If, as he's bending down, collecting their scraps, she could whack him on the back of the head … but what if she didn't hit him hard enough – she would just enrage him, *and* reveal that she was on to him, which would make things even worse.

She is shaking as she goes to lift the sardine tin.

'OK if you take that one home to your place?' Dale says. 'I can dump most of this stuff in a public litter bin, but we should really try and recycle the can.'

This is such a practical, everyday, responsible suggestion that the cogs in Bikkie's head have to creak to a halt as she re-evaluates yet again. He wants her to take home a tin can for recycling – that doesn't sound like the sort of thing she imagines a rapist would say, just before assaulting his victim. Maybe they *are* just cleaning up after themselves – maybe it was simply a nice picnic and poor Dale really does have the skin disease he claimed.

By the time the bags are packed, and Dale hasn't pulled a knife, or tried to choke her or threatened her with the corkscrew, but has simply lifted their things in both hands, Bikkie realises that she has been panicking for no reason. This is the same Dale who made her a daisy chain, shared a bag of chips, who probably missed his dream job because he was too nice to ask for a pair of protective gloves at the interview. And while she wouldn't say he sees into her soul exactly, he seems to understand that this thing between them cannot go on forever, because he recognises that she is in some kind of trouble and must face it on her own.

This is why he has not asked to see her again, has not pressed her for an address, or a phone number, or even her full name. He knows it's over. When they say goodbye, there is a moment of something, but no-one says that this is the last time they will be together, speak to each other, look each other in the eye. As she watches him limp away, in his John Lennon sunglasses and his fishing hat, she hopes, genuinely, that he will meet somebody who deserves him, that he will love and be loved. And then he's gone.

Bikkie is feeling strangely ready to face the future too. She has made many, many mistakes, taken wrong paths, gone with bad people, but that is going to stop. She will return to the flat one last time, take a long shower, then telephone the police. She will apologise to her father for everything she has put him through and she will (she dredges the word up from school assemblies) *repent*. She will work hard in prison, both at the chores they give her and at some form of education. She could get a degree from the Open University. She could train as a peer mentor, to help people who are in danger of doing the stupid things that she has done. She will prove to everyone that she is sorry, so sorry, and they will give her another chance. They have to. One day, perhaps, she will meet someone as nice as Dale, and if she's really lucky, there will still be time to have a family, bake cookies, tuck them into bed.

Bikkie heads back to the flat, still swinging the sardine tin in the plastic supermarket carrier she keeps stashed, when empty, in her shoulder bag. She has to make her way across a series of busy junctions, and it makes her think of the Jimmy Cliff song 'Many Rivers to Cross' – one of the few pieces of music both she and her boyfriend liked. Stopping at a red-man signal, she is at the front of the crowd on the kerb, waiting for the green man to appear, traffic thundering past. She glances into the buggy parked beside her and spies a chubby-faced little girl with a tiny tuft of blonde hair tucked into a pink elastic with a flowery bobble. She would like to take this little girl home with her, feed her milk from a bottle, give her a bubble bath and put her into clean pyjamas, sit her on her knee and look at a picture book together.

It is a tiny little clip, right into the back of her knee, but that's all it takes. Bikkie lurches forward just enough to catch the front hem of her maxi dress under the toe of her sandal, which sends her toppling in front of an articulated lorry.

27

There is time for Bikkie to see the lorry coming, a moment to lock eyes with the horrified driver; she feels him stand on the brakes, knows he is trying with all his might to pull it up, like a headstrong stallion. She actually thinks he'll do it, too – there seems to be so much time. But she is wrong.

She doesn't go right under the wheels, but she feels herself flying, then hitting the ground like a stone.

Bikkie can see the sky, hear the impact of two more vehicles crunching against each other somewhere and the sound of a car alarm; there are faces coming into view and what looks like the back of a man's head wearing a khaki fishing hat, but that couldn't be Dale moving off – she left him half a mile away.

She's been lucky. The lorry has thrown her clear and there are lots of people about – any minute now the ambulance will come and they'll lay her on a stretcher and give her oxygen and get her to hospital. Shouldn't some passing first-aider be putting her in the recovery position? But perhaps they fear she has a spinal injury, which is reasonable, so they mustn't touch her.

She can feel the grainy roughness of the hot tarmac under her cheek. She wishes she was at home – not the crummy flat, but her real home, lying on one of the purple velvet sofas she chose because he loved purple – Prince – which means she loves it too.

When she is mended, she would rather go anywhere than back to that flat, all alone without anyone to talk to, not allowed even to pass the time of day with the neighbours, in case it gives them some detail to remember her by, forbidden from playing her favourite music because it might tip someone off that it was Bikkie who'd been living in that flat this summer, she, the missing woman, the redhead who'd supposedly drowned while swimming on holiday in County Galway. Oh how she hated that flat, with little more than a scuzzy bed and a tiny television, tormented by the heat and the hateful, banging clanks of the plumbing pipes which started up any time anyone in the building had a shower. No wonder she took to thumping them in answer with her shoe.

Maybe all the sessions at the public pool her boyfriend made her do, so everyone would believe she was a keen and confident swimmer, will stand to her during her recovery from this disaster. It can't hurt that she was fit and strong from all the exercise, and she's only thirty-six.

It'll all come out now – her boyfriend, his scheme to fake Bikkie's death, make good on the life assurance, so they could run away together. They'd have no more worry about an impossible mortgage, no more pretence about being *more* than they were – a couple whose best stroke was to present as having it all when, in fact, nothing could be further from the truth.

Bikkie is glad now that Kevin wouldn't marry her. She took his name without asking him, just started using it, put it on her loyalty cards and her swimming pool pass – you can do that – so people naturally assumed. No wedding rings, though. No photos of the bride and groom on the wall in the purple front room at Parnell Park, but she knew everyone thought they were married.

Kevin thought Bikkie was a stupid name, babyish, and he got his way over that one, simply by refusing to say it and always calling her Kim. Babyish – ha! He was the one who insisted on treating her like a child, telling her what she was allowed and wasn't allowed to do. And he wasn't the first. But she is going to choose her men more wisely in future.

Where is the ambulance? She is getting cold. She would like a blanket.

As if he can hear her thoughts, a man gently sets his jacket over her.

At least now, due to this happening, Kevin cannot hold her responsible when everything unravels. She won't have to look over her shoulder for the rest of her days. So something good will come of it, even if she does have to go through weeks or months of physio, learning to walk again – it'll be worth it not to have to worry about him.

Her dad will come straight to the hospital when he hears – all will be forgiven. Her grandfather might even break his stony silence – Bikkie's dad brought her up determined to manage without him, yet there was always that understanding that the old boy could be called upon if circumstances were dire; what was it her dad said? '*In extremis*'.

And perhaps her mother? Bikkie hasn't completely given up on that one yet. Given time, anything is possible. Given time …

An ambulance siren cuts across her thoughts. They are here. At last.

If only she hadn't turned away when that teacher from across the road – Alice – spotted her on the train. If only she had smiled and waved – it would've had to end then and there; they would've had to drop the whole charade, she could've come back to Parnell Park, there would've been no fake drowning, no jeans and shoes and t-shirt left on the rocks in Galway, no postcard, no Facebook posts, no mystery, no investigation, no hiding out, no financial claim. She and Kevin could have gone quietly off each other, sold the big house, gone their separate ways. It only needed a smile. She liked Alice, although she barely knew her. If only.

She can sense the flashing blue of the lights.

OK. So it's a mess, and it could've been avoided. But it is what it is. The point now is to make better choices in future, repent, clean up her act, all of which she is determined to do.

That's the third thing she should've told Dale: Bikkie – and she wishes she'd confided in him, in the end, that she wasn't called Charlotte – never quits. She might not be the brightest star in the sky, but she's a trier. She gets up and she goes again.

She hears someone saying that she just seemed to trip and fall onto the road. Another voice blames the long dress. But she knows this isn't right. That's not how it happened. Someone stuck their toe hard into the back of her knee. It was no accident. She must tell them this. She must tell someone. But she cannot move, cannot speak.

Someone is kneeling beside her. He is touching her – checking her pulse, she thinks. He is speaking to her, but it is as though he is floating off and she cannot understand what he is saying.

The sound and colour are draining away rapidly now. With her last conscious thought, Bikkie relives the little clip to the back of her knee, sees the image of the fishing hat retreating from the scene, and she knows it was Dale.

And then she dies.

28

The Twelfth of July festivities seem to have gone off without incident, although the night is young.

Callum rings to check that we're good for tomorrow evening. Seeing that Joe is engrossed in a consumer programme in the front room, I sit on the stairs with the phone and say that we are. My voice is wavering like a nervous teenager's. I *feel* like a nervous teenager. He's been gardening this evening, he tells me, and I imagine him smelling of cut grass and new sweat. He's taking a breather over a beer in the rocking chair in the kitchen – with its stone floor, it's the coolest spot in the house. He hasn't heard from Kim yet, but he's sure it's only a matter of time and sooner rather than later is his guess. He doesn't know if she'll have her tail between her legs or come out fighting, but she isn't a brooder, he says – she won't leave Kevin simply hanging.

'Not sure they'll make it, though,' he says. 'Kevin likes to think he's pretty laid-back, liberated, a bit of a bohemian, but at heart he's more traditional than he admits.'

I remember Antoinette saying she'd heard them rowing, before, verging on the violent.

'You don't think he'd hurt her.' I'm doing it again, suggesting that Callum's friend of years and years has a sinister side. I've got to stop or I'll turn him off me.

'No, not physically. He'll say some hurtful things, I'm sure – words are Kev's weapon of choice, not fists. Emotional abuse? Possible, but then what would you call what she's just done to him? Anything else, no. If he really can't take it, he'll just walk.'

We agree to meet at an inn a little way out of town.

Five minutes after this call, Kate rings. She knows I'm distracted.

'What are you up to, Mrs?' she says. 'You're not even listening.'

Joe is still in the other room, so I tell her.

'Ooh!' says Kate. 'What's he like?'

'I've only met him twice, really,' I say. 'And once only for fifteen minutes. He's intelligent. He's a single dad of a teenage daughter he worries about, a lot, but he seems quite well-adjusted. He's nice.'

'How nice?' says Kate. 'What does he look like?'

'Dark,' I say. 'Very dark. Amazing eyes, actually. Not what you'd call a big man, but I'm only five-three, so tall enough.'

'You're going to sleep with him.'

'Kate!'

'Trust me, you are. George and I got together ridiculously young, I know, so it's a long time since I've been out there, but I listen. When a woman over forty talks about a man in terms of his physical features, they're definitely going to have sex. Does he seem like he has good personal hygiene?'

'Yes.'

'Then go for it – he sounds gorgeous. It's about time you got your leg over, Ali.'

'But ...'

'Don't worry about Joe. You can cross that bridge when you come to it. Live a little, Al. You deserve it.'

She tells me that George has started his new admin job, and likes the bunch of people he's working with. The extra money should tip them over from simply not enough to just about managing and I know the difference this will make.

We are talking about Conall's clarinet lessons, which I sponsor, when I hear the tone in my ear that means someone else is trying to call me. As it's twenty past ten, this can only be the care home, so I curtail our call. Kate understands.

It's Linzi.

'I'm really sorry to bother you, Alice, but Ruby's in a strop because she's wet her pyjamas and all her other ones are at the laundry. We've offered to lend her a pair, but she won't wear them and she's really quite distressed. She's asking for you to bring her in something from home – I don't suppose you could come over for ten minutes, just to settle her?'

If Linzi is ringing at this hour, it means Mum is really

kicking off, and Linzi is doing me a favour because she knows Mum is generally happy where she is and doesn't want to give management any reason to move her to another facility.

'I'm on my way. I have a drawer full of spare pyjamas for her,' I say. 'I appreciate you calling, Linzi.'

'No problem, Alice. You know why I'm doing it.'

I've been drinking, though. Two large glasses. I'll have to call a taxi.

Mum is almost sleeping. Happy in her new pyjamas, she is curled on her side, hands together beneath her cheek. I slept like this as a child and remember her telling me that she did too.

'Thanks so much for coming over, Alice. I'm really sorry to get you out so late,' Linzi whispers.

'I'm happy to do it – I'm only sorry it took me so long to get a taxi; I suppose there were quite a few revellers tonight of all nights.'

'She's usually so good – there's far worse here than her, but then they probably will be shifted on to somewhere else, and I don't think that would be right for Ruby.'

'I know, she's relatively sane, in her own way.'

'She's great. She doesn't miss a trick. No, we'd like to keep her here with us.'

'I'll be back in the morning. I've got a couple of new magazines for Mum, but I didn't think there was any point in bringing them over tonight.'

'I'll not be on, now – I've a couple of days' leave and

Lawrence and I's bringing the wee ones up to Portrush while the weather's still good. Alanis'll be here, but.'

'She's not working tonight, I suppose. I'm surprised to see you here – I thought you'd still be celebrating The Glorious Twelfth.' I can say this – Linzi knows I have no interest, but also that I mean her no disrespect.

'Twenty years ago, maybe, but you wise up, Alice. We just take the kids to see the bands now, get a burger and an ice-cream at the field, and then we're happy enough to come home.'

'Alanis still enjoys it, though?'

'No, she's away to Castlerock, to the beach. Went last night.'

'With her boyfriend?' Why am I prying?

'No, with the girls. She's not seeing anyone at the minute – even if she was, she always keeps up with her girlies. Our Alanis is very picky about men – it takes a lot to impress her. Don't get me wrong – she doesn't love herself or anything, but she'd surprise you, the ones she goes for.'

'Not the obvious suspects.'

Linzi laughs. 'No, definitely not.'

I remember the promise I made Joe – that I would ask Linzi to remind me of Kim Kennedy's maiden name. Whatever I think of the pointlessness of this exercise, I have a policy of telling Joe the truth. As I am the only ever-present human in his world, I believe it is imperative that he can trust me completely and this means no deception. How else can he have faith in the universe? This is why I have told him about my date with Callum, although I have not felt obliged to speculate about any possible relationship arising from it.

'Atchison,' Linzi says.

'Atchison, of course,' I say. 'I was thinking Atkins, Atkinson. I was close.'

'She was a funny thing at school, though; like I say, we only lived up there for a year for my dad's work. Gorgeous-looking. Beautiful red hair. But kind of lonely. Her granda owned half of County Antrim, apparently, but Kim just got on the same as the rest of us. She'd no mummy, but. That was sad.'

I will relay this name to Joe and he can do his Facebook search and he might find a secret account and he might not, and if he does, it might throw some light on this supposed affair and it might not; at least I will have done my bit.

I am making my way down the carpeted stairs, soundlessly, I think, and I mean to open and close the heavy front door as quietly as I can, when Linzi stage-whispers down after me.

'Because of her ginger hair, and because she was Kim, everyone called her Kimberley Biscuit – do you remember the Jacob's advertisements?' She sings: '"Kimberley, Mikado and Coconut Creams ..."? In the end, they just called her Bikkie.'

29

Margarida takes a good look at me.

'Alice? There's something different about you today.'

'I had my eyebrows waxed,' I say, with a blush.

'Yes, I can see that, but that's not it,' says Margarida. 'I think you've met someone.'

Good grief, is it that obvious? I must be utterly transparent.

'I have a date tonight.' Still blushing.

'How exciting!' says Margarida. '*Is* it exciting? Is it a first date? Do you really like him?'

'I met him through a neighbour, but this is the first time we'll have spent time together, just the two of us. Based on what I've seen so far, yes, I really like him. I've only just met him, though.'

'Well, he's a lucky guy to go out with you, Alice. Don't forget that.'

'I'm as nervous as a kitten. You'd think, at my age, I'd have more sense.'

'It's part of the romance, being nervous. Butterflies in your stomach – it's meant to feel that way.'

I think, to my shame, how far I am from being able to use idiomatic expressions in Portuguese – or any language other than English – and admire Margarida all over again, then I sign in and go looking for Mum.

In the courtyard, half a dozen residents, including Mum, are sitting in a row. The new activities co-ordinator, whose name I can never remember, is playing some sort of game with them.

The elderly aunt who recalls Mum and Dad coming to the little café where she used to work tells me it's called boccia, and it's a form of bowls designed for the disabled or infirm.

The activities co-ordinator is talking too much, and her voice is getting carried away on the breeze – she will lose her audience completely if she doesn't actually make something happen, and quickly.

She sits down in a spare chair to demonstrate. Her aim is poor, but at least she's giving the oldies an idea. I continue to stand back and watch, smiling at the serious expression on Mum's face. When it's her turn, she aces it, and I applaud and hoot. Her parents were champion bowlers – I guess some things get passed on. She turns at the sound of me.

'Alice! I didn't know you were there. Go and get Michael – I want him to see this.'

'You keep playing. I'll wait for you.'

Mrs Lappin is approaching on her rollator. I could run, but what would it really cost me to give her five minutes while Mum is otherwise occupied?

'Not playing, Mrs Lappin?'

'Your mummy was very sharp with me this morning,' she says.

'Oh dear, I'm sorry to hear that.'

'I only asked her does she ever get out to visit your daddy's grave. My daughter brings me to my husband's grave when she comes home from England, gets me flowers to put on. She gets the loveliest flowers in Tesco – big lilies, sometimes, or gerberas. I don't like chrysanthemums – they make me think of funerals.

'My husband's buried with his mother and father and I'll be buried with them too, but I don't know what'll happen to my son. He might want to be buried in Canada – that's where his children all are, and they'll want to visit his grave, so there's no use him being buried over here.'

Mrs Lappin meant no harm, I'm sure.

'The thing is, Mum doesn't always remember that Dad's passed away, Mrs Lappin,' I say. 'I think it's a bit of a shock to her when anybody brings it up. Most of the time, she thinks he's still alive, just not in the room. I find it easiest to play along with her and not rock the boat.'

'Oh, fiddlesticks,' says Mrs Lappin, a look of deep regret coming over her face. 'Oh, your poor mummy. I won't say another word.'

She is chastened, but only for a moment.

'So, *does* your mummy get out to visit the grave?'

'No, Mrs Lappin – since she thinks Dad is still alive, that wouldn't be very helpful.'

'Oh ... no. I'm to be buried with John and his mother and father, but I don't know who'll look after the grave when I'm gone – my daughter lives in England and my son and all his ones are in Canada.'

I would like to do something nice for Mrs Lappin, but I am not willing to give her Mum's magazines before Mum's had a chance to have a look herself.

'Let's take a walk around the sensory garden,' I say. 'If you're feeling up to it.'

Mum is given a gold plastic medal on a red, white and blue ribbon to wear, for winning the boccia. It's hard to tell if she's proud.

I give her the *Good Housekeeping* magazine. She smooths it out with both hands and appears to compose herself, like a concert pianist about to play.

'Can I look at it now?' she asks.

'Of course. It's yours.'

'I'll start at the front,' she says.

Mum turns pages carefully, taking them by the top-right corner, dampening her fingertips ever so slightly if necessary, but not enough to leave a mark.

'Jane Fonda,' she says. I look and see that she's right. It's an advertisement for anti-ageing cream. 'Don't tell me she hasn't had plastic surgery – she's older than me.'

I giggle. Mum's entirely fluid sense of chronology is never dull. At this moment, she is able to locate both herself and this film star as older women.

'I'd say that's a wig too,' I say.

'I'd say you're dead right,' Mum says.

She continues turning pages.

After a while, she says, 'When are you going to bring my wee man in to see me?'

This refers to the angelic child with the halo of curls whose photograph took pride of place on her mantelpiece, in a home that was modern and practical and not given to sentiment; it still sits on her bedside table here, in Mount Charles, beside the jug of water and the tumbler and the jewellery box containing the rings that no longer fit over her bony knuckles. Joe – the Joe I love – aged six.

My heart feels heavy. Joe and Mum could be so good for each other, even though he is no longer that sweet little boy she remembers, but it's yet one more aspect of life that has had to fall by the wayside, like so much.

'Kate and the children are coming over next month,' I say. 'Do you remember Kate?'

'Married to the boy from Kent,' Mum says.

'George, yes. Do you remember him?' I think they only met a couple of times.

'How could I forget him? He refurbished the bungalow to make it wheelchair-friendly for me – all the neighbours came round. It was on TV.'

For a moment, she has me really foxed, until I realise that

she is conflating George with Nick Knowles on an episode of *DIY SOS*.

'Did you used to use a wheelchair then?' I say.

She looks puzzled and I wish I hadn't said it.

'I'll bring Kate's children in to visit. If I tell Linzi they're coming, and you play your cards right, there might be a cake in it.'

Mum smiles, remembers her magazine, and resumes flipping.

'I could bake them a lemon meringue.'

Her lemon meringue pies were legendary. Mum was good at pastry and knew just how long to whisk the egg whites.

'That's a great idea,' I say.

'How's your dad getting on, cutting the grass?' she says.

Mrs Lappin leans in from the right. 'He's nearly finished, Ruby, and then he's just going to change his shirt.' She looks at me solemnly and I do not know whether she's being a good sort or is as much away with the fairies as Mum, but I give her a little smile anyway.

30

The taxi Callum ordered pulls up outside the house at 7.30 p.m. exactly.

'Have a great time, Mum,' Joe says. He sounds like he means it, but surely he must have thoughts about the implications for him, if I were to become involved with someone.

'It's just one date,' I say. 'And only a drink – not even dinner. No big deal.'

'If you say so,' Joe says.

The taxi driver is chatty – he wants to talk about devolution and also the EU, but is keener on preaching than on hearing from me on either subject, which is fine. When I try to pay him, he assures me that 'the gentleman' has already sorted it, which makes me feel a tiny bit of a floozy and also a tiny bit more excited.

The Bailey is a nice pub-restaurant, built with reclaimed brick and out of town. As I climb from the car, I see Callum already sitting at a table on the wooden decking area at the front. Good – it's too nice an evening to sit inside in the dark.

He stands up when he sees me.

'Ali. How are you?'

We manage to kiss each other's cheeks without too much awkwardness.

'What can I get you to drink?'

'A white wine?' I say.

'Anything in particular?'

'A Sauvignon Blanc, if they have it. But a Chardonnay would do.'

'I'll be right back.'

When Callum returns, he is carrying a little bottle of wine and a glass for me and a pint of lager for himself. Those little bottles of wine hold more than you'd think.

'Did you come by taxi too?' I say, then feel stupid – I might as well have asked him if he's planning to drink-drive or has made alternative arrangements.

'No, it's a bit far for that, so I booked a room here,' he says. He immediately looks embarrassed – 'I mean, just for me, so I didn't have to drive the car.'

I smile to show that I know the act is innocent and he visibly relaxes.

'Haven't lured you here with any wicked intentions,' he says.

I hope, at some point, he will feel just a little bit wicked.

'I hope you didn't mind me sending a cab, instead of picking you up. It's just … I didn't particularly want Kevin to know I was meeting you.'

'Oh?'

'Not that there's anything wrong with us seeing each other for a drink, and not that I won't tell him in the future; just, well, it's nice to have some privacy, at least to begin with.'

I could interpret this in a number of ways. Worst-case scenario, I'm an embarrassment. Best case, he's taking this seriously, protecting it from the start.

'So, what've you been up to today?' he says. 'Working or relaxing?'

I tell him about my visit to Mum, a bit about Mrs Lappin, about Margarida, about the boccia and Nick Knowles. I try to make it sound entertaining and perhaps I succeed, because Callum is laughing.

We talk a little about The Bailey and the surrounding area, about what makes one establishment feel nice and relaxed and another feel gloomy and depressing, and the tendency these days to hang vintage bicycles on the walls and line the windowsills with earthenware flagons, where once it was all red flock wallpaper and dark, spindle-back chairs. It's warm-up stuff and it's all right, but I hope we'll go a bit deeper than this as the evening wears on.

'Look, I don't want to kill the mood, but shall we get the updates on Kim and Rebecca out of the way now, so that then we can talk about whatever we like?'

'Sure,' I say. 'Are there updates?'

'Rebecca texted me this morning,' Callum says. 'She's in Berwick-upon-Tweed, of all places, chambermaiding in a youth hostel.'

'Berwick – is that in Scotland or England?'

'Right on the border, but currently English. She's with a friend, so at least she's not on her own, and the pair of them are living in the youth hostel and working there. Apparently she likes it, but they've decided they're only going to stick with it until the end of the summer, then come back here and do something at college – they're looking up courses online.'

'You must be so relieved.'

Callum smiles.

'I wish I could be more laid-back as a father and actually enjoy the fact that my daughter is off having adventures. I mean, part of me is quite proud that she's taken herself somewhere completely different and found work and a decent place to stay, but I just wish she'd keep me posted.'

'We're so lucky to live in the age of mobile phones, but that depends on our loved ones actually using them,' I say, although I'm in the realms of imagination here as neither Joe nor Mum goes anywhere.

'Exactly. Speaking of which, I still can't get a peep out of Kim. I just keep hearing: *Kim Kennedy can't take your call right now. Just leave your message after the tone and when you're done press hash or just hang up.*'

'It could be as simple as she's run out of battery and can't find her charger,' I say.

'It could. It's probably nothing – you haven't had any further thoughts, I suppose?'

'Nope,' I say. I don't feel like mentioning that I left Joe a note of Kim's maiden name for a Facebook search.

'If anything comes to mind – not that I'm desperately worried – you would tell me, wouldn't you?'

I think about Kevin disposing of the laptop, folding the bag and placing it in the Wrights' bin. But this is meant to be *our* night.

'Sure, of course I would.'

'I know Kevin didn't exactly welcome your interest, but I don't get the impression you're the typical nosey neighbour. It wasn't about that with you, was it? It was coming from a different place. You're caring, but there's more than that. Did something happen?'

And so, just like that, I tell Callum about Child P, as we had to call her for a time – Paige Ferguson, as she was later named in the media. I haven't talked to anyone about this since back then.

'I wasn't her regular teacher – I haven't had a permanent teaching job for years; I work as a sub. I go in where I'm needed to cover sickness, or training days or the occasional maternity. I fell into it, and I found it suited me.

'She was a funny little thing – quiet in class, didn't say much, read out the pages from her reading book in a whisper, hated circle time – she just used to pass on the talking bear as quickly as possible and say nothing – but I could see she was a daredevil in the playground.'

'What age was she?' Callum says.

'Seven. Seven years old.'

'I'd been in school for two or three weeks when my class

got their turn for swimming lessons. Most of the kids loved this – getting out of the classroom and going on the bus was a bit of excitement, on top of the actual swimming. Only a couple of them could swim already, the rest were there to learn, with two or three who were real bags of nerves.'

'I bet you were brilliant with the anxious ones.'

I tried. I urged the swimming teacher to let them keep their armbands on longer than the others, to build their confidence. I didn't like the thought of them dreading coming to school every Wednesday – there was one little boy in particular I feared could be a flight risk. I told the head so. The swimming teacher didn't like me telling her her job.

'Over the course of a month, Paige never once swam. One week, she had a note from home to say she had an ear infection and couldn't go in the water, another week she was whipped off to the dentist; one Wednesday she was absent for the whole day and another she "forgot" her swimming things.

'I knew something wasn't right, and I doubted that this child who ran and jumped and cartwheeled and, sometimes, *thumped* her way round the playground had a fear of water, but I didn't say anything to anyone.

'I mean, yes, it was a busy room with thirty-one kids, but not so busy that I didn't notice the pattern. Of course it occurred to me that Paige might have injuries covered by her clothes, which would be revealed in a swimming costume, but then she changed with me for PE twice a week in the classroom, into a vest and shorts. I could see her arms and legs and there wasn't a mark on her.

'There were no signs of neglect. Her uniform was clean and smart. Her hair was shiny and tied up in a ponytail. She had a good, warm winter coat.'

I take a large slug of wine. I'm not sure I can finish this account.

'Because I couldn't actually see any evidence of abuse, I didn't pass it up to the school's safeguarding officer. Even if I had, she said she probably wouldn't have found anything to pursue – there was nothing visible. The eventual investigation noted that I had observed the child in vest and shorts twice-weekly, and there were no signs of anything untoward. They acknowledged that I had spoken to the mother after Paige had missed four consecutive weeks of swimming and the mother had assured me that Paige would be available to swim the following Wednesday.

'Except by then Paige was in intensive care, with a catastrophic head injury inflicted by her stepfather. She never recovered. They found dozens of cigarette burns on the soles of her feet.'

'Jesus,' says Callum. 'She didn't need to change her socks for PE, but someone would have seen the burns if she'd bared her feet to go swimming. I remember this. Forgive me, but I turn away from stories about child cruelty.'

'I do too. I can't bear them. Working with children, I always knew there was the possibility I'd come across something, but when it came I missed it. The investigation said the warning signs were minimal, and added that to the fact that I was temporary staff and the injuries well-hidden, and didn't recommend any action against me – they actually said there should be no stain on my character or my professional standing, but I will carry that oversight with me forever.'

'But the soles of her feet,' Callum says. 'You couldn't possibly have thought to check there – not when her face and arms and legs all looked fine.'

'I'd know now.'

'Hindsight's always twenty-twenty vision. It's easy to be wise after the event.'

'It changed me. Ever since then, I'm constantly afraid of missing something, afraid of turning a blind eye. I have an overwhelming sense of responsibility. The safeguarding officers in all the schools I work in must be sick of the sight of me – I record and report every tiny thing that strikes me as even slightly strange. And it doesn't stop there – I freeze when I hear parents shouting at their kids in the street; I make sure they know I've taken a good look at them. I've reported erratic drivers to the police. It took me a long time to trust the carers completely in Mum's home.'

'So you're always on the lookout for the next disaster, which you believe you will be able to avert, as long as you're constantly vigilant.'

That is it, exactly.

'Hence your interest in Kim.'

'I wasn't always crazy.'

'I don't think you're crazy now. I think you've been traumatised. Were you offered counselling?'

'It was proposed. It was meant to happen, but the dots never quite got joined up and I didn't pursue it.'

In truth, I would be afraid to enter therapy. If I started to talk, I don't know where I'd stop.

We sit in silence for a few moments, and Callum's eyes drift to the next table, where an overweight couple are having food delivered. She is having fish and chips and he a large steak, topped with battered onion rings. His stomach is so huge that he is struggling to make enough space to eat, as he is wedged on a bench seat fixed to the table. The woman asks the waitress to bring a free-standing chair that can be placed at the end. When Callum sees the waitress – who could be sixty – carrying out what looks quite a cumbersome chair, he excuses himself, moves towards her and takes it, places it for the man. I suspect he is not impressed by the couple, but he cannot hide that he is rather taken by their food.

'Could you eat?' he says.

Joe and I just had wheaten bread and cheese at five o'clock, so that I would have plenty of time to get ready. 'Yes, I could eat.'

'I'll just grab a couple of menus,' Callum says.

31

'So, your mum's in a nursing home. How're you finding that?' Callum is having jambalaya, his fork casual in his right hand.

'It's not technically a nursing home – that's more for people who need a higher level of nursing care. Hers is a residential home – lots of the oldies are only there because they have such limited mobility, but they have all their other faculties; some, like Mum, have a bit of dementia, but are still fairly sociable.'

'Does she know you? Sorry – that came out more bluntly than I intended.'

'Y-yes. Mostly she knows that I'm her daughter – although not always – but she assumes I remember everything she remembers – being a child in the forties, going to dances in the fifties. She thinks my grandparents and my dad are still alive too. When she first started getting that sort of stuff wrong, I used to correct her, but it was horrible – she'd go into mourning all over again. Now I just sail along with her in whatever little boat she's in today. Much better.'

'I haven't been through it,' Callum says. 'I don't remember my mum, and Dad's still only in his early seventies. Kim doesn't see him. Did I tell you that before?'

I don't remember. I make a non-committal gesture. My mouth is full of a terrific smoked fish and cider pie.

'It's stupid. Kim was involved with a bit of a bad boy – this was before Kevin. She was too smart for it to last; it would all have been done and dusted if Dad hadn't started shouting the odds. Of course Kim threw the head up and got engaged to the guy. Dad went ballistic, Kim marched out. The bad'un was already married, for a start, so there was no need for Dad to go charging in – he should've just bided his time – and a GBH conviction soon put an end to that particular romance anyway; not involving Kim, I hasten to add. But even though the guy was banged up and off the scene, neither Dad nor Kim would make the first move and now they haven't talked for years.'

'Did he go to the wedding when she married Kevin?'

Callum smiles. 'Ah, now that's a little tricky. Please don't tell Kim that I've shared this. And perhaps don't tell your neighbour.'

'Antoinette?'

'Kim and Kevin aren't married. She'd love to be – or,

perhaps, *would've* loved to be – but he's not the type. She put one over on him by quietly changing her name to Kennedy, though.' He chuckles. 'There wasn't much he could do about that – he doesn't have exclusive rights to it.'

I'd never have guessed. It makes you wonder what other secrets lurk behind the glass-panelled front doors of Parnell Park. Do we *all* have things we want to hide?

'I won't tell Antoinette,' I say. I won't run her down to Callum, but he's right – she couldn't keep it to herself.

'How long have you lived where you are now?' he says. 'Something tells me you've been there for quite a while.'

'Sixteen years,' I say. 'It wasn't really my choice – my husband liked it, or thought he did. His enthusiasms never lasted very long. Sorry – Joe's the last person I want to talk about tonight.'

'Can I ask, is he still around?'

'No. In no sense of the term is he "around". He's been dead almost as long as I've been in that house.'

'I'm a widower myself.'

'I thought you might be.'

'Really? Why?'

'I don't know. Maybe your relationship with your daughter. And you have a car sticker for a cancer charity.'

'You're very perceptive. Now's not the time, but I'll tell you about her some day. Don't expect any hagiography, though – Juliet was my wife and I loved her once, but we'd been planning to divorce when she was diagnosed. I can see you're relieved. Don't feel guilty – no-one wants to compete with a saint,' Callum says.

'I'm not relieved!' I say. But I am.

Callum goes to the bar and I stare at his back. He's wearing black, again. A woman in tight jeans and high heels edges close to him and he takes a small step away, which makes me smile. She speaks to him and I think he must reply, but the angle of his head suggests he is not looking at her as he does so. He turns with the pint and the little wine bottle and gestures to her with them, as if to say 'Cheers' or 'Goodbye'. She watches him go and, I soon see, watches *to whom* he goes.

'Getting chatted up there at the bar,' I say.

'Not my type,' Callum says, pouring my wine.

'Oh, come on – she's everyone's type; she's gorgeous,' I say.

'Then I'm not everyone,' Callum says. 'I work on this ratio: if it looks like a woman spends more time on her make-up than she does reading, then I'm out.'

How much time does it take me to do my make-up in the morning? Fifteen minutes, max. I couldn't make do with only fifteen minutes' reading a day.

'You're doing the calculations now in your head, aren't you?' Callum says, smiling.

I throw my beer mat at him.

'Touched a nerve!' he says.

It is the best night I've had in a long, long time. I hardly notice the light fading until the waitress comes by with a box of extra-long matches and lights the candle inside a lantern on our table.

'If you get cold, come inside – there's a couple of empty tables,' she says.

I don't want to move.

I'm not sure how it happens, but I find we are talking about Kim again. Maybe it's because Rebecca has turned up safe and well in Berwick, maybe it's because Callum is getting to know me and find me credible, maybe my tale of Child P has reminded him that bad things do sometimes happen, but I feel he is growing more willing to listen to my concerns.

Despite my earlier intention to stay off this subject, we run over the 'evidence' I previously laid out for him and this time I feel him reaching out to believe me – not because he wants to think that something bad has befallen his sister, but because he is ever so slightly starting to see things my way, ever so slightly wary of missing a danger right under his nose.

'So, she took the cherry blossom photo down that night after the postcard episode, then put it back up again within hours? Or somebody did?' he says.

'Yes,' I say. 'I saw it.' It wasn't me. It was Joe. But I'm not ready to tell Callum about Joe yet. 'And how did she suddenly learn how to spell "occasion"? I know they're only small things, but the fact is nobody has been able to speak to her for days – no-one can reach her. Isn't that, added to the little things, enough reason to be worried? And there's more. It might be nothing, I don't know.'

'What more? Tell me,' Callum says. 'I want to know everything that's bothering you about this situation. I'll set aside my feelings of friendship for Kevin if you'll level with me, tell me what you've seen.'

'OK. He brought an estate agent to the house, covertly.'

'He did what? When?'

'Recently. Very recently. Since Kim disappeared.'

'They've never mentioned selling. They always talked about doing the place up, bit by bit.'

'But maybe he's not selling – maybe he's just finding out how much it's worth, if ...'

'If what?'

'I don't want to say it.'

'Say it.'

'If the mortgage was to be paid off upon Kim's death.'

'Oh, Ali, I really don't think ...'

'And there's one more thing.'

'Tell me.'

'Kevin disposed of a laptop. He left the house with it after dark in a laptop bag and an hour later he came home and the bag was empty. You said yourself he has no background in criminality – if he has ... done something ... he must have needed to do internet searches before embarking on this ... whatever it is ... and he had to be sure they couldn't be traced. He must've taken it away to drop it in the river or smash up the hard drive or something.'

For a moment, Callum says nothing. Then he looks directly at me.

'There was an incident, years ago, when we were at college, involving another student. Kevin did something strange and vindictive. I was the only one who knew it was him and I put it down to a moment of madness. I haven't thought about it for years. Look, I don't think Kevin's killed anyone, or is planning to kill anyone, but I wouldn't put it past him to have come up with some crazy scheme to make a bit of money – he's always been broke and it's always been an issue for him.

If he's got Kim tangled up in something she'd be better off out of, then I'd like to find her and put a stop to it. I'm going to give this twenty-four hours and then, if I still can't get any reply from Kim, we'll go to the police together, just to see what they suggest – agreed?'

'Agreed.'

Having eaten well, we follow one drink with another and still don't get drunk. In Callum's case, there is another reason for this – I learn inadvertently from the waitress that he has changed to low-alcohol beer.

He looks slightly flummoxed that I have found out, which makes me wonder about his motive.

Callum lowers his voice.

'Look, I'm not expecting anything, Ali. I'm not pushing any agenda. But if anything were to happen ... I mean, if you wanted it to ... if you wanted to stay, I'd want to be ... *capable*.'

I raise my eyebrows, but I'm delighted.

'Put your jacket around my shoulders,' I say, and he does so.

'Now I'm your girl,' I say.

I am nervous, climbing the staircase to Callum's room. I genuinely wasn't even considering staying the night when I set off this evening.

When he opens the door, ushers me in, I am glad to see two wing-backed chairs on either side of a low table, in the window – somewhere to sit, other than just the bed.

'I'll have to send a text,' I say.

'Sure,' says Callum.

It's because he doesn't ask that I volunteer: 'I have someone at home, housebound. I have to let them know I won't be back tonight.' Even saying the words almost takes my breath away.

'Oh. OK.'

If Kevin has told him about the Joe I love – if Kevin even knows about Joe – Callum isn't making anything of it.

I pick up a large paperback from the low table. I recognise the name as a new release, but I haven't read it yet.

'Any good?' I say.

'Really good. I finished it this evening, just before you arrived. Read the blurb and take it with you, if you fancy it.'

I don't read blurbs: too many spoilers. Instead, I open it and read the first page. Yes, this is my kind of thing.

'Sure I can have this?' I say.

'Yeah. I think you'll enjoy it.'

I don't know what to do next. I have forgotten how this works, after all. Do I send some subtle, or not-so-subtle, message to Callum to tell him to kiss me, hold me? This is all suddenly strange, unfamiliar.

Maybe it's all happened too quickly. When I hug Joe, or even Antoinette, it comes naturally. This is different. I am sliding slowly but steadily towards panic. What have I got myself into?

Someone knocks on the room door. Callum moves soundlessly to answer, speaks to a sliver of black and white and turns back into the room with a tray.

'I ordered us each a Drambuie, to settle our nerves.'

Our nerves. So he's either as anxious as I am or very sympathetic. I already feel a little better.

Callum passes me a glass, then sits down on the side of the bed, watches me.

'I want you to be happy, Ali. Any time you want me to stop, just say and I will.'

'OK,' I say.

The liqueur is sweet and warming.

'C'mere.' Callum comes across, takes my hand and pulls me to my feet. He edges back, gently, leading me by both hands, until the backs of his legs are against the bed. He continues holding one of my hands, wordlessly releases the other and softly pushes my hair back from my face. I feel spellbound. I reach to stroke his cheek. He turns my hand over and lightly kisses the palm. Then I am falling, and it takes me a second to realise that Callum is sitting on the edge of the bed again, this time with me held tight against him. He smells faintly of bergamot. Slowly, carefully, he undoes my belt, which allows him to free the hem of my top. His hands feel warm.

It is not as I remember sex with the Joe I hate, which was passionless and full of entitlement. This, with Callum, is sweet and sensuous and new.

As we lie in the afterglow, he asks me if it is my father who lives with me, who is housebound. Partly to deflect him from learning about the Joe I love, and partly because I feel my father would be so happy that I am with someone like Callum, as opposed to someone like my first husband, I tell him how Dad died.

32

'You have to understand that he loved my mother more than anything,' I say. 'But looking after her was becoming too much for him. It simply wasn't in his nature to ask for help, and he couldn't see a future for them. He decided to take both their lives.'

Callum strokes my hair, says nothing.

'He chose tablets. Hoarded them until he was sure he had enough. The plan was to give Mum hers, then take his. I had absolutely no idea about this until it was too late. When the moment came, he decided that he should be first over the top: once he'd swallowed enough pills, he could immediately feed Mum the rest and they'd float away together. So he took his, but when it came to it, found he couldn't bear to kill Mum.

If he'd called an ambulance straight away, they might have been able to save him, even then. But he dithered, and when he did phone, his organs were already shutting down. I got to see him, and he'd left a letter explaining what he'd done and why he'd done it, but it was too late.

'OK. I've told you something, now you tell me something. What's the story with the tattoo?'

Because, to my great surprise, when Callum pulled his shirt off over his head, he had a ferocious wolf tattoo on his right shoulder.

33

I wake up slowly, contentedly, remembering where I am, and with whom. I roll over and look at him. He smiles.

'Good morning,' Callum says.

'Good morning.' I smile back.

The duvet is on the floor and we are covered only by the sheet, but it's already warm so it's enough.

'What time is it?' I ask.

'Eight o'clock. Want to get some breakfast?'

'Eight o'clock. Wow. I don't usually sleep so well or so long. Are you hungry?'

'I could be.'

'I'll have to wear the same clothes as yesterday.'

'I could lend you a shirt.'

'Great. Do you want the first shower, or can I ...?'

'Be my guest.'

The little hairdryer I find in the chest of drawers takes forever to dry my hair, so we end up being ready at the same time.

'Shall we?' Callum says, and he holds the door and follows me downstairs.

There is no formal dining room or breakfast buffet, just half a dozen pub tables set for breakfast, but the cutlery is heavy and a menu offers us a choice of continental or cooked food.

We decide to have the full Ulster fry and, as we wait, the waiter brings a large pot of tea. Callum asks if there's any chance of a newspaper and, given a choice, requests the *Daily Telegraph*.

'Bored with my company already?' I say, and instantly regret how needy that sounds.

'Never,' Callum says, looking at me. 'I can read it later, if you want to talk.'

I don't want to talk. I just want to look at him. He places his hand over mine.

'There's no rush, Ali. I'm not going anywhere. We can have a leisurely breakfast, go somewhere quiet for a walk – isn't there a canal round here? A stroll along the towpath might be nice.'

I am giddy, loved-up, four inches off the ground. I am wearing his shirt! I want to be with Callum, while at the same time I want to go home, lie on my bed and think about what has just happened.

I want to tell someone, but there's no-one I can tell. I can't discuss this with Joe, and I don't want to share it with Antoinette, at least not yet. There's no way I can talk to Mum. Could I tell Margarida?

It occurs to me that the Bailey staff must know that Callum booked a room for single occupancy, then ended up having company. Do they think we just met and that I'm a one-night stand? I'm not, am I? I mean, if I was, he'd have slunk off by now, instead of sticking around for breakfast and the *Telegraph*. Wouldn't he?

'Ali?'

I look up.

Callum puts his head on one side. 'You're brooding. What's up?'

'Nothing,' I say. 'I'm just daydreaming.'

Breakfast arrives and he lifts his hand away from mine.

We spend the morning lazily reading the papers at a window table and drinking coffee. By lunchtime, I feel I must go home to see Joe – he'll be growing concerned. We agree that Callum will drive me to the street at the other entrance to the public park, and I will stroll through to the Parnell Park gates and home, without being rumbled.

When we pull up, he switches off the engine, unbuckles his seatbelt and leans across to kiss me.

'It's not that we're doing anything wrong, Ali, I just don't want to deal with Kevin's smart-arsery just yet.'

Fine by me. I don't either.

*

'I'm home!' I call.

'What time do you call this?' comes Joe's voice from upstairs. His tone is full of mischief plus the strain of lifting weights. Good, he is going for a light-hearted approach.

I sling my bag in the hallstand and pick up an envelope addressed simply 'Ali'. I tear it open. It's from Antoinette. She's reminding me she's gone on holiday to Italy, and will I please remember to put out her bins. I have absolutely no recollection of Antoinette saying anything about a holiday, but when I check the calendar, there it is, in my writing. I run upstairs. I must change out of Callum's shirt before Joe sees it, it might be too much.

'So,' I say, dropping onto the sofa. 'What did you watch?' Joe flinches. Despite the fact that he hasn't left the house in years, it still stings that I assume the only thing he could possibly have done last night is watch television.

'Some detective crap – doesn't matter. I have a bit of news. No sign of a second Facebook account under Kim Kennedy's maiden name, but two police officers called at the Kennedys' place this morning, stayed a while, and now the curtains are all drawn.'

I immediately go to the window and look over. He's right. All the curtains at the front of the house are across.

'It might be to keep the sun out. It's blistering again today. Some people try to protect their furniture from fading, too.' I think of Kevin, with his overflowing ashtrays in the purple front room, and reckon he is highly unlikely to pull curtains to prevent upholstery fabric from bleaching.

Then I notice that the Wrights' curtains are now all drawn too.

'I don't like this,' I say.

'What do you think it is?'

'People pull curtains when there's been a death. Someone's dead, Joe.'

'You don't know that.'

'Then I'm going to find out. I'll call on the Wrights.' I grab my keys and I'm out there, marching across the road, trying to compose myself, but my heart is thumping.

Marjorie Wright ushers me into her porch and closes over the front door, but not tightly: she wants a discreet place to speak, but doesn't want me to feel invited to stay.

Jim knew one of the police officers who called on Kevin this morning. Kim Kennedy has been knocked down and killed at a busy junction in south London. A tragic accident. The post-mortem revealed she had spent some hours in the sun and had alcohol in her blood and the combination of that and the maxi dress she was wearing ... the lorry's dash-cam didn't show anything suspicious and no foul play is suspected.

I cover my mouth with my hand.

'I know, dear. It's a big shock. She was only a young woman.'

It is happening again. Paige is happening, again. I should have done more. I should have made someone listen.

'Do you know when she died?'

'Thursday evening, apparently. It took the London police some time to establish her identity.'

Oh! I am almost gnawing my hand. So she was still alive when I spoke to the two officers, when I confided in Antoinette, when I first told Callum. Callum! Kevin will have called him by now, surely. He will be distraught. I must talk to him. I thank Marjorie for putting me in the picture, and tip out through the porch door onto the street.

'Call the brother,' Joe urges me. 'He has to listen now. Then call the police.'

34

Even though it happened in London, it's the lead story on the local news. Not much detail, but there's a head-and-shoulders photograph of Kim laughing, with her chin up – laughing, somehow that makes it worse – and the newsreader gives her age and the name of our town in a grave voice.

I have met Callum at the worst possible time in his life. His little sister has just died, possibly in suspicious circumstances, away from home, and his daughter has called him away over some sort of crisis he's vague about but which she can't deal with herself in Berwick-upon-Tweed.

'I have no right to ask it of you, but I need your help,' he says on the phone. 'You have to go to the police. Tell them about the computer bag – that's got to strike them as strange. Mention the other stuff too, if you want, although I'm a bit afraid it makes you look like a busybody – which I know you're absolutely not. But disposing of the laptop's got to be the big one. Make them listen, Ali.'

He goes quiet. He's thinking.

'Maybe don't tell them about us, yet. If they get wind of that, they'll think we're in cahoots, that I'm encouraging you, and they'll write us both off. It's better if you go to them first, and then I can speak to them with my own suspicions when I get back from Berwick.'

'OK. Don't worry. I'll make them believe me.'

'Oh, Ali, I'm so sorry about all this. It's a nightmare.'

'I know. I'm sorry too.'

'At least you tried. You went to the police, but they didn't take you seriously.'

The line goes quiet again.

'Ali, before I go, talk to me about something normal, something everyday. There's just too much weird at the minute.'

'OK,' I say. I stroke the book jacket on the sofa beside me. 'I started reading the novel you lent me, to take my mind off what's happening, I guess.'

'And? What do you think?'

'I like it. It's quirky.'

I turn the book over absently and touch the back. There is an old-fashioned price sticker near the bottom. In tiny print it reads: 'Beggars' Bookstore, Galway City'.

'I didn't know you'd been in Galway recently,' I say.

'What?'

'Galway City. Beggars' Bookstore – it's on a sticker on that book.'

There is a hesitation. Then the line goes dead.

He was driving as we were talking – perhaps we just lost our signal.

It's a coincidence, though, Callum being in Galway and that being the place where Kim was supposedly on holiday. He never mentioned it when I told him about the Galway stuff on Facebook, the picture of the university with all the cherry blossom. What was he doing there anyway?

My phone rings. It's him.

'Sorry, Ali. Don't know what happened there. Yeah. No, I picked it up in a charity shop. Someone else must've bought it in Galway and donated it.'

Ah. 'Lucky you, getting such a new release! When I go book-browsing in charity shops all I seem to find are old Lynda La Plantes and Catherine Cooksons.'

'Hey, I'd better go now. I'm coming off the motorway and the sat nav needs to speak to me.'

'OK. I hope Rebecca's all right. I hope you're all right too.'

'I will be, when we get to the bottom of this. The computer bag's the key, Ali, so use it.'

'I will. Take care of yourself until I see you.'

'Take care too.'

35

'**M**rs Payne?'

'Alice, please. Ali, even.' The police have come to the house. It's two different officers this time. 'Can we speak in the garden?' I slip out the front door, keys clutched in my hand, see them exchange a look.

'I need to talk to you about a suspicious death,' I say, when we are safely round the back and out of sight. 'At least, it's just a death, as far as most people are concerned, but I have reason to believe that there may be more to it.'

I have reason to believe – no-one actually says that. What's wrong with me?

'What death is this, Mrs Payne? Alice,' says the burly male officer.

'Kim Kennedy. A neighbour. She lives in the house directly opposite. Lived.'

'And what are the circumstances of her death?'

'She was knocked down. Somewhere in south London.'

The officers exchange another look.

'*Somewhere* in London?' says the female officer.

'In south London, yes,' I say.

'And were you present with Mrs Kennedy at the time of the incident?' asks the man. If they told me their names, I didn't take them in.

'No!' I say. 'I was here.'

'Then in what sense can you say this was a suspicious death, Alice?' Her again.

For the second time, it seems that the more I have rehearsed in my head what I want to say, the more muddled it comes out.

I stagger from Galway to East Croydon station, from cherry blossom to hair appointments, from holiday bookings to words once routinely misspelt then suddenly, amazingly, being spelt correctly. It is a watery soup of undernourished melodrama which, even as I relate it, I know sounds unconvincing. But Callum was sure the laptop bag would be the clincher.

'There's one more thing,' I tell the officers. 'Kevin left the house in the dark the other night, with a laptop in a laptop bag. He came back an hour later and disposed of the bag – it was empty. He must have been destroying evidence.'

'Did you see him leave the house with the laptop?' The man.

'Yes.' A lie – it was Joe who saw him – but a necessary one.

'And you just happened to see him come back an hour later?' Her.

'Yes.'

'Were you watching Mr Kennedy's house, Alice?' Her again.

'No! I couldn't help seeing: his door is right across the street from my front window. I often sit in the window seat and read.'

'If it was dark, how could you see at all?' says the burly one.

'He was under his outside light when he put the laptop in the bag,' I say. 'And the street lights were lit.'

'How do you know the laptop bag was empty when Mr Kennedy returned home?' says the man.

'Because he folded it in two and placed it in Jim and Marjorie Wright's wheelie bin,' I say. Surely that is conclusive. Surely that is an odd thing to do.

'Mrs Payne, Alice,' the female officer says, her face weary, which annoys me, 'do you have any evidence for any of this?'

They think I am a crazy old bat with nothing better to do than spy on my neighbours and dream up dark fantasies about them, or else they've checked the records of my last call-out. But this time, I have something to show them.

'Can you wait here for just a minute?' I ask. I go to the spare bedroom, open the drawer under the divan and pull out a package inside a black bin liner. I march back to the garden, where the officers are still standing, and present them with it.

'It's the bag,' I say. 'I retrieved it from the Wrights' bin. I wore a glove and I put it in a brand new rubbish bag, just off the roll, to preserve any forensics.'

If they are surprised, they give nothing away.

'Right, Alice,' says the female officer, holding the package. 'We've taken a note of your concerns and we'll get back to you.'

There is nothing in their demeanour to suggest they have taken anything I have said seriously. As they walk back to their car, I feel the truth slipping away from me. I have let Callum down. I have let Kim down.

But the police car sits by the kerb and they do not drive away. I cannot see inside, but they must be talking. Of course they could be laughing about me, or taking instructions about their next appointment or phoning in a pizza order. I let myself back into the house and hover in the front-room doorway, where I can see their car but I don't think they can see me.

'What's happening?' Joe appears at my shoulder. 'Did they listen?'

'I didn't think so, but they're still there.'

Now look: this is something. They are getting back out of the car. Are they coming to caution me for wasting police time?

It's Joe who says, 'They're going over. They're going to Kevin's.'

It's premature, I know, but I immediately ring Callum.

'The police have been. I told them everything and I didn't think they were remotely convinced, but then I gave them the laptop bag and that seems to have done something. They've just gone across the road.'

'You didn't tell them about me, though,' Callum says.

'No. You're right, it's hard enough to get anyone to listen without clouding the situation.'

'That's what I thought. I wish I could be there to support you, though.'

'Support *me*? You've lost your sister, Callum.'

'I don't think it's hit me yet. When the police look into it, properly, when Rebecca's safely home with me, then maybe I'll be able to absorb it.'

I understand. When Dad died it was days before it felt real. Then I went a bit crazy.

'It'll take time to get over it, and you don't ever really get over something like this, but you learn to live with it.'

'Wise words. You're a wise woman, Ali.'

'I wish I could do more.'

'You're doing fine. You're my little chink of normal in a very strange world at the moment. Talk to me about something mundane, something everyday.'

I rack my brains.

'It must be the ladies' singles final at Wimbledon today.'

'You follow tennis?'

'Not properly. I'll dip in if it's on.'

'Tell me something about us. Tell me what you'd like to do when this is all over.'

If he thinks grief is quick, that he'll just pick up his life in a week or two, then he's wrong.

'Something I wanted to ask you, but we got … side-tracked. How much did your tattoo hurt?'

'Ha! Not that much, actually. Modern methods are a lot kinder than in the old days. How much did it hurt getting your ears pierced?'

The police seem to stay in Kevin's for a long time. I grow tired of standing and sit on the sofa, waiting.

Eventually, they re-emerge. They turn on the doorstep to

speak to someone whom I cannot see, then they return to their car. They still have the package in the black bin liner. Again, the vehicle just sits there.

'What do you think's going on?' Joe says.

Now the car pulls away.

'I wish I knew.'

'Mum! Get in here. They're back.'

By the time I make it from the kitchen, the police car is outside our house again, and Joe is lurking in the front-room doorway.

It's the same two officers. The woman emerges from the driver's door and the man lumbers from the front passenger seat. He has the black bin liner.

They are coming back to our house. I feel sick.

The bell rings. Joe has already fled upstairs.

'Alice. Can we come inside?' The male officer.

'I'd rather we spoke in the garden,' I say.

'We'd prefer to come in,' says the woman.

'And I'd rather you did not,' I say, and pull the door behind me.

They follow me to the bench on the patio, but none of us sits down.

'Did you ask him about the laptop bag?'

'Mr Kennedy is extremely distressed, Alice,' the female officer says. 'His wife has just died very suddenly and very unexpectedly and in a public place, among strangers. Mr Kennedy has yet to see the body and he is currently having to contact friends and relatives to inform them of his wife's death and also make funeral arrangements.'

'But did you ask him?'

'Mr Kennedy left his laptop computer in for repair with a gentleman on Park Road two nights ago,' she says.

'And you believe that? What repair shop stays open at night?'

Now the burly officer sighs. 'Mr Kennedy has a receipt for the laptop and we have just come from Park Road where we spoke to the gentleman who does repairs from home. He confirmed Mr Kennedy's account.'

'Then why did he try to hide the bag in the Wrights' bin?' My voice is shaking. This is slipping away from me, again.

The woman takes over. 'Mr Kennedy discarded the bag because it was broken.' She slides it from the black polythene and shows me the catch – half of it is missing. I hadn't noticed. 'He put it in the Wrights' bin because his own was full – he'd forgotten to leave it out a fortnight ago, so it had a whole month's rubbish in it.'

She continues, 'Alice, I have spoken to our colleagues at the Met about your concerns and they are confident that this was a sad, but not unusual, road traffic accident. Now we would advise you to put your worries to bed and give Mr Kennedy peace to grieve for his wife.'

'Not his wife.'

'What?' Her again.

'Kim Kennedy wasn't his wife – she was his partner.'

'All right, his partner.'

I have failed. I am now actually worse off than before, because even if I succeed in turning up more, better evidence, the police have made up their minds that I'm a busybody, a time-waster, a fantasist, doolally, demented, not worth listening to. I am defeated. How will I tell Callum?

As I go back inside, Joe waits to hear the front door slam, then crashes downstairs.

'I heard you through the bathroom window. Mum, we've been set up. It was staged, and I fell for it. Think about it: why did Kevin put the laptop *in* the bag, *on* the doorstep for me to see? Why didn't he just pack his bag inside the house? And the bag wasn't broken then – I saw him fasten it. I *remember* seeing him fasten it. He must've tampered with it deliberately. I don't know how he knew I was watching – or maybe he waited until he knew I was watching – but he must have done something, shone a light, made a noise, to get my attention. He wanted you to go to the police. He wanted you to accuse him, because he'd set the whole thing up to discredit you. We've been played.'

We sit and stew in the heat, me on the sofa, Joe on the big chair. I don't know if Joe is right or if we're both going slightly mad. If what he says is true, then who was so keen for me to big up the laptop bag to the police? Callum. I think about that paperback novel, bought in Galway, and how the line went dead when I mentioned it, then he suddenly reconnected with that explanation about picking it up in a second-hand shop. What was a well-dressed man like Callum doing in a second-hand shop? *Was* he in Galway? Why lie?

I feel suddenly cold, which seems impossible on this, another sweltering summer night. Callum. How much do I really know about him?

36

If, on dark winter evenings, after a long day at school, I don't feel much like driving to Mount Charles to see Mum, then in the midst of this disturbing summer it is actually very grounding and I am glad of it.

I wish I could take her some snaps of Joe, show her how her special boy is now, but of course Joe would not let me photograph him. Instead I bring her some Scottish butter tablet they had on the counter at the garage shop when I was paying for my petrol.

A different care assistant lets me in. I explain that I am Ruby's daughter and she is delighted to meet me.

'The teacher! Ruby's told me all about you,' she says. 'You

must be a real brainy family. She was speaking French to us, before.'

Was she, indeed? Never a dull moment.

I sign in, then stand in the doorway of the day room and watch. Mum is studying the television intently, even though the volume is so low that she cannot possibly hear what is being said. Phyllis, the arthritic former coffee shop waitress, sees me and waves, which alerts Mrs Lappin, who gives me a big smile, then turns away and pulls the outer corners of her mouth down in a bizarre grimace, which I imagine has something to do with adjusting the position of her false teeth.

'Mum,' I say, pulling a chair alongside her.

She notices me for the first time.

'I was just thinking about you,' she says. 'I was just thinking: what did that lovely girl ever see in Joe Payne?'

This is surprising. I'm not sure Mum has ever called me a lovely girl before, and she never said a word against Joe, even back when I sometimes wished she and Dad would.

'Oh?' I say.

'We never thought you were the marrying type. You were a free spirit. Your father worried you'd end up in prison on the other side of the world for protesting against the government or trying to start a revolution.'

'Well, I didn't,' I say.

'No. Once you met Payne, that was it. True love.'

'I never said it was true love.'

'I know. I was being sarcastic. It was your hormones.'

Even by Mum's standards, this is a strange conversation.

'Women are slaves to their hormones – they're the reason

we're the second sex. Even the brightest girls, like you, can throw it all away for a man and a baby.'

'You didn't. You had it all, Mum – a happy marriage, a child, a career.'

'I was exceptionally lucky. Your father was a nurturer. Not so Joe Payne. He sucked the life out of our daughter.'

'Well, he's dead and gone now.' It can't hurt, reminding Mum of that – it doesn't sound like she'd miss him.

'Yes. I saw the notice in the paper this morning. I'd say that'll be a big funeral. Donations in lieu of flowers to Cancer Research.'

Where does she get this from?

'Your father's favourite song was "Bridge Over Troubled Water". We had it at his funeral.'

It very possibly was, but we didn't.

'I miss him, Alice.'

'I know. I miss him too.'

The new care assistant brings round a tea trolley. It isn't the usual time, but they're trying to make sure everyone's getting enough fluids.

I'm offered a cup, which I gratefully accept.

'Hi, Alice.'

It's Linzi.

'What's this Alice's brought you th'night, Ruby? Fudge? Oh, lovely.'

'Would you like a piece?' Mum asks.

'Don't tempt me. I'm trying to lose weight,' Linzi says.

She turns to me and lowers her voice. 'Here, Alice, I heard

about Kim Atchison. Terrible. And me and you was just talking about her the other day. Did you hear what happened?'

'Only that she was knocked down at a busy junction in London.'

'I seen it on Facebook. I was just checking again there on my break and it said she was hit by a lorry and died at the scene. Was she on holiday?'

'I don't know. I haven't heard. Hit by a lorry?'

'That's what it said.'

'Were there any other details?'

'Just that the house is private, but her husband has said he wants people to feel free to bring flowers to the funeral, because Kim loved all kinds of flowers.'

'But nothing about why she was in London?'

'No, I didn't see anything. Alice, are you all right? You're very pale.'

'Am I? No, I'm fine.'

'Have another wee cup of tea. This weather's very close – it would give you a headache. Here, give me your wee cup and saucer and I'll get you it. Ruby, do you want yours heated up?'

As Mum drinks her tea, I find myself a little trembly, my cup rattling ever so slightly in its saucer. I don't ask to be involved in events like these. I didn't ask to be Paige's teacher; I didn't ask to see Kim Kennedy at East Croydon station. Why me? Why not Antoinette, who has gone off on holiday, no doubt carefree, while I remain here, riddled with worry, beset by questions, weighed down by the suspicion that something very bad has just happened and I am the only person who knows about it but cannot get anyone to listen.

I will take five minutes to compose myself, finish this tea and go home.

Linzi is talking to Phyllis and the new care assistant. She indicates me, and I realise she is telling them about Kim Kennedy.

'I always remember her,' I overhear her saying, 'because we were doing them Venn diagrams in maths and Kim and me was the only people in the class in the middle section, you know where the hoops overlap, because we were both left-handed, and we both had attached earlobes – look, mines are so small, I wanted to get them pierced twice, but the jeweller said there wasn't enough room – and neither of us had a brother.'

What? My heart feels as though it actually leaps in my chest.

'What did you say there, Linzi? About Kim's brother?' I am trying to sound normal. I am trying not to have some sort of cardiac episode.

'No, I was just saying she had no brothers, same as me. 'Member I told you about us and the Venn diagram?'

I do remember, vaguely. But I don't recall brothers being mentioned.

'Are you absolutely sure Kim said she had no brothers? Not even one quite a bit older?'

'I'm dead sure 'cause that got us talking to each other, for the first time, really, and we were discussing whether it would be better to have a wee brother or a big brother and we both said a big brother, definitely, 'cause then he'd bring all his friends round to the house. I was commiserating with her and she was commiserating with me and then sure didn't my mummy fall pregnant at thirty-eight and didn't I get a wee brother and he was a wee shite.'

My mind is exploding with images of that first night Callum turned up at Parnell Park when Antoinette and I were sitting out front, how we walked to the off-licence and seemed to pair off so easily. I remember the flowers, the invitation, my excitement. Joe's words about the laptop bag incident come floating back: 'We've been played.'

I rush to the front door, fling it open just in time to vomit on the step. Linzi approaches.

'I knew you didn't look well, Alice. Look, you go on home. I'll tell Ruby you said goodbye. It's just, if you have a wee bug, we don't want it going all through this place.'

'But this mess.'

'Don't you worry about that. I'll fetch your wee handbag and you get on home and lie down.'

Linzi does as she said and I climb shakily into the driver's seat. I hear my mobile ringing from the depths of my handbag and I scrabble for it among my things. I freeze when I see it is Callum calling. I let it ring out.

37

I drive around. I don't go home. I don't know what to say to Joe. I stop and retch over the grass verge, but there's nothing left to come up.

However anxious I was an hour ago, I am ten times more worried now. At least I could choose to walk away, before – stop meddling and try to blank out my suspicions that Kim's death was somehow Kevin's doing. But not now. Now I am caught. Because if Callum isn't Kim's big brother, *who the fuck is he*?

He's in cahoots with Kevin – that much is undeniable. But is he part of a murder plot? Is he a professional? Then I must be in danger. I remember the Galway bookshop sticker. Good new titles like that don't just turn up in second-hand shops.

Which means he's been in Galway very recently, I'm sure of it. Why, though? It's relevant, I'm convinced, but I can't put this puzzle together. And now he's caught me in some sort of honey trap, and encouraged me to bust my flush with the police so that I can't go back to them.

What if I rang them now, told them I was having an affair with someone who claimed to be Kim's brother, except she doesn't have a brother? They'd look at my last two call-outs and push me to the very bottom of the pile. Wait, though – it wasn't just me to whom Kevin and Callum lied – Antoinette was there too. But Antoinette is in *fucking* Italy.

As I sit at the side of the road, my phone rings again. I'm afraid to look, but when I do it's OK – it's Joe.

'Hi, Joe.'

'Hi, Mum. Where are you? It's late.'

'I just got talking to some people at the home. I didn't notice the time. I'm on my way now, though.'

'OK. I was going to ask you to bring home some milk. We're almost out.'

'Sure. No problem.'

'You OK, Mum? You sound weird.'

'I'm fine. Just tired. I'll be home in ten.'

As I set down the phone on the passenger seat, it pings to announce the arrival of a text.

> Should be back from Berwick tomorrow. How did things
> go with police? I must see Kevin, of course, and I'll just
> play along with him until I hear what PSNI said, but then
> thought you and I could meet. Let me know if you're free.
> Callum, x.

Shit, shit, shit. I want to run. I could go to Kate's, but I can't leave Joe – what if whoever killed Kim decided to target my son, as a means of shutting me up? And that's what the whole Callum façade has been about: keeping tabs on my thought processes and then ensuring that my accusations and my evidence are discredited so no-one will listen to me. But will they stop there or do they mean to silence me permanently? Will I fall under a lorry too? Or slip by the canal, or meet with some other little accident?

Like a tonne weight it dawns on me that Antoinette knowing about the Callum lies is actually the gravest danger – when she returns from holiday, she could corroborate my story on that matter at least. The police couldn't so easily ignore two of us. Kevin and Callum know this, which means I must be silenced before Antoinette returns. With me out of the way, by the time she comes back to Parnell Park, no-one will be asking if Kim has a brother – why would they? As far as everyone else will be concerned, she was the victim of a simple traffic accident and the focus will be on her grieving husband. Her murderers will have got away with it.

With shaking fingers, I text: Down with horrible bug. Just threw up at Mum's care home, so taking tomorrow in bed. You don't want to catch this one, believe me. Maybe meet up Monday? Ali, xo

I drive very carefully to the garage shop. I will go inside in a minute and pick up milk. But first I just need to sit here. I can't think what to do. I can't think what to do.

38

'Kate?'

'Ali! Hi! How are you?'

'Not bad. Just at a bit of a loose end, so I thought I'd call for a chat.'

'Sure. Let me grab a chair. So, how's things? Joe all right?'

'Yes, Joe's good. He's joined some online forum, so he's making new friends all over the planet through that. There's a Norwegian girl he seems to chat to a lot.'

'Well, that's something.'

'Not the same as real friends.'

'No. But we'll be over soon, take him out of himself a bit.'

'Kate, I don't suppose you saw anything in the paper about a woman from Northern Ireland being knocked down and killed last Thursday – over there, I mean, somewhere near you.'

'I did hear about that, actually. Not in the newspaper – who has time to read, these days? – but it was on the local news. *Look in the fridge, Pip. Middle shelf, I think.* Sorry, Ali – yeah, it only happened down the road. They put up a picture of her. She was lovely. Why? Did you know her?'

'She lived just across the road from me. She's the one I saw in the train station when I was visiting you – I told George about it, remember?'

'You're kidding!'

'It was her. What did they say on the news?'

'Not much. It was a short item, but my ears pricked up because of the County Armagh connection. She died at the scene. The lorry driver was treated for shock. They're calling it a tragic accident. There was the usual local council rent-a-quote advising people to stand well back from the kerb at busy roadsides. I'm always telling the kids that – the traffic flies through some of those junctions when the lights are green. I'm sorry, Ali – did you know her well?'

'No. Not well.'

Kate talks about the kids and about George's job and an opportunity she might have to help out with a new youth theatre – paid, if not well paid – but I am only half-listening.

'But this is all just chit-chat, Al. What I really want to know is how your hot date went.'

'That's a tricky subject,' I say. 'I don't think it's going anywhere. The guy wasn't what he seemed.'

'Oh, that's too bad. Sorry about that. But hey, never mind, there's plenty more fish in the sea.'

'Kate, if anything were to happen to me ... I don't know what would become of Joe.'

'Ali? What's up with you? Are you ill?'

'No, I'm not ill.'

'I know you're not! When I saw you a week ago you were as fit as a flea. So, nothing's going to happen to you.'

'I've left the house to Joe, and my main insurance policy, but there's a second one for you. It's not huge, but it'd be a deposit on a house.'

'Ali, you're worrying me now. It's not because of this bloke, is it? C'mon, you're not going to let some stupid man get you down.'

'Bye, Kate. Love you.' I'm going to cry.

'Ali? Ali?'

I can't explain. If I tell her anything, I don't know what the consequences might be. They might go after her too. I hang up.

39

There are a few perfect seconds when I wake up, in bed, on Sunday morning, and I haven't yet remembered any of my problems. There is the pleasure of having actually slept, for once, the delicious sensation of being just a little too warm under my duvet, the softly diffused light coming through the curtains.

Then, *Bang!* I remember, and it all goes dark and heavy.

I have bought a day's grace, I remind myself. By feigning this stomach bug, I can hold them at bay for today. I can't go anywhere, of course, in case I'm seen, but I can hide away and try to think.

It occurs to me to look on the *Belfast Telegraph* website, to see if there's anything about Kim's accident. Here it is.

Her uncle, whom it says brought her up like a daughter, has issued a statement. It's mostly the usual – deep sorrow at her untimely death, regret that she died away from home and among strangers, the joy she brought to all the lives she touched. There is also this: her grandfather is the nonagenarian retired property developer Max Atchison, but it is understood Kim was completely estranged from Atchison Senior and from her mother, Margaret. However, the uncle-slash-father says the family would always come together *in extremis* and it is only so very sad that they now find themselves united in grief.

I take a long, hot shower, wash my hair, clean my teeth, pull on clothes, slot my feet into my flip-flops.

Joe is in the kitchen, drinking coffee and reading. He is in jeans and a t-shirt too, and barefoot. I still think he looks beautiful, no matter what.

'You look refreshed,' he says.

'I actually slept. You were in bed when I got home last night. That was early for you – feeling all right?'

'Yeah, fine. I was up at five yesterday, to chat to someone in New Zealand.'

'Ah – your forum.'

'Yep. Coffee?'

'I think I'll make myself a decaff.'

I flip-flop round the kitchen gathering together a mug, coffee, milk. I'm not hungry but I put a slice of bread in the toaster and hope the warming smell will give me an appetite.

Joe says, 'So, do we talk about the obvious, or ...?'

'We have to talk about it. There's been a development. We

could be in danger, Joe, and the police aren't going to listen to me, so, somehow, we have to sort this out for ourselves. It might mean we have to be brave, do things we wouldn't ...'

'Mum, I'm not leaving this house.'

'Joe, these people have killed.'

'I don't care. I'm not leaving this house. I'd rather die ...'

'Please don't say that.'

'You go, if you want to.'

'You know I can't leave you.'

'That's not my fault.'

'None of this is your fault. That doesn't mean it's mine, either.'

'So what's this development anyway?'

'This man I've been seeing – the one who sent the flowers ...'

'The one you spent the night with, who set you up to make a fool of yourself with the police.'

'Yes, well, he's not Kim's brother. She never had a brother. One of Granny's carers went to school with her and she mentioned it; more than mentioned it, in fact – I asked her to repeat it and she's absolutely sure there was no brother because she and Kim talked specifically about it.'

'Then who is he?'

'I don't know, Joe. But, since Kevin was in Parnell Park when Kim died, I'm very much afraid he might be her killer. Based on when I saw him, he had enough time for flights to and from London. He could've done it.'

'Does he know you're on to him?'

'I don't think so. But we know he's aware of my suspicions

about Kim – that's why he's trying to manipulate me. He's got no guarantee I won't keep on snooping, so I don't think he and Kevin will feel safe with me still around. Plus, when Antoinette comes back, she could expose him as an imposter, if I was still here, making waves.

'I was thinking, if I can hold him off until Antoinette comes back, if I appear to have dropped all suspicions and just accepted that Kim died in an accident, then I could speak to Antoinette the minute she returns and she could go to the police. She doesn't have a history of time-wasting and they told her too that Callum was Kim's brother.'

'You really think he'll give you the opportunity to do that?'

'No.'

'Then you've got to think of something better.'

'Help me, then. What can I do?'

40

Callum texts: Feeling any better? I'm seeing Kevin at the house later – I could bring you some Lucozade.

I reply: A little better, but no thanks to the Lucozade. I'm sticking to water, for now. You don't want to come down with this, when you've just got Rebecca home. Will let you know when improved.

I wonder whether anything Callum told me was true. Does he have a teenage daughter? Did his wife die of cancer? How do he and Kevin know each other? Are they really old college buddies or is Callum a hired assassin, dramatic as that sounds?

'Mum, come quickly.'

I go to the front room, where Joe is standing at the window, looking through the slatted blinds.

'An ambulance just pulled up, outside Kevin's.'

We watch, as two paramedics approach Kevin's front door. One of them pushes it and it swings open.

'What do you think's going on?' Joe says.

'I don't know. He must've made a 999 call, but I didn't hear a siren.'

'No, there was no siren, but the blue lights were on. I suppose there's no traffic to clear in a cul-de-sac.'

'Let's sit here, see what happens.'

Joe puts on a CD, but it does nothing to help.

After about fifteen minutes, Kevin's front door opens again, and he appears with the two paramedics. Joe grabs the binoculars he's been wearing all day and watches through the slats.

'Shit.'

'What is it?'

'Look.' He thrusts the binoculars into my hands and I try to put them to my eyes without pulling Joe's neck.

There is Kevin, in pyjama bottoms and a t-shirt, ashen-faced, and with his two wrists bandaged.

'He's slashed his wrists,' Joe says.

Kevin looks utterly, utterly terrible. He looks old, like he can barely make it to the ambulance. A female paramedic puts an arm round the back of his shoulders and her male colleague is talking to him all the time.

'Does this make our situation better or worse?' Joe asks.

I understand that he does not care, at this moment, for

Kevin's welfare, because neither do I. What I want to know is how this will affect what Callum does next.

'He's got to be worried, now, that Kevin will tell all. Maybe Callum will decide to cut and run and just disappear back to wherever he came from. It could all be over, Mum.'

'But he'd still be out there,' I say. 'I'd never know if he was going to come back. I'd be looking over my shoulder forever. Listen, why do you think Kevin slashed his wrists, anyway? Guilty conscience? Cry for help? Running away?'

'Everyone else will reckon it's a broken heart, won't they?'

'Probably,' I say.

'But whatever the reason, he's pulled back, dialled 999, saved himself. Maybe he always intended to call the ambulance. Maybe it's a way of getting a safe bed in hospital, away from Callum.'

'You think he might be frightened of Callum too?'

'I think it's possible that, even if Kevin thought he wanted someone dead, he wasn't prepared for what that would actually feel like when it came to pass.' My own father thought he could take Mum's life, but, when the moment arrived, he couldn't. Imagining it isn't the same as doing it.

'He did look terrible just now,' I say. 'I assume hospital will hang onto him at least for tonight.'

'If he's deemed a danger to himself, they might keep him a lot longer than that.'

'But you hear all the time about suicidal types being discharged too soon and then going on to finish what they'd started.'

'We're just speculating. The truth is, we don't know what

the truth is, in any of this. And Kevin cutting himself doesn't make it clearer. Mum, keep a hammer beside the bed and I'll try and remember how to reset the old intruder alarm, if it's even still working.'

It feels strange, not going to see Mum. The home has a rule that staff and visitors must be forty-eight hours free of vomiting before they can go back. You can understand why – trying to manage the spread of anything in that place would be difficult, and the residents don't have the defences to deal with illness. Of course, I don't actually have a bug, but I can hardly explain to Linzi and Co that I vomited from sheer revulsion.

Instead, I phone, to hear how Mum is.

Alanis answers.

'She's grand, Alice. A hundred per cent. She ate all her dinner and she's at her tea now. What about you, but? Feeling any better?'

I assure her I'm fine, and will drop in tomorrow evening.

'No worries, sure. We'll see you then. Take care of yourself.'

I have been taking care of myself all my adult life, I think as I hang up. First as a backpacking nomad, crossing seas on rickety boats, hitching the highways and byways; Joe Payne certainly never looked after me, and then, when he died, I was on my own again, with not just myself but my young son to look out for. Even then, I didn't know what tricks fate still had in store for us. I always thought there would be time to work it out, though. I thought there'd be a breakthrough in treating

Joe's condition – the Joe I love – or that the right psychiatrist could help him find a way to live with it, or that he'd simply grow used to himself, to his appearance, and one day decide he could face the world, walk into town, go to a coffee shop, buy a newspaper, talk to people.

This is why I cannot come to harm at the hands of Callum – not because I am too young or because I deserve longer or even because there would be no-one to visit Mum, but because Joe isn't ready yet. He isn't fixed. I cannot die until he is back in the world again. Someone said grief is the price we pay for love, but they meant that we, the living, grieve for those we love who have passed. I have grieved these ten years for my beautiful boy who still walks and talks yet is calcifying in this prison of a house, day after day, year after year. He should be out there lying on the beach in this weather, plunging into the waves to cool down, lazing outside a harbour bar with a cold pint, laughing with friends, falling in love. He is so lonely – he must be so lonely. Once, I found him listening to 'I've Fallen in Love', that sweetest Bap Kennedy song, on the stereo and just looking at himself in the mirror above the fireplace. I was in the doorway, and at first he didn't see me, then he caught my reflection. Without turning round, he gave me a little smile, and a shrug, and I felt my heart would break for him.

41

Joe has spent the last half-hour fiddling with the intruder alarm, trying to get it to work. I have been thinking. If Kevin really has hatched a murder plot, then there must be some sort of record, somewhere. He can't possibly have set all this up without using a phone number or a password, at the very least, and surely he must have written these down. There must be a secret notebook, or a Word document, or even a Post-it with these scraps of evidence, which would show what he's been up to, and connect him to the killer.

'He can't have stored anything on the laptop he left with the guy on Park Road,' I say. 'An expert would be liable to find it, especially if he's been looking at criminal websites. So any evidence must be in the house.'

Joe doesn't look up from his tinkering at the keypad in the hall cupboard. 'Mum, it takes us half a day to find the scissors when we've lost them, and we know what they look like – what are the chances of locating a minuscule piece of information in a strange house, and which Kevin may well have encrypted?'

'That's why the timing is perfect – with Kevin in hospital, I could have a free run of the place.'

'You're going to break into Kevin's?'

'I don't know if they have a burglar alarm, but I'd say it's highly unlikely that Kevin thought to set it, the state he was in when they took him in the ambulance.'

'That's not what I mean. I'm saying, it's a big thing breaking into someone's house.'

'It's a bigger thing killing someone!'

'How would you do it?'

'Go round the back. Put a brick through the patio door – it's the same as ours, with a handle on the inside; I've seen it. Reach in through the hole and *voilà*.'

'Smashing glass makes a lot of noise – what if the Wrights hear you, or the family on the other side?'

That's true.

'It is a good opportunity, though, with Kevin away,' Joe says.

We kick around a few ideas, but conclude that, unless Jim and Marjorie and the neighbours on the other side all choose to go out, simultaneously, then we're stuck.

Unless. I go to the hallstand, open the drawer, push through a bundle of string and a stapler, a hole-punch, and keys for the garage and the garden shed.

'Ta-da!' I hold up a Yale key on a red plastic fob. 'It's their front-door key. Kim gave it to me last summer when they went to Portugal – I watered their plants. So, all I have to do is wait until dark, then I can simply go across the road and let myself in.'

'What if he comes, looking for Kevin?'

'Callum? I could text him, tell him Kevin's been taken to hospital – then there'd be no point in him coming.'

'He'll know you've been nosey-parking out the window again. And it might make him nervous, knowing that Kevin's having some sort of crisis. I'm not sure we want to make him nervous.'

'He should be nervous – we're closing in. But to get any closer I have to get into that house.'

'OK, but take your phone with you. Anything strange, ring 999.'

I am feeling much, much better. I am not cowering, waiting for the bad guys to make their next move: I am taking the game to them.

42

It seems to take forever to get dark. I have been hanging about in my black clothes for ages, looking like a stage hand, Joe says, waiting until I'm confident I can merge into the night.

Joe is having another go at the alarm he failed to fix earlier. Neither of us has had anything to drink.

'OK,' I say, at last. 'I think it's time.' I have my phone in my jeans pocket, a rubber torch in one hand and the Kennedys' key in the other. 'Wish me luck.'

'Good luck,' Joe says. 'And if anything odd happens, it's a straight 999, right?'

'Yep,' I say. But nothing will go wrong. With the epiphany over the likelihood that Kevin must have left some telltale crumbs of evidence, added to his absence at just the right moment, the tide has turned in my favour, I'm sure of it.

I let myself out of the house and Joe quietly closes the door behind me. There's no-one about and I pad across the Park and nip into the Kennedys' driveway. As I approach the door, it suddenly occurs to me that this key is a year old – what if one of them found themselves locked out since then, called the smith and had the locks changed? My key will be no use on a new model. Heart thumping, I slide the key into the lock. It doesn't turn. I close my eyes, take it out. Thwarted. What now? Just turn and go home? But I was ready for this. I was ready to fight back. With little hope, I give it one more try – slide it in, turn it, yes! It's a bit stiff, but it works. I push the door gently and it swings open with a slight creak. I can just about make out the shapes of a coatstand in the far corner and a rack of shoes by the radiator. I'm in. This is it.

The Kennedys are people just like us, so I should think like us. Where would I hide secret information? I used to keep my diary in the gap behind my husband's chest of drawers – I reasoned he'd never look in a location that seemed to be his already. I actually go there – I reach my hand in behind Kim's chest – I deduce that hers is the one with the jewellery box and the dish of lipsticks and Kevin's has the two mugs and the biography. I find nothing and pull the chest out from the wall to be sure, but there're only dust bunnies.

I don't feel good about this, but I open every drawer of Kim's chest, rummage under her things, hoping for a notebook, even a little scrap of paper; there's nothing. Today, these clothes are still personal, chosen by Kim, paid for on her card, probably, and worn every day or on special occasions, making her feel good about herself, I hope. In a few months, they will be just another bundle of landfill, or may hang anonymously in some charity shop. I stop and stroke one item carefully, wanting to show some mark of respect. Then I continue with my quest for clues.

I remind myself that this isn't like looking for lost scissors, or even for something hidden from a spouse – when Kevin stashed this information, he would've had in mind the possibility that, at some point, police might come looking for it, so it had to be so cleverly concealed that even seasoned detectives didn't find it easily.

I look inside shoes, inside socks, I unfold sheets and pillowcases from the hot press. I open a soap dish, shake out boxes of tampons, headache tablets and vitamins. I go through every single CD case and every vinyl sleeve. I check that all the cans in the larder are real cans and there isn't one which is a secret money box. I peek into the open box of Cup-a-Soup sachets and the tub of parsley sauce granules. I climb up and look inside the lampshades, I look in the cleaning caddy under the sink. Nothing, nothing, nothing, nothing. Finally, I look in what I consider the least likely place – least, because it is the most obvious – the desk in what appears to be Kevin's study.

This is an intriguing piece of furniture – what is called a secretaire, I believe. Possibly not well-enough maintained to have come from an antique shop, more likely an auction find. The desk folds down to reveal pigeonholes for different stationery items, an inkwell and two little drawers. Is it possible that Kevin was so casual as to leave incriminating evidence in his own desk? Was he that confident that Kim's death would never prompt much of an investigation? I've searched everywhere else, so why not?

I begin with the large underneath drawers, which are crammed with file blocks and printer paper and newspaper cuttings. There are also leads and chargers in the bottom one.

I flick through the pigeonhole contents, find nothing and try the little drawers. One contains paperclips and drawing pins. The other is locked. It may have been locked when Kevin bought the secretaire. He may not know what, if anything, is in it, if the key didn't come with the piece. On the other hand, it may contain a few digits or a web address that could put Kevin and Callum away for twenty years. I have to know.

I unfold one of the paperclips from the unlocked drawer and try poking it into the lock, with no success. I tap the locked drawer, hard, and again, with the heel of the torch handle, but it doesn't help and I'm afraid of losing my light, so I stop. I go back to the kitchen, to where I remember seeing a screwdriver in a drawer, and bring it to the desk. I don't care any more. I whack and thrust at the little locked drawer with the driver. I'm not in a frenzy, but I'm determined. Suddenly, I hear a key in the front-door lock, and I recognise the creak as it slowly opens. I flick off my torch, pull out my phone and crouch behind the secretaire in the dark.

43

Someone is in the hall. I hear them close the front door, stop and pause. Why? Are they an intruder, like me, trying to discern who else is in the house?

It's not inconceivable that it's Kevin – people discharge themselves from hospital care, or simply fail to find a bed. Whoever it is goes into the front room – I can hear them gently bumping into furniture in the dark. Why don't they switch on a light? My knees are starting to ache, crouching here.

I hear a creak on the stairs and reckon my visitor is heading up. This is my opportunity to run for it. I straighten up as soundlessly as I can manage, test the strength in my legs and prepare to flee. Only now, I realise that I have forgotten to change my stupid flip-flops. I vacate Kevin's study, see the front door just down the hall, and hurl myself towards it. It is like trying to run into a headwind. Some unseen force seems to be pushing me back and a journey of a few steps feels like it takes a lifetime. I grab the front door, pull it open, but I'm not quick enough. I'm not quite quick enough and a gloved hand clamps over my face and drags me back across the threshold. I cannot see anything, but I smell bergamot and I know who it is.

44

I have been overbalanced, and although I do my best to struggle, I cannot resist much when I have lost my footing. Callum drags me easily back into the hallway.

Joe will have been watching. Did he spot Callum at the front door? Will he call the police? We didn't discuss this in advance. I was to ring 999 on my mobile if things went awry. Joe doesn't speak to anyone in authority as it would make him visible and he largely lives his life as a non-person. This, though – this is different.

My phone is no longer in my hand – did I drop it? Put it back in my pocket before I ran? I'm not sure, but it wouldn't matter – Callum's grip is like iron. All I can think of is Joe – what will happen to him if I'm not around? How many times have I thought that I did not bring him into the world to live like this, condemned like this, isolated and diminished in every human way? But to think of him suddenly alone ... perhaps it is the hand over my face reducing my oxygen intake, for I imagine myself back in the labour ward, the gas and air mask hard yet soft over my mouth and nose, and the cold, white light above the thing on which I am lying, which is called a bed but doesn't feel like a bed. My nightie is bundled up around my chest and the midwife must keep changing the large bloody pad beneath me and I am howling in pain, and pushing for all I am worth. Bringing Joe into the world is the hardest, bravest thing I have ever had to do and I didn't go through all that, and produce all the milk and the love and blot up all his pain, just to leave him now. I suddenly find the strength of a labouring mother and I bite and I kick and I tear myself from Callum's grasp and spill out onto the driveway and I try to roar from the depths of my desperate lungs.

'Joe! Joe! Help me!'

Joe will be watching – will it be enough?

I think I have actually knocked Callum off his feet, because it is seconds before he is upon me and I have time hoarsely to scream 'Joe! Joe!' again.

I will Joe to be brave, to leave the house, to run out into the road and save me – he is strong and there would be two of us against one. I will him to do this not only because I fear Callum, but because if Joe left the house just once, let people see him just once, then maybe, just maybe, his lonely nightmare might start to come to an end too.

Callum has thrown his arms tightly round me, pinning mine.

'Joe! Please!' I call again, more weakly. If he doesn't come now, it's going to be too late. Callum has his hands round my throat. He's squeezing the life out of me. I try to summon up the labour ward again, tap into that super-strength, but all I can do is claw at his hands. It is no good. Joe isn't coming. I am going to die as I lived – silently, unnoticed in this quiet street.

Woy-woy-woy-woy-woy-woy-woy-woy!

It's our intruder alarm. Joe must have fixed it. He has set it off to draw attention.

Yap-yap-yap-yap-yap-yap-yap!

Ruff-ruff-ruff-ruff-ruff-ruff-ruff!

Wa-oo, woof-woof-woof, wa-oo!

It rouses all the neighbourhood dogs into a cacophonic chorus.

With a scamper of nails on tarmac and a good bit of snarling, the two escape-artist terriers from round the corner arrive. One of them grabs Callum's ankle.

'Who's there?' I hear footsteps running towards us from the other direction. The grip on my throat loosens, then releases me completely and when I fall to my knees, Callum is gone.

Two new figures appear beside me in the darkness.

'Mrs Payne? Mrs Payne, it's Weston. Are you all right?'

I am choking, gasping, trying to get air into my lungs, trying to think straight.

'I'm not sure what happened,' I say. I have to decide what to reveal – this isn't over yet. 'I think he was trying to mug me.'

'You poor thing,' says the other figure.

'This is Darius,' Weston says. 'He's my ...'

'I'm his boyfriend,' Darius says. 'But his mum thinks I'm his personal trainer, which is why we had to go down the garden for a snog. Is that your burglar alarm as well, Alison?'

'Yes. I must go and switch it off before I annoy half the town.'

'Do you want us to come in with you, take a look around?' Weston says.

'No, he didn't manage to get in,' I say.

'But you'll phone the police – tell them he attacked you when you disturbed him,' Darius says.

'Yes.' Not yet. I haven't got him yet.

A muffled version of Van Morrison's 'Glad Tidings' rings out. It's my phone and yes, it is in my pocket. It's Joe. I switch it off.

I glance back at Kevin's front door, see that Callum has coolly pulled it shut.

The two young men insist on seeing me home.

'Are you sure you don't want us to come in for a while?' Weston says.

'There's no need. I'll ring a friend. She'll come over.'

I don't ring a friend. When I go inside, I check all the doors are locked and I call the number on the folded scrap of card I took from underneath the back foot of the secretaire, and which I only spotted because I'd had to crouch beside it. Somehow I have held onto it, screwed up, tight, inside my fist.

45

I tap the digits in with a shaking hand. My phone recognises the number.

'Ali, hi. All well?' Callum.

His nonchalance chills me.

'I'm going to get you,' I say.

46

Joe is struggling. I could've died out there and we both know it. And he didn't come. I want to tell him I understand, that it's not his fault, but I fear making things even worse.

I slept, fitfully, with the intruder alarm on and, as Joe proposed, a hammer in my hand. Callum didn't come back, but presumably it's only a matter of time.

Joe and I thought about calling the police, but we haven't yet got enough to dispel their belief that I am some mad menopausal bitch with a fanciful notion that my neighbour has been murdered. Weston and Darius didn't actually see Callum, so if asked they could only say I *told* them I'd been attacked, and our burglar alarm wasn't set off by an actual break-in – no broken glass, no jimmied door.

So we have to do this ourselves.

Callum might have the element of surprise, but only slightly – after all, we know that he's coming, we just don't know when.

'It's like *Home Alone*,' Joe says, in a brighter moment.

We close all the windows as well as locking the doors, but we feel sure he won't come in daylight. Later, we'll sleep in shifts. We each have a claw hammer and an aerosol deodorant to spray in his eyes. We have a rope to tie him up until the police arrive. Callum knows that a housebound person lives with me, because I told him as much, but I reckon he's expecting someone elderly and infirm, not a strapping lad who works out on a home gym for hours every day.

I don't see any reason why I can't visit Mum and, in fact, I decide I must – I need to give the home Kate's contact details and I need to tell Mum I love her, just in case anything should happen to me. Just in case.

'Drive straight there,' Joe says. 'Keep the car doors locked and don't stop off to buy anything. Definitely don't pull over if you see something that looks like a breakdown or someone tries to flag you down – it could be a set-up. And watch your rear-view mirror – if you think you're being followed, then drive to the police station.'

'OK.'

'And when you get back, be careful getting from the car into the house. Sit in the car for a few minutes, if necessary, until there's someone else passing by. Don't get out if the Park looks deserted.'

I do everything Joe says. I wait until the dog-walkers fill

the roadway on their afternoon stroll to dash to the car, jump in, lock the doors. I drive straight to Mount Charles, not even stopping to pick up a treat for Mum, and checking my rear-view mirror constantly. There is no dark Volvo and what vehicles there are keep changing. Callum is not tailing me.

It is Margarida who answers the door.

'Hi, Alice. I heard you were sick. Better now?'

'Much better. How's Mum?'

'Belligerent.'

'Oh? Do we know why?'

'You didn't come yesterday. We told her you were sick, but I don't think she believed us.'

'Sorry.'

'Why are you sorry? You were unwell, Alice – it happens. No-one else has a visitor who comes every single day, like you. Your mother's very lucky.'

Margarida is trying to be nice, trying to be fair to me, but I cannot regard my mother as lucky, when other women her age are still playing golf, posting on Facebook, even having a love life.

I sign in and venture into the day room. Linzi is kneeling in front of Mum, taking Mum's bare feet out of a bubbling foot spa. They are so good to her here. Linzi stands, picks up the foot spa levelly, so as not to slosh water over the sides.

'Och, Ruby, here she is now. It's great to see you back, Alice. You were missed. Feeling better?'

'Much, thanks. I hear all wasn't sweetness and light.'

Linzi smiles, lowers her voice. 'She's been a bit cranky all right. She might take a wee minute to come round – I think she's in a bit of a huff with you, with all of us, in fact.'

'OK. I'll tread carefully,' I say. 'Here, give me that.' I take the towel with which Linzi was about to dry Mum's feet.

'Oh, thanks, Alice. Her wee pop socks and slippers are just there, under her chair. All right, Ruby? I'll leave yous to it, then.'

'Great. Hi, Mum. How are you today?'

'Pissed off,' Mum says.

'Oh!'

'Absolutely pissed off.'

'Why's that?'

'Wouldn't you be pissed off if you were stuck in here, all the time?'

'And where would you rather be?'

'In the bungalow, of course, with you and your father, with my own kettle and my own toilet. You can bet Michael won't have done any washing while I'm in here and I'm going to go home to a mountain of ironing. I need a new iron anyway – that old one's started to leak.'

'I could do some of it for you, if you want.'

'You shouldn't have to iron your own school shirts.'

'But it's the holidays – I have bags of time.'

'And they made me miss my visitor.'

'Oh, did you have a visitor?'

'A gentleman came here to visit me, but they wouldn't let me see him. They just wanted to keep him for themselves – that blonde one's man-mad.' Mum uses language she would never have used when she was well, and even has thoughts I don't believe she had back then. She was what some people still call 'a lady' – discreet, measured, not prone to terms like 'man-mad'; 'pissed off' possibly, but exceptionally.

'It was probably just the man to read the meter.'

'It wasn't. They asked me did I know who it was, but how could I know when they wouldn't let me see him?'

'Well, never mind, I dare say he'll call again if it's anything important. Anyway, how have you been eating?'

'So-so.'

'Really? What did you have for lunch?'

'I hardly ate a bite. Just two fishcakes, potatoes, carrots and peas.'

'No dessert?'

'Trifle.'

'And you ate that too?'

'Yes.'

'And a cup of tea with a biscuit?'

'Yes, but it was a fig roll.'

'And that's all you were able to manage.'

'Yes.'

'You must be hungry now then.'

'No. I don't get hungry. It's these tablets I'm on. They kill your appetite.'

'Evidently.'

The tea trolley approaches and Alanis offers Mum the plate of biscuits.

'Take two or three, Ruby,' she says, and Mum does. No appetite, indeed.

'Oh, by the way, a man called looking for Ruby this afternoon,' she tells me.

'I was wondering about that. Mum said something, but'

– I lower my voice and turn to Alanis – 'I wasn't sure if it really happened. Was he a red-haired guy, stocky, glasses?' I'm thinking of my cousin Kenneth, who has popped in occasionally in the past.

'No, this was a different fella. He seemed lovely. Ruby was in the shower, but, and she'd only started. It takes us a good while to get her in and wash her hair and then get her out and dressed again and her nails cut and her hair dried and all. He waited a wee while, but then he said he had to go on.'

'Oh, that's a shame. I wonder who he was.'

'I'll check the book, sure. He signed in.'

Alanis fetches the book while I join Mum in a cup of tea.

'Here it is,' she says. 'Oh, here, it's hard to make out, he's written it that quick. You look at it, Alice. Is that a D? I think that's David.'

'I think you're right.'

'David what, though?'

'Is it Ogilby? David Ogilby? Doesn't ring any bells.'

'He seemed real nice. Medium height, dark hair, late forties, I'd say. Good-looking.' She gives me a wicked smile. 'You wouldn't kick him out of bed, Alice.'

Alanis is laughing, but I feel my cup start to rattle in my saucer.

'Drove a big, dark Volvo. We saw it through the front window. I'd say he's worth a few pound.'

47

'Alanis, I need to talk to you. And your mum and Margarida. But I need to do it in private and I need to do it now.'

Alanis looks into my eyes. She must see something there, because she says, 'We can't leave this day room unattended, but I'll grab Mum and Maggie and we can go into the corner. No-one'll hear. Is it about that man? Is he trouble?'

'He's dangerous,' I say.

I don't know what Alanis tells her Mum, but she and Margarida appear in a second, looking concerned.

'That man who called here, he's someone I know – Margarida, he's the guy I had the date with, remember?'

'I remember.'

'Look, it's a long story, but he is not a good person. Last night he attacked me ...'

'He attacked you?' Margarida says.

'Have you been to the police?' says Linzi.

'I can't go to the police yet, because he has very cleverly made me look a fool to them already and I need to get some better evidence before they'll believe me. He's a manipulator.' I turn to Linzi. 'I think he killed Kim Kennedy and made it look like an accident.'

'Fu-u-ck,' says Alanis.

'Is this the woman you were telling me about?' Margarida asks Linzi.

'Yes,' Linzi says. 'Alice, do you not think you're out of your depth here?'

'I am *way* out of my depth, but I know the only way I'm getting out of the water is if I get enough to expose that bastard.'

'What can we do?' Margarida says.

'Well, stupidly, stupidly, I must've told him which care home Mum's in.'

'Now that you mention it, he never said Ruby's second name, he just asked for Ruby, Alice Payne's mother. I didn't think about it at the time,' Alanis says.

'Promise me, if he comes back, you won't give him access to Mum. Don't identify her to him and don't give her the chance to identify herself. Don't act weird, just keep Mum safe.'

I look away, and see that Phyllis the ex-waitress and Mrs Lappin are both watching us and listening. I don't know how much they heard or followed. Nothing, I hope. Alarm could spread through this place in no time.

'Alice, I understand your wish to gather evidence about this man, but if you believe he has killed someone, then we must go to the police,' Margarida says.

'I've already been to the police. Twice,' I say. 'At first I looked crazy, and now they think I'm a pest.'

'Then let us talk to them,' Margarida says.

'And say what?' I say. 'A man called here and attempted to visit a resident? So what?'

'We could say we see you every day and you don't seem like a crazy pest to us,' Margarida says. 'If this man is capable of murder, we have to think of all our residents, and we have to think of our own safety too, Alice.'

'Aye-aye. We'll have to save that decision for another time,' Alanis says. 'Look who it is.'

Outside the front window, a long black car has just pulled up.

48

With the lights on inside the day room, Callum could see right in. I am saved by the fact that the other three women are round me in a huddle, but there is no running away or he might spot me. Alanis shoves me behind the long, patterned curtain at the back window and Linzi answers the door.

I can hear voices in the hall, but cannot hear what they're saying.

Margarida is over at Mum.

'Let's go for a little walk,' she says.

'A walk? Where to?'

'Would you like to see the kitchen? See where all the magic happens?'

They are bound to meet Callum in the hallway, but providing Mum doesn't take it upon herself to announce, 'I'm Ruby', Margarida can escort her to safety.

'Sit there, sure,' I hear Linzi say. 'I'll just ask Alanis to fetch it. Alanis, could you get this gentleman a glass of water, please?'

'Coming right up.'

'I'll have to leave you here a wee minute – there always has to be one of us in the day room with the wee residents.'

'Of course,' Callum says. 'Don't mind me. I'll come in with you.'

'No, you don't have to. It's fine.'

'I'd like to see where Ruby spends her time. I'm just sorry I've missed her. Again. But Alice is here.'

'Alice? No.'

'But I saw her car.'

Shit!

'Oh, yes.'

'She went to the hospital in the ambulance with her mother.' It is Phyllis's voice.

'Sorry. We're not really meant to give out details like that, only to family,' Linzi says.

'Of course. You have to be so careful these days. I work with a lot of personal records and data protection would be a big thing for us. I'd like to make sure they're both all right, though. I'll pop over to the hospital. See what I can find out there.'

'They didn't take her to Craigavon. They took her to the Royal.' Mrs Lappin!

'Mrs Lappin, we're not really allowed to give out that sort of information. Only to family.'

'And are you not family, dear? I thought you had the look of Ruby about you.'

Oh, dear Mrs Lappin, you have just played a blinder, but please do not engage this man in any further chat. I am trying so hard not to shake this curtain, but I don't know how long I can keep it up.

'Here's your wee glass of water.' Alanis is back.

'Thanks.'

'Flip, you were ready for that. It's a powerful summer we're having, isn't it?'

The voices move back into the hall and I cannot make them out again, but I hear the beeping of the keypad that releases the front door and then the door itself shut. He is gone. At least, I think he is. I don't move from my hiding place. There is the sound of a car engine and then Alanis comes and gets me.

'All clear, Alice.'

'Thank you. Thank you so much,' I say.

Linzi re-appears. 'He's tore the page out of the visitors' book when I wasn't looking, the shite.'

Has he, indeed? Is it possible that 'Callum' has blundered, on his first visit, when unexpectedly asked to jot down his signature? Is that why he came back this evening, to remove the evidence? David Ogilby. Your real name. Gotcha.

49

As I leave Mount Charles, I feel sure the girls will discuss what has just happened and conclude that they must call the police. This is fine. It makes little difference. The officers on duty may decide that, as nothing has actually happened at the care home, other than an unknown visitor calling and asking for a glass of water, the call can be filed under 'bin'. Or they might decide to ring me again, or call at my house to ask what I have been saying and why.

The main thing is that Callum is on his way to the Royal Victoria Hospital in Belfast, a place all the better for me to meet with an accident, as it has no connection to Kim or Kevin or Parnell Park. I could 'fall' from the hospital's multi-storey car park or be the victim of a hit-and-run in the dark.

Except this time the trick is on him and I will be safe and on my guard at home before he realises he's driven twenty-five miles on a wild goose chase. Thanks to Mrs Lappin's excellent bit of embellishment, I even dare take time to stop at Nicholson's and pick up something for supper. I concentrate on getting round town in the right lanes and easily find a space in the car park.

There's no real hurry, and I pause to look at the display of soft fruit. Am I sick of strawberries yet? Who gets sick of strawberries? I pop two punnets in my basket. It's too hot for proper cooking, but I can find something good in the deli fridge.

'Mrs Payne!' It is a smiling woman in her forties, and I have no idea who she is.

'Hello!' Should I know her? Is this another fact that has fallen out of its proper box inside my brain and floated off, like happens to Mum?

'You won't remember me, but I'm Ellie's mum, from Dovecote Nursery. You came and filled in when Mrs Grant went on maternity.'

Oh, yes! That was a few years ago. It was demanding, but lovely. The children got to play all day, and we'd have a little snack and a story and rhyme-time and sing-songs in a side room we called The Den. No homework to set and mark, lots to make me smile and an assistant who backed me up in every possible way. A dream job, really.

'Ellie absolutely loved you. She still talks about you.'

I try desperately to remember who Ellie was.

'What age is Ellie now?'

'Seventeen. Doing her "A" levels next summer, providing she does well in her ASs.'

No. Dovecote couldn't possibly be that long ago.

'Ellie was the one who insisted on wearing a nurse's outfit to nursery every day.'

Ha-ha! Now I remember her, of course. An absolute pet, so caring of everyone.

'And does she still want to be a nurse?'

'Oh, yes. She's got her heart set on doing her degree at Queen's, specialising in paediatrics, and then going on to be a health visitor. Ellie has it all worked out, so long as she gets the grades.'

'And is that looking good?'

Ellie's mum looks like she doesn't want to boast, but she can't resist telling me that her teachers are predicting an A and two Bs.

'Then she's all set,' I say.

'And we're so grateful, every day. She has a wee friend, Victoria, who would just love to be going with her, but she's in a chair, disabled, and she hasn't even got great use of her hands; she left school and went to the further education college to try and find something she could do on computers. She's ended up studying travel and tourism, but it's not what she really wants to do. You don't realise how lucky you are, when your kids have all their options. Actually, you might have heard … Victoria – the wee girl in the chair – her assistant at college was the woman from here who was killed in that road accident in London. Her mummy says Victoria's devastated. That child has no luck, no luck.'

Kim, an *assistant*?

'The woman who died was a *tutor* at the college, I thought,' I say. The piece on the *Belfast Telegraph* website hadn't specified – just said her colleagues at the FE college were heartbroken.

'No, their tutor was a young man, as far as I know. I was talking to Victoria's mummy when I was in getting my roots done – they only last about three weeks now; they're pure white – and she was telling me. This woman took notes for Victoria and put her bits and pieces in and out of her bag. I think she helped her with toileting and that as well. Och, it's very sad, now.'

So Kim was *not* married to Kevin and was *not* an FE tutor and Callum is *not* her brother. Is anything what it seems?

'But what about your boy, Mrs Payne? I remember him being in the nursery with you a couple of times when his school was on holiday and the Dovecote was still on. He's up and away, I suppose.'

'Actually, he's home right now. That's why I'm looking for something nice for supper.'

'Oh, lovely. You have to make a fuss of them when they come back, don't you? But I'll let you get on. It was nice to bump into you. My name's Andrea, by the way.'

'And I'm Alice.'

'All the best, Alice, although you'll always be the famous Mrs Payne to us. Enjoy your supper.'

'Give Ellie my best wishes.'

'I will.'

I pay for my purchases and carry them out to the car, set them on the passenger seat and do my belt. Putting the car in gear, I check behind before reversing out of my space. A large saloon comes up behind me. Suddenly my heart is beating fast again. It's Callum.

50

I immediately lock the car doors. Somewhere along the line, Callum must have decided not to go to Belfast. Did he sit on the road outside Mum's home and wait to see if I appeared? He must have. What to do? I can't think. Maybe if I just drive, I can lose him in traffic, not that there's very much of it. That way, I could beat him to Parnell Park, get into the house and be ready.

I thrust the gear stick into reverse and swing the car out of its space. I almost drive into a white BMW and the driver blares the horn. 'Sorry! Sorry!' I mouth.

I turn left down to the traffic lights and they are green as I drive towards them, still green, still green, now amber – can I make it? – now red, but only just: I'll chance it. It works. I get through and Callum, who was on my tail, has to stop.

A lucky break, and I must make the most of it. But wait, if I drive straight home, he'll know where I'm going, he'll be seconds behind me and I might not have time to get into the house, grab my claw hammer and my spray. I remember his hands around my throat, how quickly I ran out of air.

No, frightening though it is, I have to slow down, let him follow me now, lead him away, then somehow, somehow, escape him and dash home. Years ago, this would have been better for me, as I know all the side streets and back roads and Callum doesn't. But sat nav means, as soon as he realises he's lost me, he can find the quickest route back to Parnell Park just as easily as I can. But what else can I do? I have to try.

I pull in at the bus stop, where Callum will see me, and I look as he pulls in across the road. I text Joe that I think Callum's real name might be David Ogilby and then I pull away again and he follows.

51

It takes all my concentration to drive through town, making sure I'm in the right lane when I am beyond stressed. Maybe if I head out the dual carriageway, another car will come between us and I can choose a turn-off for a speedy getaway before he knows it.

I get in the correct lane at the roundabout and it's busier than I expected, so when I slip into the flow a couple more cars come round immediately after me, change into my lane and I am shielded.

Normally, I'd sit at fifty and the cars behind me with more confident drivers would fly past, leaving me in their wake. But I've got to keep a couple of vehicles between Callum and me, so I sit in the outside lane at eighty. I have never driven at eighty in my life.

About two miles along, there is a slip lane on the right for leaving this carriageway and effectively making a considered U-turn into the opposite-running traffic. I indicate right. Shit! It's the double-blinking sound that means my right-hand indicator is not working again. How can I pull out to my right at eighty miles an hour without indicating?

I slow down in the outside lane. The driver behind will be incensed, but these are desperate times. I swing right into the space where I can leave the dual carriageway and angle back towards the way I came. The driver behind blasts his horn, at being taken by surprise, with no indication, and I am sure that Callum will slow down too, behind us, and follow me again.

Suddenly, the car behind is flashing its lights and I recognise it as a police vehicle. I am to pull over. In my rear-view mirror I see, to my relief, Callum's saloon car continue on its way out of town. They have frightened him off. I complete my manoeuvre onto the town-bound carriageway and hastily move onto the hard shoulder, where I get a quick ticking off for my faulty indicator light, which I fib had been working perfectly until that moment. I demonstrate that I know how to use hand signals until I can get to a garage. All the time I am watching for Callum to return, but he does not come this way. I have shrugged him loose. For now.

I fly back to town – I must, must, must stay ahead of Callum. I find my correct lane at the roundabout – I'm so focused now – and I drive straight to Parnell Park.

My heart is in my mouth as I unlock the car doors – what if I'm wrong? What if he passed me on the dual carriageway after all? What if he's here now? – and I lug my Nicholson's bag of food across the driveway and up the front step with shaking hands. My keys are bunched in my fist and I fumble for what feels like ages trying to locate the door key. I struggle to match it to the lock, such is the tremor from my shoulder to my fingertips. Quickly, quickly, please. As it finally turns, I sense a presence behind me and swing round with a gasp, but there is nothing there. I push open the door and stagger into the hall, close the door with my back and breathe.

52

We are ready. The house is in darkness, but Joe and I are wide awake and lying in wait.

'When this is over, we won't have anything to talk about,' Joe says. 'It's almost been enjoyable.'

'I'm glad you think so. A woman is dead, and I've spent a night with a killer. Not my idea of enjoyment.'

'That's not what I meant. I meant the challenge of figuring it out.'

'We still haven't really done that. We know who; we don't know why.'

'That's the missing jigsaw piece we're going to put right tonight.'

'When this is over, Joe, we have to talk.'

'About what?'

'About everything. About you.'

'Mum ...'

'You can't go on like this, Joe.'

'Why not?'

'It's not good for you. I'm not being a good parent, just letting you ...'

'So this is really about you.'

'No.'

'You don't have to be a good parent. I'm not a kid. I'm an adult.'

'Yes. Exactly. So you should ...'

'I thought we didn't like the word "should" – didn't we agree it's a word that invariably makes people feel worse about themselves?'

'Could you feel any worse?'

'Fuck you, Mum.'

'You can be as abusive as you like, we *are* going to talk, when this is over.'

No-one says anything for a while. Then I say, 'It's strange, sitting here, without any music.'

'We don't always have music – sometimes we have Radio 4.'

'But there's always something. We never choose silence, do we? We always fill it up. Stop talking for a minute and just listen.'

We do. A deep-voiced dog barks somewhere in the distance, then there is nothing. We sit in the quiet, for once. Then comes a low crunching from down the hall. Someone is working at the front door. I feel ... composed, poised, ready. I do not feel weak.

'Go!' I whisper to Joe, and he disappears without a sound.

53

There is a deeper, wooden crunch and then I hear the front door swing open. I'm not surprised it's this easy for Callum – we still have the original 1930s front door, with wood that's well on its way to rotting around the basic Yale lock. Yet another little household job I'd put off. I stay where I am, stay very still, but my heart is pounding.

'Alice.' It is Callum's voice. 'Alice, I'm home!'

I say nothing.

'Alice, I'm going to stand here for a minute, because I'm guessing you have a few little surprises in store for me, and I don't particularly want to be ambushed. When I saw the house in darkness, I guessed you'd cut the power. Yes, it meant you lost your burglar alarm, but you didn't care about that. A little bit of fuss over an alarm is no use to you, is it? You want this finished. You want *me* finished. I can sit here all night, if need be, and then I'll have the benefit of daylight, won't I?'

I still say nothing.

'Alternatively, I could just use this.'

From where I'm standing, I can see the beam of a torch partially lighting up the hall.

'Why did you kill Kim?'

'And why should I tell you that?'

'Because you're proud of it. Because you want me to know how cleverly you've done whatever it is you've done. What harm can it do to tell me now? You're going to kill me anyway.'

'I'm not sure anyone does appreciate quite how clever it was, actually,' Callum says. 'Because it didn't start out as a murder at all. At first, Kevin wanted Kim – aka Bikkie, aka Charlotte – to fake her suicide, like the canoe guy – remember him? – only better. She was to appear to be on holiday in Galway, go swimming in the sea and drown. Then she'd disappear into hiding in London, live in secret for a few years, with clandestine visits from Kevin, he'd collect a whopping great insurance policy, the mortgage would be cleared and they'd eventually be reunited somewhere nice and hot and far away, live happily ever after. The whole thing was his idea, of course. She had to be talked into it.'

'So where did you fit in?'

'I was the facilitator, the fixer. I set up the Galway end of things, found the bedsit in London, made the necessary arrangements. It was a fine project and I executed it immaculately. And then you saw Kim at East Croydon station and things got a bit tricky. But I like a challenge, so I spun it to Kevin – who only really wanted the money, anyway – that she could meet with an accident. We'd drop the fake suicide plan, get rid of Kim for real, and he could keep the insurance money and the house all to himself. Well, share a good chunk of the dosh with me, obviously.'

'Are you sure that's what he wanted? Are you sure that wasn't just your warped fantasy?'

'Oh, he agreed to it all right. Kev was fine with it. Until it actually happened. Now that she's dead, he's gone to pieces. Some people just can't take responsibility for their choices.'

'And were you really old friends from college?'

'Oh, Alice, haven't you realised yet? Nothing *Callum* told you is true. Not a word of it. So, no teenage daughter, no ex-wife with cancer. It made for an endearing story, though, didn't it? And you lapped it up. That Volvo I've been enjoying belongs to Kim's head of department, who, Kevin was good enough to tell me, is spending the summer in Greece with his family, so he won't miss it until the end of August. No, I'd never met Kevin before in my life. He found me online – you can find anything online these days.'

'You're a psychopath.'

'I tend to think you're right, although this is my first murder. I just wanted to see if I could do it and get away with it. Turns out I can. There were any number of ways I could've killed Kim, and I had to resist the urge to stage something really stylish, but I reeled it in and kept it so simple. Just one little kick to the back of her knee was all it took. Dozens of people there, and I simply walked away. It helped that I'd already decided to befriend her in London, when she was merely going to be a fake suicide – I wanted to get a little peek at this woman I'd been spending all those hours on.'

'What if Kevin talks?'

'Kevin won't talk. When he got the heebie-jeebies I made it quite clear to him that, if anything happened to me, I'd take him down with me – joint enterprise and all that. He's shaken up by what we've done, but he's not up for twenty years in prison.'

'So you've succeeded.'

'With just one little "i" to dot, and that's the "i" in Alice. Part of me thought you were a damned nuisance, spotting the cherry blossom in the photograph I took of Kim months ago, undermining all the little things I told Kevin to do to indicate future plans with Kim. The other part decided you actually made it more fun. You were dead right about booking the holiday and buying paint for the study – it was just as you said, a trail of crumbs to a happy couple who were looking forward to things. Kevin panicked when you started sniffing about, speaking to the police – that's why he took down the cherry blossom pic, until I told him to put it back, leave it, let things play out just a little differently to what we'd first intended. Possibly I should've called a halt when I saw how unreliable he was – he got his days of the week wrong over that hair appointment; honestly, one simple little thing and he couldn't get that right, and it didn't get past you, did it? I admire that, I really do. Ditto the change of style in the Facebook posts – Kevin's efforts were all a bit too literate. That morning in the park, when you set it all out there, I was impressed by your detective skills. And then you spotted the price sticker on that book I lent you too – I can't blame Kevin for that one. You were right about everything, Ali. Too bad no-one was listening.'

'How will you do it?'

'I thought you might disturb a burglar – your neighbours can vouch that your alarm went off last night; perhaps the culprits came back to finish what they started.'

'And they, what, strangle me, like you tried to do before?'

'Could do. Or stab you with something they grabbed from the kitchen – they didn't set out to kill you, they just panicked.'

'I see.'

'You seem remarkably calm, for someone who's about to die.'

'I'm fifty-one years old, I live with my elderly, housebound husband, I visit my demented mother in her care home every single day and in a few weeks I have to go back to work with a lot of children who are hyperactive, or uninterested, or just gobby or, if they're five-year-olds, are increasingly turning up in pull-up nappies, if you can believe it. The only date I've had in years was with you. What have I got to lose?'

I'm also recording this conversation on my phone, and have no intention of dying here, tonight.

'But, Alice, Alice, I'm forty-nine and I'm only just opening a whole new exciting chapter of my life.'

'Meaning you'll do this again.'

'Of course, and better. I've learned so much from this experience.'

Although I didn't think he'd made a sound coming down the stairs, I can now discern Joe standing in the hall, behind Callum. Joe must have done something just perceptible, because Callum turns and in that second I fly at him from the darkness with the claw hammer. It hits the side of his head. I think I've landed a good blow, but he still makes a grab for it and he's so strong. I try to keep hold of the metal shaft but he tugs and tugs and it springs from my grasp. One strike hasn't been enough and now he has the weapon.

'Yaagh!' Joe suddenly springs, but Callum is swinging the hammer he took from me.

'His eyes! Get his eyes!' I hear my voice, even though I hardly feel I am forming the words.

Callum is staring at Joe. 'Jesus, what the fuck …?'

Joe sprays the mist – but he's not very close to Callum's face. It makes Callum stop, stagger, put his arm to his eyes.

'Joe!' I shout and we charge for the back door.

But Callum is at our heels.

I stumble on the uneven concrete, drop my phone and it smashes. Joe is smarter – he has ducked round the side of the doorway and, as Callum emerges, he hits him, hard, with his hammer. The blow misses his head, lands on his shoulder. Callum seems to shrug it off, crushes my fallen phone with his heel and looks for me.

Our scheme hasn't worked. Joe still has his hammer, but Callum has one too. I am more frightened of Callum hurting Joe than hurting me. If I can get up, if I can run, if I can lure him out of our yard and onto the street, just maybe someone will come and Callum will run and Joe will be saved. If he brings that down on my head with the strength he's capable of, I don't stand a chance, but perhaps Joe can survive – for what, to live how, I don't know, but at this minute I have to do what I can. I scrabble on the concrete, urge myself forward, but I feel Callum grab my leg, pull me back. He's going to win. He's going to kill me like he killed Kim and then go back to some other life, posing as a normal person, while I am dead and Joe is abandoned and the recorded confession is destroyed and then he's going to emerge some day and do the same thing all over again. This knowledge is unbearable. It is worse than mere fear.

'DAVID! POLICE! Stop right there!' It's a woman's voice, cool, calm, authoritative, close by, though I cannot see her in the dark. The police are here. They're actually here. Margarida must have called them, or Linzi, made them come. They will save us.

'Mum!' Joe lurches for Callum, or David, who has leapt at me with the hammer. I shouldn't have relaxed, I should've realised that this was personal now, him and me.

Joe misses. But only because someone else has brought Callum tumbling, tumbling through the air and against the old mattress, dragged out to the back for now, because I didn't want to display it at the front until the council were due to take it away next week. 'Aaagh!'

The exposed corkscrew spring has gone into Callum's eye.

George, for it was he who rugby-tackled Callum, faints. Kate grabs Callum's hammer and throws it up the garden, then kicks his legs out from under him and he collapses on the ground.

I start to shake. *Really* shake. I wrap my arms round myself and try to hold it in, but I can't.

Kate is making a 999 call. But I thought the police were already here?

'Police, please. Armed intruder apprehended at 25 Parnell Park. Postcode, Ali?'

I tell her and she passes it on, listens again.

'Do we need an ambulance?' Kate looks at me, gives the whimpering heap on the ground a kick. 'No. Not necessary.'

54

While the police are dealing with Ogilby, Kate sits me down with a cup of tea.

'Kate, not that I'm not grateful – you saved us, you and George – but why are you here?'

'Well, first we had that weird conversation on the phone, where you were practically telling me the contents of your will, then I had a peculiar text from Joe, saying that if anything unusual happened to either of you, I was to go to the police with the name David Ogilby. I remembered you telling me once about a first aid trainer who said that the best test of when to call an ambulance for a child, even if you weren't really sure that anything big was wrong, was if you just weren't happy. And I just wasn't happy.'

'So you didn't simply ring me – you got on a plane and flew over.'

'Yes.'

'Who's minding the kids?'

'George's mum was up from Kent. Try and eat a Digestive with that. The sugar might do you good.'

'He would've killed me.'

'Yep.'

'What if he tells the police he was just a simple burglar – or a stalker-slash-intruder, which would explain him turning up at Mum's home as well? I still don't have anything to prove his connection to Kevin, at least not until Antoinette gets back. What if they charge him with something minor, he gets bail, and then just disappears? I think he loved making all the arrangements to hide Kim, and he'll be even better at it now. I could be looking over my shoulder for the rest of my life.'

'Surely the neighbours must have seen him hanging about at the Kennedys'.'

'Even so, he could say it was just an acquaintance he struck up in order to stalk me. If he makes out he's merely a bit of an oddball with a thing for me, maybe they'll believe him. He can say *we* attacked *him*. He makes a very credible witness, Kate. He knows how to play people.'

'Well, he won't be going anywhere tonight. He'll be in hospital, which is more than he deserves.'

Hospital doesn't sound secure to me.

'You made an awfully good police officer. You had me fooled.'

'I am supposed to be an actress.'

'Poor George.'

'Yes, he's extremely squeamish at the best of times and, to be fair, it wasn't pretty.'

'How come you were in the garden, anyway? Why didn't you just ring the doorbell?'

'When we got here, the house was in darkness and there was a strange car parked outside. You and Joe always have soft lamps on all over the place, and you don't bring visitors in, except us, so I had a bad vibe. We went round to the garden to see what we could see, and then you lot all came tumbling out. Which house was the dead girl's?'

'That one, just facing us,' I say.

'Ah, that explains the old biddy outside it when we arrived, watering the hanging baskets. She said her neighbour was away but she couldn't let his baskets die of thirst – he'd always been so good to them.'

'That'll have been Marjorie Wright, their next-door neighbour. The Wrights are salt of the earth – I don't know what they'll make of all this. Yes, it's true, Kevin was very attentive to his hanging baskets.'

And then it comes back to me what Mum said about Joe Payne never having been a nurturer, as my dad was. Well, Kevin definitely wasn't a nurturer, and suddenly I have a hunch.

'Kate, come with me. Quickly. There's something I have to do.'

'Ali, sit down. You're going nowhere.'

'It's just across the road. Come on.'

I grab the old milk crate I climbed on to cut the privet and I stride across Parnell Park.

'Ali, what are you doing ...?'

I place it under Kevin's hanging basket, stand on it and dig under the plants with my fingertips. My nails hit something plasticky – it could be the basket's lining but I don't think so. I give it a tug and it comes away.

'What've you got?'

I knew Kevin's frequent attention to his hanging baskets was out of character. I hold out what seems to be a plastic sandwich bag, folded over and over, with something inside.

'A memory stick.'

55

Kate and I are lying side by side on two sun loungers at the bottom of the garden. Joe and George are playing cards on the patio.

'So that's it, then,' Kate says. 'Ogilby and Kevin both behind bars, awaiting trial. Job done, Ali.'

'Yes.'

'You don't really want to talk about it, do you?'

'Not especially. I think I'm still in shock, or traumatised, or something.'

'You'll recover. You're a tough old bird, Al.'

'I wasn't always. I didn't know you had to be. Living with your uncle Joe, I discovered it was essential to find a vein of resilience to mine, somehow. Street angel, house devil – isn't that what they say? That was him, and you were one of the few people who saw it. And then, when he dropped dead playing golf and I found out he'd cancelled his life insurance and there was absolutely no money, I had to dig a little bit deeper, again. At least the mortgage protection meant I got to hang on to the house.'

'That's one good thing among some shit-awful luck.'

'I love having you here. This house is a sanctuary, but it can also be a kind of prison. You can't imagine what it's like jumping every time someone comes to the door, and Joe scurrying off upstairs. I'd love to get somebody in to sort out this garden, but he can't feel free to move about indoors when there's anyone out here who might see him.'

'Interesting you should say that. George and I have been talking a lot recently – and this isn't just in light of what happened with Ogilby – about what exactly we want to do with the next ten years of our lives, and where we want to do it.'

'Oh?'

'Ali, we're tired of having absolutely no money for a car or holidays or just going for a night out. George's new job's all right, but it's not really going to change much. So, we thought – why don't we move here? If we did, the kids could walk to and from school and we wondered if maybe Joe would be willing to be their childminder, so I could return to work properly, knowing there'd be someone who really cared about them to look after them after school and in the holidays or if they were sick.

'There's a thriving arts scene in Belfast, and, even if we

couldn't get work there, we thought we might set ourselves up as a drama project for children and young people – doing workshops for schools and youth clubs, you know, fostering creativity and self-confidence and stuff.'

'But you've only just moved to Croydon.'

'I know, but we've not settled there, not really, and we have no friends or family nearby. If the kids are ill or we just want a babysitter, there's no-one to turn to – whereas if we came here, we'd have you and Joe, and we might actually be able to buy a place. We've thought about this, Al.'

'I'd love to have you around, of course I would, but wouldn't you feel you were giving up on your dreams?'

'Dreams change.'

They do.

'Whatever you choose to do, I'll support you in any way I can.'

'Thanks. I knew you would. Could we live with you guys for a while, until we look around, see what's what?'

'I'd love that.'

We lie there for a while, in silence.

Then I say, 'I've tried talking to Joe about reviewing his whole situation. I want us to find out if there're any new avenues for treating his disfigurement or, if there's absolutely nothing happening there, then having some sort of therapy to help him live a more normal life.'

'How did that go?'

'He gets angry when I suggest any kind of facing up to it. He was so brave in agreeing to speak to the police, but now he's terrified I'll pressure him to see other people, because he's done it once. If it was just simple agoraphobia … but it's not. He feels like some sort of Gothic sideshow. I can't promise him that there won't be stares, and worse, if he ventures out, but is it really any better living as "the freak in the attic"?'

'Would you like me to try talking to him?'

'Oh, would you, Kate? He might listen to you.'

'He might, and then again he might not, but I'll give it a go. What time are we seeing Ruby?'

'Oh! Are you coming with me?'

'Try and stop me. Visiting Ruby's like rehearsing Beckett.'

56

'H ello, Alice. How are you?' It is Linzi who lets us in.
'Hello ...' She looks expectantly at my companion.
'This is Kate, my sort-of-niece. More my friend,
though, really.'

'Oh, pleased to meet you. Come on in.'

'You've got a new signing-in book.'

'Yeah. The police took the other one.'

'I'm really sorry you all got dragged into that ...'

To me, Linzi says, 'Would you stop apologising?' And to
Kate, 'She's always apologising, and there's no call for it.'

'Did the police interview you?'

'Yes – me and Alanis and Maggie. Told them what we
thought of them leaving you to face yer man on your own.
How are you now?'

'Pretty good, actually. I saw my GP this afternoon and he's checked me over and given me a clean bill of health. I talked to him about something that's been bothering me – it's to do with Mum, really; I've found I've been forgetting things a lot, lately, and I was worried I was heading the same way as her, but he doesn't think so. He says it's not the right sort of forgetfulness to denote dementia and it's more likely to be related to my insomnia, so he's sending me to a new sleep clinic.'

'And had you been panicking about that?' Linzi asks.

'I really had.'

'Well, I'm glad he's put your mind at rest.'

'So. How's Mum?'

'She's in good form, so she is. Since this new chef came, I think all the wee residents are in better form, 'cause they're all enjoying their grub.'

Kate follows me into the day room. 'Hi, Aunt Ruby, do you remember me? Kate.'

'Of course I remember you. Phyllis, this is Kate Middleton. Do you recall her wedding? We had a marquee in the garden at the bungalow. It was a beautiful day, just like this, and we had jugs of Pimm's and salmon en croûte and Elton John played the piano.'

Sometimes I wonder if Mum knows she is making this up. She can say anything she likes, indulge any fancy, lie through her teeth, and we all smile and go along for the ride. Sometimes I catch a little glint in her eye and I think: *you know exactly what you're up to, Mum*, and I kind of wish she did, but in the end I decide she's just confused, or wishful, and not really, truly lying.

ACKNOWLEDGEMENTS

Thanks go to Faith O'Grady, my lovely agent, who cast the first professional eye over the manuscript and saw promise, to my gorgeous editor and publisher, Ciara Considine, who made publication a reality and endeavoured to get the book into its best possible shape, and to Aonghus Meaney, sensationally sharp-eyed copy editor who kept me right. Thanks are due, too, to the fab Lucy Crichton, who has supported and encouraged my writing endeavours in a very practical way in recent years. I also appreciate the patience and encouragement of my parents, Robin and Myra, and of the individually and collectively wonderful Keir, Clem and Nye, and of my husband, the inimitable Niall, all of whom have had to put up with blank looks and 'Could you say that again?' on a daily basis, because instead of listening to them I am thinking about my book.